Dear Reader,

Thank you for joining me on this journey. I hope you enjoy *Without a Trace*. I really enjoyed writing it.

As Anne chased down the villain, I found my own heart pounding, hoping she would figure out the mystery before it was too late. One thing I really enjoy about this series is the contrast within Anne—a woman who serves her friends and community even as she struggles with the pain of losing her husband and the challenges of parenting two young children alone. It's a life so much like our lives, complicated, not perfect, yet tinged by grace. In *Without a Trace* Anne is starting to let go of her past, trusting that God can help her learn to live again even though the future is something she never envisioned.

It is my hope that you will find that same strength to go on after hardships, looking to Him for the strength that He longs to give you. He loves you so much.

Warmly,
Traci DePree
writing as Emily Thomas

Secrets of the Blue Hill Library

Without a Trace

Secrets of the
BLUE HILL LIBRARY

EMILY THOMAS

Guideposts
New York

Chapter One

"And in that moment," Lucas Miller read, "I knew I had said too much." The writer's voice was quiet yet infused with tension as he glanced around the room. By the smirk that lifted the corners of his mouth, he obviously knew he had them.

Anne Gibson, the town's librarian, sat in the circle of chairs, her arms crossed in front of her as she gazed at the critique group. Each face was transfixed, lost in the story.

"Anger in his eyes," Lucas went on, "he turned to me. I knew I had two choices—stay and face whatever wrath the man had to dole out or run for my life."

His eyes flicked to the clock on the wall and then to Anne as he straightened and closed the pages of his manuscript. "It looks like I've used up my time."

The group gave a groan.

"We have to wait till next time to find out what he does?" Wendy Pyle complained. The mother of seven and regular volunteer at the library lifted an irritated brow. "This just won't do! You have to finish it, Lucas."

But Lucas was shaking his head. "I'm sorry, Wendy, you'll have to wait until next week." He gave her a wink.

Lucas's smile was a bit crooked and, despite his joking, Anne noted dark circles under his eyes. She wondered if he'd been up late working on this latest masterpiece, as he was known to do, sometimes staying up all night writing, then heading out in the morning to work his full-time job.

Of those at the meeting, Lucas was the only published writer. He had sold a book to a New York publishing house and, though he only had one published crime novel to his credit so far, his publisher had contracted him to write a four-book series. He was gathering a loyal following already—at least among his local fans in Blue Hill, Pennsylvania, and the surrounding area.

"So." Mildred Farley shifted in her seat, her attention still clearly on the excerpt Lucas had just read. The older woman wore an aqua pantsuit with a large peach-colored brooch in the shape of a rose on its lapel. The colors set off her gray eyes and stunning white hair. The seventy-something woman definitely dressed with flair. "Your plots are so complicated I never know what's going to happen next. How do you figure all that out? Do you write a long outline before you start?"

Anne hadn't known Mildred was interested in writing until they started this critique group, at Lucas's prompting. Although, of course, she knew of her friend's love of reading. All of Anne's dearest friends shared that love—it was part and parcel in being a friend of the town's librarian.

The group met once every couple of weeks in the Reference Room of the Blue Hill Library. The old Victorian house had been Anne's great-aunt Edie's home for as long as Anne could remember. And while the place still carried the essence of Aunt Edie's home, decorated with some of the photographs and artifacts she'd collected over her lifetime, now, as Blue Hill's library, it had become a perfect gathering spot for the small town. The homey library beckoned visitors to sit for a while and enjoy a good book, with comfortable chairs and nooks and a decent selection of the classics, as well as new books.

Lucas was nodding. "Oh yes, I create very detailed outlines." He swiped his hand through his blond hair. "First I decide what the crime was and who did it. I create a whole outline for that, and then I pull possible clues from it, trying to time things between what the perpetrator is doing offstage and what the hero is doing on. And of course I create my cast of characters." Anne's glance took in Alex Ochs to Lucas's right. A local contractor and longtime friend—and high school sweetheart—of Anne's, Alex seemed particularly interested in hearing what Lucas had to say.

"I always find several sources on any particular subject," Lucas went on. "I've even taken various jobs as part of my research. I've milked cows on a dairy farm, baled hay, worked on power lines with master electricians…you name it. The only way to get into the skin of a character is to experience their life. I'll take several weeks or even months researching my protagonist's life before I begin my outline, that way the nuances that only someone in their shoes will appreciate can become part of the plot."

Mildred seemed impressed. "That's quite a commitment."

"My wife says I take it too far," he admitted a bit sheepishly.

"Well, I am just so impressed," Mildred went on. She had read her piece earlier, a poem from a collection she'd written in her younger days about watching from her window while the snow fell and being mesmerized by the patterns it created on the glass.

"Your poem was pretty awesome too, Mildred," he said sincerely.

She blushed and said, "Oh, go on. You're just flattering an old woman."

Anne said, "I think it was wonderful too."

Each member had read a portion of their work, except for Anne, who'd chosen to participate only in the discussions. As a widowed mother of two young children with a full-time career, she didn't have much time for serious writing. Though she certainly enjoyed these creative sessions. She'd never known some of her neighbors had a bent for putting word to paper. It was eye-opening to hear what they wrote, especially Lucas Miller. He was deeply gifted and so humble about it.

He was also the father of Remi and Bella Miller, eighteen-year-old twins and two of Anne's employees. Lucas was often around the library to pick his daughters up from work or to stop in and give them a hard time. He was famous for that.

Anne looked around at the rest of the room.

Wendy, who had become one of Anne's closest friends, hadn't settled on a particular genre. She said she was still dabbling, trying to figure out where her interests lay when it came to writing since she liked reading so many different kinds of books. Tonight she'd read a children's story she'd written about a camel who was self-conscious of her knobby knees.

Douglas Pauthen, a retired military man who enjoyed history and biographies, was writing a history of Blue Hill with Garret Jones, curator of the Blue Hill Historical Society. The two men were often in their own world, talking about items of interest from Blue Hill's past.

Rita Sloan, the thirty-something manager of the bank in Blue Hill, attended as well. She wrote contemporary inspirational romances. Charlotte and Henry Jordan, the new owners of the Blue Hill Inn, rounded out the group, writing collections of short stories.

Mildred seemed to be the only poet in their midst.

Marta Henshaw, a local photographer, hadn't come tonight. Anne wondered why. She was usually a faithful member of the writers' group. Like Lucas, she wrote crime novels, though she had yet to be published.

Chairs scraped the floor as people reached for bags and purses, stretching muscles that were tired from sitting for an extended time. The men gathered in a small circle to chat. The ladies moved to the side table, where the remains of a coffee cake laid in state. Anne cleared paper plates and plastic cutlery from the white tablecloth.

"I couldn't believe it," Anne heard Rita say to Mildred. "It was obvious someone had been in the house. The door was ajar. I was so frightened."

Anne couldn't resist joining the conversation. "When was this?"

"Last Sunday, when I got home from church," Rita was saying. "I was so scared. I felt…invaded."

"Did you call the police?" Wendy asked, her brow furrowed.

"I did, but they didn't have any answers for me since I wasn't there when it happened and hadn't seen anything. They told me to keep my doors locked from now on."

"That's scary," Charlotte Jordan said.

Rita nodded. "You're telling me! The thing is, nothing was stolen. Whoever broke in rooted through my stuff, but I didn't find anything gone." She turned her gaze toward Anne. "So what could they have been looking for?" She shivered and hugged herself.

Anne glanced at Lucas, who seemed deeply troubled by the story.

"Did you see anyone hanging around your place before you went to church?" he asked.

Rita shook her head. Then she lifted her purse and said, "Well, I'm staying with a friend for a couple of days. It all gives me the creeps. I'm not going to take any chances." Then she waved and left. "I'll see you all next time."

Lucas looked around the emptying room. "That concerns me," he admitted to Anne. "That kind of thing shouldn't happen, especially to young single women in Blue Hill."

Anne agreed, but she was curious about Lucas's vehemence. It was as if he took the offense personally.

"I wonder where Marta is tonight," he said rather absently. Finally, his gaze returned to Anne's. "She edits for me, has a good eye. I have a few more chapters for her to go over." He held up the paper-clipped pages, a good two inches of writing.

"How long did it take you to write that?" Anne asked, impressed.

"Oh, not long. I write quickly."

"I didn't hear anything from Marta," Anne admitted.

"It's great to get the feedback of everyone here," he explained. "Don't get me wrong. But people who write poetry and children's books don't have the same insights as someone who writes crime novels."

"I can understand that," Anne said.

Mildred joined them as Wendy said good night from across the room and escaped through the side door.

"Poor Rita!" Mildred said, then turning to Lucas she added, "I am just so glad I came tonight." The septuagenarian had a huge smile on her face.

"We're glad you came too, Mildred." Lucas reached for the trash can next to the table of snacks and coffee. He tied the bag shut and pulled it out to take downstairs to the trash bin.

"You know..." Mildred turned to Anne. She had been a dear friend of Anne's great-aunt Edie. "Your aunt Edie would have liked these sessions."

Anne smiled. Though Anne was well aware of her aunt's love of writing, she'd discovered much that she hadn't known about her deceased aunt since moving to Blue Hill from New York. Some secrets she never would have imagined in her earlier days.

Mildred turned back to Lucas. "So tell me. What was it like the first time you found out a publisher wanted to buy one of your books?"

Lucas smiled at the memory, his blue eyes twinkling. "That was pretty special," he admitted. "I'd just returned from four months of driving truck in the oil fields of North Dakota. Another research thing." He waved a hand. "Anyway, I'd sent my proposal out months before, heard nothing from any of the publishers I'd sent it to. Joyce and the girls and I were sitting around the dining room table, just happy to be together again...That was the longest time I'd been away from them, and I thought it would kill me! So being home was just...sweet." He paused, obviously content with the memory, before going on. "Then the phone rang. Bella got to it first, like she always does. Of course she was joking around but then her face got all serious." Lucas's eyes took on a faraway look. "She turned to me while she was talking into the phone and said, 'Are you serious? Like you're a real publisher?' That was when I knew." He chuckled. "I reached for the phone and chills went down my arm."

He shook his head. "The editor said he wanted to take me on—and not just for the one book," he added, "but they wanted to commit to growing me into a best seller. A person doesn't hear those words all that often, so I was blown away." He exhaled. "That day changed everything."

"How so?" Anne asked.

"Well," he cleared his throat. "I guess I always thought once I got published, everything would be different—and it has been. Just not in the way I imagined. I'm not famous or wealthy. My life is far from glamorous. Hey, I still have to work a day job and take out the trash!" He held up the bag in evidence. "Only now I have deadlines to meet for a publisher on top of everything else—so I'm working double time. No one tells you about that. And I thought I'd feel more secure in my writing…that I'd *arrived*, but I've come to the conclusion that we never really arrive. We're always striving to do better, to not be found out a fraud. There's always that element of insecurity, wondering if other people will like what I write or not."

Mildred placed her hands on her hips and lifted an eyebrow. "I'm still waiting to arrive too, son, so you aren't alone!"

"Well, that's encouraging, Mildred!"

They all laughed.

"You worked the oil fields in North Dakota?" Anne had to investigate that bit of information.

"I was living in my car in North Dakota in the middle of winter, then driving on those icy roads during the day. You tell me how bright that was!" He was so good-natured about it all, so down to earth. Anne liked that about him. It explained a lot about why his girls were so likable.

"Wow," Anne mouthed, amazed at the lengths Lucas would go to make sure his readers were fully immersed in his stories.

"Well, I better get home," Lucas said, meeting Anne's gaze. "Joyce will wonder what's keeping me."

"Thanks for everything," Anne said. "Oh, Bella said something about getting a new cell phone, but she never gave me the number. With my in-laws coming, she said she could come in and help a bit more this week. Do you have it?"

"Sure do." He pulled out his phone to look the number up. "Want me to just text it to you?"

Anne felt her pockets and then looked around for her purse. "Oh brother. If I had my phone *on* me. I left it upstairs."

"I'll just write it down for you." He grabbed a blank piece of paper from his notepad, then reached into his shirt pocket and pulled out an expensive looking pen — gold plated with the initials JSM engraved on its side.

"That's quite a pen," Anne remarked.

Lucas held it up for her to examine. "It was my dad's. A Waterman." Then he patted his shirt pocket. "I like to keep it right here." He winked and wrote down the phone number, handing it to Anne.

He waved good night and followed Mildred down the stairs to the first floor of the library. Anne followed them, locking up after they were gone and returning to the second-floor meeting room. She glanced around the dark-paneled room. All the chairs had been put away by the writers, the table cleared. All that remained was to rinse out the coffee urn and head upstairs to her sleeping children.

But when she got upstairs she knew immediately that no one was asleep. The television was on a bit too loudly, playing a children's show that had five-year-old Liddie enraptured. Anne flicked it off, and the kindergartener let out a disappointed, "Aw, Mom!"

Anne shook her head. "I told you—in bed by eight o'clock." She turned to Ben, who was buried deep in a book in the adjoining chair. He lifted startled eyes, then realized his mother was talking to him.

"Uh, sorry, Mom. I guess I didn't notice the time."

Anne smiled. "Obviously." She turned to Liddie and said, "Go brush your teeth and get your pajamas on." Liddie grudgingly got up to obey, and Anne gave her a playful swat on the bottom. Liddie giggled and quickened her pace.

"How was your meeting?" Ben said, setting his book down and rising to his feet.

He had hazel eyes and brown hair like his mother, while Liddie had golden brown curls with blonde highlights curls and brown eyes like her father. Eric had been gone for three years, yet Anne could see him every time she looked at their little girl's face.

Anne rubbed the back of her neck as she realized how very tired she was. "It was okay."

"I was thinking about when Grandma and Grandpa come…" Ben changed the subject.

Anne's in-laws were coming in a few days to spend some time with their grandchildren, and the kids were excited. They hadn't had any substantial time together since Eric's funeral, a few quick visits here and there but never any vacations. This would be a chance for Liddie and Ben to spend some quality time with them.

The plan was for Byron and Marlene to come from their home in Ithaca, New York, in their brand-new motor home. They would take day trips with the kids for the next two weeks and spend evenings with Anne, since she couldn't get away from work with the summer reading program just about to begin. They explained that the RV would provide a private place for them to stay without invading Anne's third-floor apartment above the library.

"And?" Anne waited for Ben to finish his sentence.

Ben grinned. "Do you think that we could go fishing? Remember, Dad and I used to go?"

"Of course I remember. You can always ask them." She smiled at her son's enthusiasm as he nodded a little too vigorously.

Anne was glad for the boy's excitement. She was looking forward to catching up with Byron and Marlene too—even if their presence would bring back painful memories of Eric's passing and another sharp reminder of the man she'd loved so much…and lost much too soon.

If Liddie looked like Eric, Eric's father, Byron, wore his personality like a comfortable sweater, finding opportunities to laugh, teasing his wife and Anne at every opportunity. Yet, like his son, he was brilliant too. Anne remembered Eric and his father often talking late into the night about philosophical and spiritual things, passionate in their zeal for learning and for debate. She hadn't always appreciated the similarities, and now she worried that they would send her into that cavern of self-pity for missing Eric.

She brushed the thought aside. She would have to deal with that when the time came.

* * *

Tuesday had been a busy day at the library. It was always busy when Anne was gearing up for the start of the summer reading program right after school let out. Anne had everything set to go for the following week. Decorations of construction paper cut-outs gave the old Victorian house a festive feel, especially in the Children's Room on the second floor with its bright colors and youthful theme. The tagline for the year was "Get Caught Reading" with photos on the walls of Blue Hill kids reading here and there—on the bus, under a blanket with a flashlight, holding a fishing rod in one hand and a book in the other, even one shot of a boy fully clothed and reading in the bathtub, plus so many other fun spots. Anne put a lot of effort into making the program fun, not just for the kids but for their parents as well. She knew that their interest would keep the children coming.

She had weekly activities and crafts lined up, plus monthly events with speakers and musicians and zookeepers with animals from local zoos, not to mention the occasional children's authors who would read their books to the children.

Anne was immersed in her work when Alex Ochs came into the library. Her back was turned to the checkout desk as she readied a bin to go to a sister library in their system. The courier would pick up the requested items the next time he stopped by.

"Are you always so intense?" Alex's deep voice broke into her thoughts.

Anne jumped. "Don't do that!" She pressed a hand to her chest as a smile grew on her face. Alex laughed.

"I guess I was preoccupied, wasn't I?" she admitted.

Alex nodded, his blue eyes twinkling and an eyebrow raised. At six feet one, he towered over Anne.

"I thought I should return these." He held up several books on interior design. "But your bin is too full." He pointed to the book drop's slot where several tomes stuck out.

"I'm a bit behind. Can you tell?" She reached to take the books from him. "Wendy is on her way to help out today or I'd be sunk." She glanced at the covers as she laid them on the counter. "What are you using these for?"

"I've been renovating Ryan's room. Or I should say *we* have been. Ryan is learning how to use power tools."

"He's ten!"

Alex shrugged. "I didn't say he was doing it alone. I'm with him, showing him how to do it safely." He chuckled at her. "Mothers!" Then he added, "We built in a loft bed and a sort of preteen man-cave area. We're far from done, but we're having fun. He's been living with me long enough now that it was time he made the space his own."

Alex had been raising his sister's son, Ryan, for the last four years, since she and her husband had been killed in a car accident.

Anne knew that Alex loved his nephew and did everything in his power to make up for the boy's losses.

"So what theme does Ryan want in his room?"

"If I let him have his way, he'd go for neon and racing stripes. That's why I needed the interior design books—to show him that we can both be happy with how it turns out. There were several possibilities in there."

"Well, if you need any help picking fabrics for curtains or painting, just give me a call. I can't do much on the building end, but you know I'm not too shabby with a paintbrush."

Alex smiled. "I'll keep your offer in mind."

As they were speaking, Remi and Bella Miller came into the library. Anne heard the sound of the heavy front door opening and closing, followed by the twins' frantic sounding voices. She and Alex turned toward the two regular library employees.

Both girls looked as though they had been crying. Their faces were blotched with red, their eyes puffy. "What's wrong, girls?" Anne said as they neared the checkout desk.

"It's Dad," Remi said, pushing her thick brown hair back off of her shoulders. Her brow was lined with trouble. "He never came home last night."

"What?" Anne immediately thought of Lucas's parting words the night before — *"I better get home. Joyce will wonder what's keeping me."*

"We've been looking for him all day," Bella added, her blue eyes meeting Anne's. Bella was shorter than her twin by six inches, and where Remi's hair was dark brown and straight, Bella had light brown hair that curled past her shoulders.

"You mean he didn't come home after the writers' meeting?" Alex said in obvious disbelief.

They nodded as one.

Anne glanced at the clock on the wall. It was already late afternoon. Where could the man have been all that time?

"Do you think he was injured, or…?"

"We don't know!" Remi was shaking her head. "We've tried his cell. He doesn't answer."

"It's not like Dad to not come home," Bella added. "Some dads are…you know…whatever. But Dad just doesn't do this — even when he's taken jobs far away, he always calls, and we always know where he is. Something had to have happened." She broke into sobs, and Anne went around the desk to comfort her.

"Oh, girls, I'm so sorry," she murmured. Alex sent them sympathetic glances.

"We had to come ask you if you noticed anything last night at the meeting. How long was he here? Was he acting weird? Anything?" Remi asked frantically.

Anne paused to think back. He seemed himself, at ease, laughing, offering advice to the other writers. "He didn't say anything unusual that I can think of." She shrugged. "He seemed…normal." She paused. "He left here around nine thirty, I'd say, and he mentioned needing to get home."

Just then Wendy came in. She must've heard the news around town because she didn't seem surprised by the Miller girls' appearance. She tilted her head and offered a sympathetic look as she bent to place her purse behind the checkout desk.

"It really doesn't sound like Lucas," Alex agreed. His gaze met Anne's. His brow was furrowed. He pulled out his own phone and dialed Lucas's number. There was no answer. It went straight to voice mail.

"Mom is being so brave, but this is hard. She's been calling everyone she knows." Bella shook her curly hair. "Dad needs to come home!"

Just then Joyce Miller came into the library. She was a petite thing, birdlike, with dark brown eyes and a short pixie haircut, the epitome of the word *cute*. Her usual smile was gone, replaced by hollow eyes and a drooping smile.

"I'm sorry to hear about Lucas," Anne offered when Joyce neared the rest of them. "Do you have any idea where he could be?"

Joyce shook her head, but her attention was on her daughters. "The police found Daddy's car," she said quietly.

Both girls straightened as she went on, "It's crashed into a tree outside of town near the Wilson farm."

CHAPTER TWO

I s Daddy okay?" Remi asked, her eyes turning to her sister.

Joyce was shaking her head. "The police haven't been able to find him. They want us to come."

The girls turned to follow their mother, then Bella looked back at Anne. "Can you come with us?" Her glance included Alex. "Please?" Bella mouthed, looking desperate.

"Well, I have the library...and my kids," Anne started to say, and yet, the twins had become like Anne's own children since they'd started working for her.

"I'll take care of things here," Wendy interjected, followed by a nod. "You go ahead. I can manage a couple of tame kids." She winked.

"Okay." Anne turned back to the hurting teenager.

"Can you drive us? I don't know if Mom is safe," Bella added.

Anne agreed, knowing it would be better for the family if someone else drove.

Alex said, "I'll follow in my pickup."

Joyce was shaking by the time they made it to the site of the accident, and Anne was glad she'd driven. Tears streamed down Joyce's face. She swiped at them with the back of her hand.

They got out in silence as the sight of Lucas's broken Honda Accord hit them full force. The front end of the car was twisted around a massive oak alongside the field approach to the Wilson's farmland that was on a little-driven dirt road just outside of Blue Hill. Skid marks on the road verified Lucas's attempt to avoid the crash.

As they neared the car, Anne could see the white of the airbag hanging from the center of the steering wheel, like some phantom remnant of the horrendous thing that had happened there.

There were many official vehicles already on site, including an ambulance off to the side. Officers stooped and inspected, stood and talked, scouted the surrounding countryside. Grace Hawkins from the *Gazette* was there too, talking to Officer Michael Banks, an old friend of Anne's and high school classmate. Even Reverend Tom was there. He nodded in greeting and started to make his way over.

The five of them went first to the car, bending to look inside. The Honda Accord was a mass of twisted metal and broken glass. Anne knew the family hoped somehow, some way that Lucas might be there, sitting inside unharmed, irrational as that thought was, that the officers might have missed him. Anne hoped it too. But of course he wasn't there. The inside was covered with shattered glass. The dash was oddly shaped—it met the front passenger seat, though the driver's side was more intact. Wires and mechanicals stuck out here and there. Anne noted that the clock had stopped at 12:31. The interior was mostly bare, with only a few items still scattered about including a pencil and a wrapper from a fast-food restaurant. The trunk must've popped open upon impact. It seemed odd sitting there exposed that way. Anne moved toward it to take a look. Inside was typical trunk paraphernalia—a tire iron and a spare tire. Nothing much beyond that.

"How are you holding up?" Reverend Tom spoke to Joyce. The fifty-eight-year-old pastor of the Blue Hill Community Church reached to give her a hug, a look of concern on his face. He was a slim, lanky man, fit unlike most men his age.

Joyce shrugged. "I don't know how I am, to be honest, Reverend."

He patted her shoulder. "That's why we're here—to help you get through this right now."

Officer Banks came up to them. Anne saw that he had something in his hands, a slip of yellow legal paper.

"Thanks for coming so quickly," the officer said to Joyce. "My men found this in the cup holder between the front seats." He shook his head as he handed it to her. Joyce turned it over to look at it, and Anne recognized Lucas's handwriting, though it seemed sloppier than she remembered it. The front read simply, *Joyce.*

The petite woman closed her eyes, then wiped them with the back of her hands before unfolding the sheet of paper. Her eyes met Anne's as she read out loud.

"Dear Joyce, Bella, and Remi…" Joyce's left hand moved to her chin as she read.

"I'm so sorry to tell you this in such an impersonal way. But I can't go on like this. I'm tired of the arguments. Of not making you happy. I haven't been happy in our marriage for a long time now. I'm leaving to start a new life. I'm not sure where I'll go, so don't even try to come looking for me. Just know that I had to leave. It's something I have to do."

It was signed simply, *Lucas.*

Joyce's face crumpled and her hand moved to cover her mouth. Bella reached for the note and read it silently, her eyes moving across the page in disbelief.

Joyce moved like a robot to scan the countryside. She gazed across the woods that meandered along a rocky ravine with a stream between the steep banks. Joyce walked there silently, no doubt to have a good cry. Anne didn't blame her. Then the girls followed, like cubs following a mother bear.

Anne, Reverend Tom, and Alex moved away and to the side so the officers could continue their investigation.

"I don't understand it," Anne said, trying to reconcile the man she'd been with just the night before to someone who would leave his family such a letter.

Reverend Tom looked at Anne. "This doesn't add up. You know Lucas. That letter sounds nothing like him." He shook his head. "Lucas went on missions trips. He was active in church, a good father."

"He wouldn't be the first person to have such struggles," Anne reminded. "To keep his feelings a secret." Though even as she said it, she didn't believe it about Lucas.

Alex seemed to take that in. "He was my friend. I'm not buying it."

"I agree," Anne confessed. That note doesn't sound like the Lucas I know. But how many of us know other people, really? Their deepest, darkest secrets?"

Alex shoved his hands into his back pockets. "Look at that car—how did he survive that? And where could he have gone afterward? He can't have gotten far."

"You're right about that. I hope he isn't hurt," Anne said.

The full cadre of Blue Hill police officers was searching the area. K-9 dogs sniffed the ground, leading into the woods. Anne watched the animals for a few moments before her gaze returned to Lucas's family standing in a huddle, arms around each other as their shoulders shook.

Grace Hawkins was walking up to them, a notebook and pen in her hands. She looked at the family and then turned back to Anne, Alex, and Reverend Tom. The pretty blonde reporter from the *Gazette* had become a good friend since Anne moved back to Blue Hill. She greeted Alex and Reverend Tom, then said to Anne, "Can you believe this?"

"Do the police have any idea what happened?" Anne asked.

Grace shrugged. "Not really. Officer Banks just said they're looking into it...but they are as clueless as the rest of us."

Anne could see the officer reading the note Joyce had handed back to him. He stood talking to her and the girls. Reverend Tom excused himself to join the family.

Once Reverend Tom had moved off, Alex scratched his head. "I just don't get it. I know Lucas. He's a decent guy. It's one thing to split up a marriage—though I never heard a peep from Lucas about him not being happy. But to do it this way? It just doesn't make sense. And why would he leave the note in the car that he was supposedly leaving in?"

"Maybe he was going home to leave it there when he crashed," Grace offered.

Anne had to agree that it was a weak explanation.

"It's as if he vanished into thin air," Anne said. "To escape an accident of this kind..."

"Was he at your writers' meeting last night?" Grace asked. She was jotting notes, in reporter mode.

"He was and he seemed his usual self too. I..." She paused to think back. "He gave no clue that he was thinking of leaving."

Joyce returned to the smashed-up car, speaking with an officer, while the girls remained huddled in their spot by the woods, their bodies moving with the grief of tears as Reverend Tom spoke quietly to them.

Officer Banks was walking up to Anne, Alex, and Grace. Michael had gone to high school with Anne and Alex. His blue eyes met Anne's hazel ones. He held out a hand to shake with each person in turn, then he lifted his police hat and scratched the top of his balding head before settling the hat back in place.

"Thanks for bringing Joyce and the girls out," he said to Anne. "As hard as this is, any clues they can offer will help us figure out what happened."

"What do you make of the note?" Anne asked.

"Hard to say," the officer said. "Our main objective right now is to determine if he made it out of that accident alive. Or if he's stranded out there somewhere." He motioned toward the farmland and woods. "If he did survive unscathed...Quite frankly, that note will limit our search."

"But the accident?" Anne asked, alarm growing at the thought of the police not putting full effort into finding the lost man. "Surely that's enough to keep you looking for him. He could be disoriented, hurt badly out in the woods."

"We already have an APB out on him. If he's hurt and needs help, we definitely want to assist, but he's a grown man,

Anne…and sadly grown men make the decision to leave their families all the time."

Joyce returned to them then, and the officer grew quiet. Joyce's dark eyes met Anne's. She held a ream of paper in her hands.

"Is that Lucas's book?" Anne asked.

Joyce nodded. "He never would've left this for someone else to find. He's very protective of his works in progress."

"We'll find him," Anne assured her, trying to infuse confidence into her voice.

"I hope so," Joyce said, turning toward her daughters who were taking a final look at the crash site. "For their sake, I hope so."

* * *

After Alex said farewell, Joyce and the twins took Anne back to the library. Alex had offered to take her, but Anne told him that she felt Joyce needed some time to talk.

"Why don't you come up for something to eat?" Anne suggested. "You don't need to be cooking right now." They were parked in front of the old Victorian. Wendy's van was off to the side.

"Okay," Joyce conceded, gratefulness in her gaze.

Remi and Bella trudged up the stairs to the Gibsons' private entrance, followed by their mother and Anne. Anne could hear Ben and Liddie talking with Wendy as they reached the top floor. Hershey came up to sniff the twins. Remi and Bella petted the chocolate Lab's head.

Wendy lifted her head as soon as Anne and Joyce entered the room. "Any news?"

"There's a search party scanning the area right now," Anne replied, her gaze turning to Ben and Liddie, who were showing the girls some of their dog's tricks. "It seemed best to come back here…" She let her words trail off.

Wendy looked to Joyce. "So he wasn't at the car?"

"No."

Anne glanced at the clock as she noted that Liddie and Ben had their pajamas on. How had it become eight thirty?

"Sadly, I have to head home," Wendy said apologetically.

Anne said, "Thanks for taking Ben and Liddie. You have your own crew…"

Wendy waved a hand. "I put a plate of sandwiches in the refrigerator for you just in case you were hungry when you got home. There's enough for everyone," she directed the last sentence to the Millers. "I don't think Hershey has been out lately," she added. Then she picked up her purse and headed for the back stairs.

Once she was gone, Anne turned to Ben. "Can you take the dog out, honey?"

Ben nodded wisely, as if he knew the big people needed a little alone time. "Come on, Liddie," he said. "You can help."

The five-year-old twisted up her freckled nose and said to her mother, "You're telling me to go in the backyard in my pajamas?"

Anne nodded, and Liddie gave her a grin. "Fun!" Then she bounded after her brother.

Anne moved to the kitchen as Joyce and the girls took seats at the small table. Joyce sighed heavily and placed her face in her hands. Remi placed a hand on her mother's shaking shoulder.

"He didn't even take any of his clothes," Bella said to no one in particular. "This is all a big mistake. He wouldn't have left his clothes behind if he was really leaving us."

Joyce's heart-wrenching sobs filled the room as tears streamed down Bella's and Remi's faces. Anne felt helpless to comfort them, so she did what she could—she gathered the food Wendy had so graciously left them and set it on the table alongside plates and mugs of steaming coffee.

Finally, Joyce lifted her tear-stained face. Anne handed her a box of tissues so that Joyce could wipe her eyes.

"I knew things hadn't been going well lately," she confessed. "But this…this completely blindsided me. I figured these things pass. It was a phase. We'd come out the other side of it and be just fine. You know, that's just how marriage is. Ups and downs." She blew her nose again. "I feel so"—she lifted devastated eyes—"betrayed. And if he's hurt somewhere… Well, he still wrote that note! So where does that leave us?"

Anne took the seat across from Joyce. "I wish there were something I could do."

"I don't know," Joyce murmured. "I just don't know."

"You can help us find him," Remi said to Anne, her brown eyes vehement. "You're good at that kind of thing. I've seen you get to the bottom of puzzles and mysteries before." She turned to her sister who was younger by only three minutes. "Haven't we, Bella?" Bella nodded agreement, and Remi went on, "Mrs. Gibson, you know how to put clues together, how to figure out what happened even when no one else sees the connections. You can do that now."

Anne shook her head. "That's a job for the police."

"But you heard them!" Remi declared. "They said that Dad was an adult who probably left of his own free will. Without proof that he was injured, there's nothing that they can do. They won't keep looking for long."

"He didn't report the accident," Joyce said. "And how badly could he have been hurt if he was nowhere near the site?"

"That's true," Anne said.

"But maybe he wasn't in his right mind," Remi said. "Maybe the accident caused him to act erratically."

"And what?" Joyce said. "Write me a Dear John letter? Girls, we have to be reasonable here."

"Mom," Bella said, a deep tenderness in the word. Anne could see that the girl didn't want to hurt her mother any more than she'd already been hurt. "We can't just give up on Dad. There's a reason he wrote that note—and it's not because he was leaving you! Dad loves you." Her voice rose with each sentence. "I know he does."

Remi was shaking her head. "The police will look for a few days or a week…but how hard?" She reached for Anne's hand. "Please, Mrs. Gibson. Please help us find Daddy! He wouldn't leave us like this—Bella's right. I know he wouldn't. He *loves* us!"

"Girls," Joyce said, "he wrote that note—there's no doubt about that. It was his handwriting. And he didn't exactly come home or call us after he hit that tree."

Anne could see how it pained her to say it.

"Maybe he couldn't. Maybe something happened to him," Bella insisted.

But Joyce was shaking her head. From the look on her face, Anne could see that the woman had made up her mind. She bent down toward the floor and lifted a large canvas tote bag she'd brought upstairs from the car and pulled the manuscript from its depths. She laid it on the table, running a tender hand along the cover page.

"This is the only thing that makes me think you might be right," she admitted, her gaze moving from Bella to Remi. "He wouldn't have left it."

That she thought he would have left her more easily tore at Anne. She placed a comforting hand on the woman's hand. Joyce sighed.

"I want you to have it, Anne." She pushed the manuscript across the table. Then she looked lovingly at her two daughters.

Bella said, "Remi's right, Mrs. Gibson. If anyone can figure out where Lucas went, it's you. Maybe the manuscript will offer some clues as to what he was thinking. In the meantime, we need to figure out what life will look like now. Without Dad."

Anne finally agreed to help look for Lucas, if—and only if—the police were unable to give them any satisfactory answers. The Millers left after Officer Banks called to tell them that their search still hadn't turned up any signs of Lucas in the ravine or the surrounding farm fields. Yet, even after the Millers had gone, the look of defeat in Joyce's face kept haunting Anne. Hope was a thin thread for her. Anne could see it in the slump of Joyce's shoulders. Just how to bring that hope back, that would be the hard part—and likely something only God could accomplish.

* * *

The floorboards of the old Victorian creaked under Anne's feet as she padded from Ben's bedroom to Liddie's. Anne had sent the kids to their rooms earlier, when the Millers were there, to read until they fell asleep. She hadn't wanted the impressionable nine- and five-year-olds to worry that she might disappear someday like Lucas Miller had. They'd already had enough of that in their young lives, losing their father to a heart attack three years ago.

Liddie lifted her cute face when Anne opened the door. She'd obviously fallen asleep, and her brown eyes drooped with the late hour.

"Sleepy?" Anne said as she sat on the side of her bed and reached for the large picture book that was still pressed into Liddie's hands.

Liddie nodded as a yawn took over. "Uh-huh." Then she added, "Are Remi and Bella going to be okay?"

Anne placed the book in the bookcase, then returned to straighten the blankets over Liddie's small form. She brushed her daughter's curly locks from her forehead. "It's very hard for them to lose their father," Anne said.

"Oh, I know all about that," Liddie said, sounding much older than her five years.

"Yes, you do, don't you?" She smiled into the little girl's eyes.

"Do you think their daddy will come back?" She folded her fingers together over her chest.

"I hope so, honey."

Liddie was silent for a long moment as she thought. "They're lucky," she finally said.

"What do you mean?"

Liddie shrugged. "My daddy can't come back ever but theirs could."

Anne reached to touch her hands. "I guess that is something to be thankful for," Anne admitted.

"Are you going to help them?" Liddie asked.

Anne studied the child's eyes, so expectant. She nodded. "As much as I can, I guess."

"That's good. They need you."

"I thought *you* needed me."

"I'll always need you. But their kind of needing is just for a little while."

"How did you get so smart?"

Liddie shrugged.

Anne held her daughter's hand and Liddie fingered Anne's wedding bands, twisting them around her finger several times, feeling the smoothness of the gold, touching the diamond and staring into its depths. It was something she did on occasion. Anne knew it was a comfort for her.

Finally, she said, "Will you always wear those?"

"My wedding rings?" Anne looked down at them. Aside from taking them off to clean, she'd never thought of not wearing them. It simply hadn't occurred to her.

Liddie nodded, her tired eyes reaching up to her mother's.

"I don't know," Anne confessed. "I never really thought about it."

"Is it like you think Daddy might come back if you keep them on?"

"Of course Daddy can't come back," she answered sadly.

* * *

Liddie's comment stayed with Anne as she moved to turn off all the lights before heading to her room. Was she subconsciously believing that wearing her rings would somehow keep Eric with her? She supposed in some small way that was true. She didn't want to let go of the precious years they'd had together.

She thought of the first time they'd gone ice skating at the rink in Rockefeller Center in Manhattan. The gold-plated statue of Prometheus bringing fire to mankind hovered above as lights from the enormous Christmas tree reflected across the ice. It had been one of their first dates. Anne had never gone skating before. She'd been so nervous, wanting to impress him. She'd wobbled on her blades, her ankles like jelly, so Eric took both her hands in his and skated backward across the ice.

"Concentrate on me, not on your feet," he'd said, pulling her to him, that beautiful grin spread across his handsome face. His eyes held such life, such joy. She'd wanted to stare into them forever.

"Does it seem odd to you that the statue is a god bringing fire to an ice-skating rink?" Eric joked. "Wouldn't that melt the ice?"

She laughed, but when she did her feet flew out from under her so quickly she barely registered what had happened. Eric fell alongside her. He lay there motionless for a long moment and she panicked. "Eric? Are you okay?" She leaned over him to check his breathing. Puffs of steam rose from his nose and mouth.

He opened one eye and pulled her in for a kiss.

It was sneaky, she had to admit, but she loved it. She loved him.

Anne sighed as the memory faded, replaced by the ringing of her cell phone.

"Hello, Byron," she said as she hit the Talk button. She knew from the display it was her father-in-law calling.

"Hey, kid," he said. Her father-in-law had called Anne "kid" since she and Eric had first started dating. Anne smiled. When she was fifty years old, the man would still call her "kid."

"All ready to hit the road?" Anne said as she pulled her slippers off and climbed under the covers of her bed.

"I think so, if your mother-in-law would stop cleaning the house. It's not like anyone's going to be staying here while we're gone."

Anne could hear Marlene's protests in the background. Their constant banter never failed to bring a smile to Anne's face. Married for almost forty-seven years and both highly accomplished professors at Cornell University, they still loved each other deeply and were best friends. It was what Anne had hoped her later years with Eric would have been like.

"Don't give her a hard time," Anne said. "I understand why she's cleaning. Who likes to come home to dirty dishes?"

"Dirty dishes?" Byron said. "She's dusting the attic!"

"I am not dusting the attic!" Marlene's voice rang in the background. "Byron, you give me that phone!"

"I just wanted to check in with you," the man went on undeterred, "to let you know our itinerary."

"We can go over that when you get here," Anne assured. "The kids are in their last week of school. Next week they are all yours."

"That's perfect," Byron said. Anne could hear her mother-in-law pick up the extension.

"What was that, honey?" Marlene asked.

"I was telling Dad that next week the kids are off for summer break so they are all yours."

"I can't wait," the older woman said, excitement in her voice. "It's been too long. And I've been baking! You can tell Liddie I made those cream cheese brownies she likes."

"She'll love that," Anne said.

"We won't go hungry, that's for sure," Byron said.

"The kids are very excited to see you," Anne said. "I am too. I'm sorry I can't get off of work. I'd thought I'd be able to get away at least a little, but my part-time help is going through a rough time, and since I am the only full-time employee, that makes it almost impossible for me to take time off. Plus, with our summer reading program starting up…"

"We already talked about this," Marlene said. "Don't you fret, honey. We understand how that is. Anyway, a little alone time with those two darlings will be wonderful."

Her love for her grandchildren ran strong. Just as her love for Eric had. The thought sobered Anne. Oh, how she wished he were here to laugh with his folks, to see the joy of them with his children. To tease his mother the way his father still did. Anne sighed.

"Now, don't be doing that," Byron said. The man knew her too well. "We aren't going to think about sad things this week— you got that? We just aren't going to."

"Okay," Anne said. "It's a deal. No dwelling."

"Good."

"We're planning on leaving here about seven o'clock. We have a stop in Williamsport to see Marlene's sister — that woman would never forgive us if we drove into Pennsylvania without visiting her. Who knows how long she'll want to visit. But I told Marlene we have to get out of there by four thirty. That will put us in Blue Hill early Thursday evening, say around seven?"

"That sounds perfect to me."

"That's the plan anyway. You know how that goes when women are involved."

"Byron!" Marlene scolded. "Anne, don't you listen to that man."

"We can't wait to see you, kid."

"I can't wait to see you either."

When they hung up, Anne was pulled back in time to the first day they'd met. She'd traveled with Eric to Ithaca for a chess tournament. Eric was a genius at chess. Marlene and Byron had welcomed her into their home as if they'd always known her. Marlene was always cleaning, making their modest home comfortably classy for "her boys" as she called them — Eric and his brother, Ted, as well as Byron. Byron liked to joke about this and that, yet he was the kind of man who enjoyed a deep conversation. Just like Eric.

Anne sighed, remembering Byron's scolding. "Okay, Anne," she said out loud as she pulled back the sheets of her bed. "No dwelling."

But that was about as likely as holding back the tide.

* * *

Anne tossed and turned for several hours before she finally sat up and switched on the bedside lamp. Her mind wouldn't shut off. At first it had been thoughts of Eric's folks coming and memories of them with Eric. But then her thoughts turned to Lucas Miller and the faces of his family.

Liddie was right.

There was one big difference between the two losses — Lucas's could still be remedied. She hoped. She could still see them gazing into Lucas's wrecked car. Had he survived? Or had he wandered off to die alone? Injured and disoriented in some ditch?

Anne shook her head and wrapped her arms around herself. If he had survived, where would he have gone after that? Had someone seen the accident and picked him up? She wondered if the police had called area hospitals.

This was getting her nowhere. Especially where sleep was concerned.

Anne rubbed her forehead as a prayer bubbled up. She closed her eyes and told her heavenly Father about her concerns for the man, for his family. She understood the mountain of uncertainty that Joyce would face in days to come, decisions to be made whether she wanted to make them or not, new skills to learn, bills to pay, and children to guide through it all.

Anne had developed a long habit of talking to God as a dear friend about all kinds of things. Even when she was upset with Him she told Him about it. She knew God understood, that He wasn't threatened by her fears and worries. That He loved her. Saying it to Him allowed God to comfort that lonely place, let Him in to the deepest wounds of her soul so He could heal them.

"Lord, help Joyce to do the same through all of this," she added. "Because more than anything else she needs You right now, to fill the questions with Your peace. Even if she never learns the answers."

When Anne was done praying, she lifted her gaze across the cozy bedroom, its windows still darkened with the night outside.

Had she allowed God to do the same for her? Fill the lonely places where unanswered questions taunted? Probably not. And yet His love for her made that all right. He would keep guiding her. He wouldn't give up.

Her eyes landed on the manuscript Joyce had given her. Joyce would want that back someday, or at least her daughters would. Maybe not soon but someday. Climbing out of bed, Anne crossed the room and slipped her bathrobe on. Then she moved to the dresser where she'd placed the stack of pages. She carried it to the corner armchair and nestled in to read. She flicked on the lamp, its yellow glow surrounding her.

She unclipped the thick black clasp and turned to the first page. It was a good two inches of pristine white paper. Why would he have printed it—wasn't that expensive? The last time she'd purchased printer ribbons for the library she'd been amazed at the expense of the things.

Couldn't he have simply e-mailed the story to his publisher? Or to his critique partners? He had mentioned wanting to get it to Marta Henshaw at the writers' meeting—had he ever gotten ahold of her?

Anne paged through, still wondering why Lucas would have left it. If he intended to leave his family, why wouldn't he have taken his manuscript, not to mention his clothes? Remi had been right about that—it didn't make sense. And why not call a tow truck for his damaged car? He couldn't have just disappeared into thin air.

As she looked through, she noticed small handwritten notes in the margins—numbers and letters. Perhaps phone numbers? But they weren't written out like phone numbers, and the letters didn't spell anything in particular. She studied them for a long while. Maybe car licenses? There were probably half a dozen such pages with the odd code, spread out throughout the manuscript.

Maybe it was simply something for Lucas to use in revisions— some kind of personal code. Anne frowned, feeling herself getting tired. She thought about trying to read the story, even though Lucas had read some of it out loud during their critique nights.

Her eyes soon grew tired. She gave up reading and crept back to bed, where sleep finally took over.

CHAPTER THREE

A nne called Officer Banks first thing the next morning just after Ben and Liddie left for school. Hershey padded up to her and watched curiously as she punched in the number.

"Michael, how are you?"

He gave a sleepy sounding reply. He clearly hadn't gotten enough rest last night.

"I'm just calling to ask if you checked area hospitals to see if Lucas might've gone there?" Anne finally said.

"Of course," he said simply.

"I'm sorry." She suddenly realized he could take her call as interference. "That's your job...I just thought of it last night and thought I'd—"

"Hey, I'm not above taking suggestions. We need all the help we can get on this one," Michael said good-naturedly. "Not one of the area hospitals or Urgent Care clinics saw him, and the K-9s came back empty last night too."

"That's disappointing."

"We're still looking," he assured.

* * *

That afternoon, Anne put the finishing touches on the calendar of events she'd created for the summer reading program. She had one for each month of summer—June, July, and August—jam-packed with fun reading-centered things to do. She'd just hit *print* and was watching the colored sheets come out of the printer when an elderly woman asked if the library had any new biographies Anne could recommend.

"I prefer the political ones," the sweet gray-haired woman said, "like about presidents' wives and those kinds of people."

"I have several." Anne led the way to the adult Nonfiction Room across from the checkout desk. While the Children's Room was whimsical in its theme, the Nonfiction Room was more serious in demeanor with soft taupe-toned walls trimmed in white, and shiny polished wood floors. Anne pointed to the shelf of books. "See, there's both Laura and Barbara Bush, Nancy Reagan, Rosalynn Carter. Oh, and look here—Eleanor Roosevelt."

The woman picked up the volume, a satisfied expression on her face. "This will do just fine," she said, adding her thanks. Then she turned to browse some more.

Anne made her way back to the checkout desk as the twins arrived. Bella held a stack of flyers in her hand.

"How are you two?" Anne said.

"Well, we're doing everything we can to stay busy and useful," Remi replied. She tried to sound cheerful, but her eyes betrayed her troubled heart. "We've made flyers with pictures of Dad to put up around town. You just never know—someone might've seen something. We need some kind of lead."

Anne offered her a sympathetic smile.

"Yeah," Bella added. "I've been thinking. Where was Dad during those hours between when your meeting ended and 12:31, the time on the dashboard clock? Surely someone saw something in that time."

The girl made a good point, one Anne had thought of when she first saw the time frozen on that clock.

Just then the doors opened on the old cage-style elevator and Betty Bultman wheeled the book cart off. Betty often helped out in the library. The mayor's wife was a tall woman with broad shoulders. She wore a calico print dress, simple, unadorned, with a white cotton collar and a gathered waist.

Mildred Farley was with her, talking about the happenings of the last two days. When their eyes turned on the Miller girls, she was instantly silent. Then she said, "How are you two holding up?"

Bella shrugged, and Remi said, "We're okay. We've decided to put up some flyers, so people know to call the police if they saw anything." She held up one of the flyers. A nice photograph of Lucas filled its center.

"Can we put one up here?" Remi asked Anne.

"Of course." Anne reached for a sheet and then pulled out a roll of tape from the drawer in the checkout desk. She moved to the doors that led to the History Room.

"How about here?" she said. "Everyone goes past here."

"That's perfect," Bella agreed.

"I can put one up at town hall," Betty offered as she reached for one of the flyers. "I'm sure Mayor Bultman wouldn't mind."

Bella handed her a sheet.

"Can you think of anywhere else?" Remi asked.

"We could head out together and look for places," Mildred suggested to Anne and the girls.

"I can manage things for you here," Betty offered.

"Sure," Remi agreed. "We can also ask around if people saw anything."

"Well…," Anne said to Betty. "If you don't mind."

"Everything is under control here."

Anne reached for her purse, and the four of them set off.

* * *

Fowler's Auto Repair had been a part of Blue Hill's landscape since 1957. It was the sort of place you took your car if you wanted it repaired right the first time. It wasn't fancy like the car dealerships up on the highway with their showrooms. The foyer was tight, with barely enough room for the four of them to stand. A tall counter with a white Formica top ran the length of the room.

Anne dinged the bell on the counter, where a note had been taped. It read, *Ring for Service.* An ancient Pepsi machine glowed red, white, and blue in the corner behind them. Next to it was a stand with two gumball-type machines that dispensed peanuts on one side and M&Ms on the other.

After a minute or two, a man came from the back, wiping his hands on a rag as he moved behind the counter.

"What can I do for you ladies?" he asked, his brown eyes moving from one face to the next. He wore a blue jumpsuit with dark smudges here and there.

"Is Shaun around?" Anne asked.

"No, he's on vacation, and I'm filling in. I'm his brother, Scott." He reached out for a handshake but stopped himself and chuckled. "On second thought, I don't think you want me to share this grease."

"We were wondering if we could put one of these up." Remi handed him a flyer.

He bent his head to study it and lifted a hand to knead the back of his neck. "Sure, you can put it up."

"Have you seen him?" Anne said, curiosity rising at the odd change in his demeanor.

He lifted eyes to Anne, then shrugged. "Probably. Everyone comes into Fowler's at one time or another, right?"

"Hey, that looks like Dad's pen," Bella said, pointing at the low chrome-edged desk behind Scott. Anne's eyes followed to the Waterman pen Anne had seen the night of his disappearance.

The man's face flushed red.

"Oh yeah...," he hedged. "Someone left that here." He moved to the spot and picked it up. He handed it to Bella who confirmed that it was indeed her father's pen. The initials JSM were easy to see.

"How did you get it?" Remi said. She leaned in, clearly excited that they were onto something.

Scott's hand finally stopped its kneading, and he said, "I was working late. Lucas—your dad—came in wanting gas. I told him we were closed, but he was pretty insistent. I found the pen on the floor after he was gone."

"Did he say anything about where he was going?" Mildred asked.

Scott shook his head. "Nothing."

"He didn't say anything about heading out of town?" Anne added.

"Sorry."

Remi reached for the pen from her sister. "This is definitely Dad's pen. He has a whole collection of them. He wouldn't just leave it behind. This one was the first—it was Grandpa's Waterman." She pointed to the initials, then looked Scott in the eyes and repeated. "He would never have just left this behind."

Anne placed a hand on the girl's back to calm her down. She felt the sigh that left Remi's lungs.

"Like I said, I found it on the floor after he left." Scott lifted his hands like a victim in a holdup. "It might've dropped out of his pocket or something after he wrote the check for gas. Listen, I've got to get back to work. I'll put your poster up if you want to leave it there on the counter."

Bella laid a sheet on the counter and they filed back outside.

"He knows something!" Remi was adamant.

"If your dad was here to get gas, it had to have been before the accident," Anne reminded. "That doesn't strike me as suspicious."

Remi's face fell. "I guess I was just…"

"It's okay," Anne said.

* * *

The group was quiet as they drove back to the library, having posted all of their signs around town. Other than Scott Milhouse's story of seeing Lucas late that night, there had been no other leads. Anne called Officer Banks to tell him of the encounter and to see if the police had any new developments.

"I'm afraid to say, no, there's nothing new," he told her. "The trail is starting to go cold."

"It's only been two days," Anne said.

"Even so, it seems apparent that he couldn't have been injured significantly," the officer reasoned. "If one of our officers should come across him, we'll stop him to make sure he's okay, ask him about why he left the scene of an accident, but that's really the extent of what we can do legally."

"But don't you think it's suspicious that he would leave the car like that?"

"Of course I do," he confessed, "but since Lucas wrote the note to Joyce that he was leaving, it ties our hands." He sighed, clearly as frustrated as Anne felt. "I wish I had more I could tell you."

"I understand," Anne said, looking at the Miller girls, worry so clearly etched in their faces.

"Unless we know there's foul play or that he's injured in some way, it's out of our hands. We just don't have much to go on."

Anne told him about their conversation with Scott Milhouse.

"That had to have happened before the car accident if he was getting gas," Officer Banks said, basically repeating what Anne had said to Remi.

Anne said good-bye, then hit *end* on her cell phone.

"So they're just giving up?" Bella said, shaking her head and running her hands through her thick curly hair.

"That's not what he said," Anne said. "They'll keep a lookout. If they see him they'll stop him."

"But that's not the same as searching for him," Remi said.

No, it wasn't. Not the same at all.

* * *

That afternoon, when Anne returned to the library, she and the twins made a list of everyone they could think of who might be able to offer them insight into what had happened to Lucas Miller. They sat around one of the small tables in the Nonfiction Room. First on the list were the members of the writers' group—Marta Henshaw, Wendy Pyle, Mildred Farley, Douglas Pauthen, Garret Jones, Rita Sloan, Charlotte and Henry Jordan, and Alex Ochs.

"How about Dad's friend Mitch?" Remi added. Mitch Bach had been a friend of Lucas since high school days. "He and Dad do everything together. If there's anyone he'd confide in, other than Mom, it'd be him."

Anne added his name.

Betty Bultman came over. "I need to get home soon," she said, motioning to the desk. "Bob invited some of the city council members over for supper, so I need to get started on that."

Anne rose to her feet. "Thanks for everything, Betty."

The woman's gaze turned to the teenagers. "It's my pleasure."

"I'll check those books in," Bella said, moving to the big desk and reaching for the stack alongside the computer, "while you start calling."

"Deal." Anne smiled at the pretty brunette.

Remi moved toward a pile of DVDs that needed to be set straight and returned them to the drawer where they were stored.

Anne's first call was to Charlotte and Henry Jordan at the Blue Hill Inn. They were fellow members of the writers' group.

Charlotte picked up. "Blue Hill Inn. This is Charlotte." She was all business.

"Good afternoon," Anne said, telling her the reason for her call before adding, "The Millers have asked me to help them find Lucas. I was wondering if you remember anything from that night, anything Lucas might've said or done that seemed unusual."

"*Hmm*," Charlotte paused. "Do you have some time? I'd prefer to talk in person."

Anne glanced up at Mildred who was watching expectantly. "Like now?"

"Uh-huh," Charlotte replied. "I don't have anything pressing that needs to be done, so…"

"Go!" Bella whispered.

"Sure, I could come over," Anne said, "Is it okay if I bring Mildred along?"

"Of course."

Anne was surprised the twins didn't push to go along, but they insisted Charlotte might talk about their father more openly to just Anne and Mildred.

On the drive from the library to the Blue Hill Inn, Anne took a side road that meandered up a hill overlooking town. The view was breathtaking—the water tower glinted silver and the historic buildings of downtown Blue Hill looked like a quaint New England village.

"What a view," Anne said as she made her way down to Main Street and parked the car in the small gravel lot alongside the three-story brick structure.

Mildred seemed lost in it too. "I sometimes forget what a pretty place we live in."

The grounds of the Blue Hill Inn were well manicured. Tall oak trees circled in hostas surrounded the stately bed-and-breakfast, and a wide wraparound porch hugged three sides. White wicker rocking chairs lined the front, separated by thick Boston ferns on wicker tables that looked like they'd always lived there. The image could've been a photograph from a magazine.

Charlotte Jordan came out the front screen door, which slammed shut behind her. She was a trim woman with short-cropped white hair, and she wore wire-rimmed glasses. She nodded as she walked down the tall front stairs of the porch.

"Thanks for coming out," Charlotte said. "I just hate talking on the phone." She motioned toward the chairs on the porch. Mildred and Anne took seats, pausing to take in the beautiful view of the valley and enjoy the warm breeze.

"Would you like something to drink?" Charlotte offered. "I just made some fresh lemonade."

"That sounds lovely," Mildred said. As Charlotte returned inside to gather their beverages, Mildred turned to Anne and said in a loud whisper, "I could get used to living like this."

Henry, Charlotte's husband, came up the stairs from the yard. "What do we have here?" he said as the corners of his gray eyes crinkled up. He pulled off some gardening gloves and slipped them into the basket he'd carried up the steps.

"We came by to talk to you and Charlotte about Lucas Miller," Anne explained. "See if there is anything you can think of that can help us figure out where he went."

Henry gave his head a shake and stuffed his hands into his pockets. "It's a sad, sad state of affairs."

Charlotte returned with a tray that she set on the low wicker coffee table in front of them. It held a glass pitcher of lemonade with slices of lemon and pale butter cookies on delicate china plates.

"Anne told you why they're here?" she addressed her husband. He nodded, though he remained standing, arms crossed in front of him as he leaned against one of the white columns.

"The only thing that comes to mind is when he and Joyce came to stay here at the inn," Henry said.

Charlotte bent to pour out the beverages, handing one to each person, then offering the cookies.

"It wasn't that long ago," he added, "maybe a couple of months?"

Charlotte lifted her head to look at her husband. "It was in February, right around Valentine's Day. Her folks gave them the weekend here as a gift." Finally, she took a seat on an adjoining chair.

"So what was it about that weekend that caught your attention?" Anne said.

"They're a very nice couple," Charlotte put in first, as if apologizing for what she had to say next. "It was that night, though—they got into a very loud argument. Disturbed our other patrons." She took a sip of her lemonade before her husband picked it up.

"We almost called the police," Henry added. "They seemed to calm down on their own. But we don't get that a lot here. People come to celebrate, they're relaxed..." He reached for one of the butter cookies, then straightened back up as he took a bite. "It just seemed unusual."

"Did they ever say anything about it?" Anne asked.

Charlotte shook her head. "We were all too embarrassed to say anything. They left early the next day, didn't even stay for breakfast."

"I didn't know the man all that well," Henry added. He crossed his ankles and placed a hand on his hip. "I'm sorry to hear that he's missing and all, but he never really seemed the writer type, did he?"

"What do you mean?" Anne asked.

"Well, he didn't fit the type. He always struck me as too…" He searched for the right word, finally coming up with, "pretty."

He did have a bit of a Beach-Boy look, Anne had to admit, but that didn't preclude him from being a writer, or from being intelligent.

Charlotte didn't seem to agree. She shook her head. "We all know how good the man was at writing. His pieces were always very impressive, but if you met him on the street you never would peg him as a writer—that's what I think Henry is saying. Am I right, dear?"

"I can see your point," Anne said.

"Well, anyway," Charlotte added, sighing as if to take a moment to think. "Oh! There was something else." She snapped her fingers. "Didn't Rita say something about someone breaking into her house last week?"

Mildred sat forward and met Anne's gaze, her thin eyebrows lifting. "She did."

"When we got home from the writers' meeting, we could see that someone had tried to get into our private residence. We always keep it locked with so many guests coming and going. We would've assumed it was one of them if Rita hadn't just told us the story of her place being broken into. And the thing is none of our things were missing, that we could see."

"But the door had definitely been jimmied open," Henry added.

CHAPTER FOUR

It's not unusual for couples to argue," Mildred said as they made their way back toward the library.

"No," Anne agreed, "but the break-in. That has me concerned." She glanced at her watch, realizing it was almost time for her children to get out of school. She dropped Mildred off at her house, then returned to the library just as Wendy dropped Liddie and Ben off at the door.

Once the library was closed for the day and Anne fixed a quick supper, the Miller twins offered to stay and help Liddie pack for her time with her grandparents. Why the five-year-old thought she needed to pack anything mystified Anne—they would be home each night. Still Liddie had said it wouldn't be a vacation unless she could pack a bag.

"Mom's working the late shift at the hospital anyway," Bella said. Joyce worked as an RN at the Emergency Room in Deshler. "Being with Ben and Liddie will distract us from that big, lonely house."

Anne had to admit her kids seemed to like the attention of the older girls.

"She's already back at work?" Anne asked.

Remi shrugged. "She says there's nothing else she can do. She might as well keep her job."

"It's better than staying in bed all day," Bella added.

"What do you mean by that?"

"Just that if Mom isn't pushing herself to keep going, that's her usual response."

Then Bella and Remi headed into Liddie's room in search of items to add to her backpack.

As she tidied the cluttered living room, Anne could hear the girls laughing. Yet, she couldn't get Bella's comment out of her head. Was Joyce prone to depression? Was that what the girl had implied?

Anne picked up the phone and called Reverend Tom.

The man knew her well enough that small talk wasn't needed. Anne got right to the point. "Has Joyce Miller ever come to you for counseling? Or maybe Joyce and Lucas together for marriage counseling?"

"Anne, whether they had or hadn't, I wouldn't be at liberty to say, for confidentiality's sake, without permission from Joyce," he said. "Although, evidently, you must believe they were having trouble."

"Well, considering that he just left her — yes. But even before that…like in February…"

"As I said, I really can't say…" Reverend Tom drew a deep breath. "But frankly, I didn't see this coming…"

"Neither did their daughters."

"Lucas and Joyce have come on missions trips with us. They came on that trip to Haiti — you should've seen Lucas with the kids at that orphanage in Cap-Haïtien …" His words trailed off. "I'm sorry," he finally added. "I realize I'm not much help."

* * *

Since Ben and Liddie were enjoying the attention of the Miller twins, Anne decided to head to Wendy Pyle's to talk things through. Her friend often had a way of seeing things from a different perspective than Anne, and she needed her insight.

When Anne knocked on Wendy's front door, Wendy waved her inside adding, "Don't mind the mess." Piles of shoes lay just inside the door, with a smattering of clothes, toys, and stacks of books next to a bowl full of keys on the entryway table.

Anne smiled to herself. It wasn't as if the house looked much different on "clean days." Wendy simply had more important things to attend to than scrubbing and vacuuming. Her home was a crazy-busy place with kids coming and going, as well as dogs and cats and an assortment of pet rodents. That was just how it was with a large family, Wendy would say in her easygoing way, usually followed by a chuckle.

Wendy offered Anne a seat on the midcentury white sectional couch and asked her daughter Hannah to bring them some tea. The fourteen-year-old gave her mother one of her "*You owe me, Mother*" looks, then moved into the kitchen to put the kettle on.

"I talked to Charlotte and Henry Jordan today," Anne said. She told her friend about the argument the couple had overheard, as well as the alleged break-in at the inn the night of Lucas's disappearance, adding Bella's comment about her mother sometimes not getting out of bed.

Wendy's brow furrowed the way it did when she was having a serious thought. Several of her kids bounced past, but she paid them no mind.

"It sounds pretty simple," she finally said. "They were having trouble. How many of us really know what's going on in our neighbors' houses? I mean *really?* We all put on happy faces and try to impress everyone else with how well we're doing. We try to sound perfect on Facebook, but the truth is, there isn't a one of us that isn't going through *something*." She shook her head, then added, "Sure, they were struggling. We're *all* struggling!"

"Struggling enough for Lucas to leave his family?"

"The jury's still out on that one. All I know is, I thought Lucas was a nice, decent guy. He adored those girls of his. Almost as much as Chad adores our girls."

"You thought he was a nice guy?" Anne said.

"Honey," Wendy said, reaching across the span that divided them and giving Anne's hand a squeeze. "He couldn't have raised such wonderful girls if he wasn't a solid father."

Wendy's words stayed with Anne as she drove home. She was right—Bella and Remi were wonderful girls—both 4.0 students, and they excelled at everything they did. They were confident, sweet, kind, and most importantly their faith in God was strong. Those traits didn't happen by accident. They were the result of parents who took time with their children, who showed them they were valued and loved. Lucas was a father who taught his girls self-respect—a rare thing in this day and age.

And yet he'd left them.

Anne shook her head as she turned onto the street that led to the library. None of it made sense.

Remembering that she had wanted to get ahold of Marta Henshaw, Anne dialed the woman's number. She would connect with the other writers from the critique group tomorrow when she could find the time. Marta had missed the meeting on Monday, though Anne had no idea why.

Finally, after several rings, her breathy voice came on the line. "This is Marta."

"Hey, Marta. This is Anne Gibson."

"Anne, what can I do for you?"

From her casual tone, it didn't sound as if she'd heard the news. "I don't know if you heard – Lucas Miller has gone missing."

"Lucas Miller? Are you sure?"

"It happened Monday night after our writers' meeting. He disappeared without a trace."

Dead silence filled the line.

Anne waited, wondering why Marta wasn't saying anything. Finally, Anne said, "Marta? Are you there?"

Marta cleared her throat. "I'm here. I'm just so shocked. Do the police know anything?"

"The police found his car wrapped around a tree on Tuesday, but Lucas hasn't been heard from since. He left a note telling his wife that he was leaving her."

"Leaving?" She seemed truly stunned. "I don't…" She seemed at a loss for words. "So why are you calling me – do you think I know where he is?"

"I'm wondering if Lucas might've said something to you. Maybe something that seemed odd…anything really that sticks out in your mind."

Again there was a long silence. "No…nothing."

"He mentioned that you edit his writing…"

"Um…uh…yeah," Marta said, sounding uncomfortable. "They were just manuscript pages. Lucas wasn't always the best speller…" Her words trailed off. "You know" – her voice suddenly got louder—"I really need to get going. I forgot I have an appointment."

"Oh," Anne said, a bit startled. But by the time she had a chance to say anything, the line had gone dead.

Anne told herself that Marta was just upset that an acquaintance had gone missing. Yet, a niggling sense told her there was more to it. What was it about those manuscript pages? She thought of the odd codes in the margins. She'd have to ask Marta about those the next time they talked. She guessed the woman wouldn't pick up if she called her back right now.

So she dialed Joyce instead, forgetting that she was working that night and likely wouldn't have her cell turned on. Anne left a message asking if she had talked to Lucas's boss about his disappearance, then she hung up as she reached home.

The Miller girls had set up a giant tent of blankets in Liddie's room. Anne smiled at the sight from the doorway as sounds of giggling emerged from its lighted depths.

"If I find you, I'm going to eat you!" Remi said to Liddie's obvious delight, telling an old campfire story that Eric had often told Ben when he was little.

"*Ew!* That's gross," Liddie complained, collapsing in a pile of giggles at the story's end. Bella tickled her and the girls looked up, realizing Anne was watching them.

"Hey, Mommy!" Liddie said, hopping to her feet. "Remi was just telling me a story."

"I heard." Anne smiled at the girls. "But it's time for this girl to get ready for bed."

The five-year-old's shoulders slumped. "Do I have to?"

"Yes you do, young lady. You have a full day ahead of you tomorrow."

Liddie turned to the twins and informed, "My Grandma and Grandpa Gibson are coming!" Her little eyes shone.

"Well, you better get your sleep then," Bella said. "You'll want to be well rested for that!"

Liddie turned back to her mother. "Can I sleep in the tent?" She motioned to her bedroom, where one blanket was clipped to another and draped across every chair and bedpost.

"I don't see why not."

Liddie jumped up and down, then rushed to get her pajamas out of her dresser. She stopped in front of Bella and Remi and said, "Thank you for the fun night!" and kissed them each on the cheek before she bounded off for the bathroom.

"How do you keep up with her?" Remi asked, slumping back into a chair.

"I don't even try," Anne said. There was a long moment of quiet before Anne added, "This meant a lot to her—thanks."

"Oh, no problem," Bella said. "You're already doing so much for us…"

"Hey, I tried your mom. Do you know the phone number for where your dad works? Do you know if anyone called them?"

"I have no idea. But I'm sure I have the number in my cell." Remi reached into her back pocket for her cell phone and, once she'd brought up the number, handed it to Anne.

It was after eight o'clock in the evening but Anne dialed it anyway. She knew no one would still be at work, but she figured she could always leave a voice mail for someone to call her back. A man's voice came on the line after a couple rings. Anne introduced herself and discovered that she was talking to the owner.

She said, "I'm calling for Lucas Miller's family. They asked me to look into what might have happened to him."

"I already told the police everything I know.

"I thought perhaps he might've said something at work that could help us track him down."

"It looks like I'm not going to be a whole lot of help, ma'am. Lucas quit his job last week. Didn't even give a notice, just came in and said he was done, then packed his desk."

"He did?"

"I begged him to stay, even offered him a raise if he would stay. He's a good web designer. I told him that if he wanted to work remotely I'd be open to that..."

"And he still left?"

"He seemed to like working here too. I just don't understand it."

"When did you say that was?"

"A week ago."

"He didn't mention a word to me," Anne confessed. Joyce and the girls hadn't said anything about him quitting his job. Did they even know?

"How long has Lucas worked for you?"

"Lucas just started with us a few months ago. It was a big step up from his job at the casino in State College."

"Casino?" Anne repeated, surprised by this bit of information. She didn't realize Lucas had worked at a casino—it seemed an odd fit for the man who went on missions trips.

Had he been that desperate for a job that he would take something like that? Or was it simply writing research? He'd said he'd done that kind of thing before.

"I think he was a blackjack dealer there," the man went on. "Considering how brilliant he is, that seemed odd to me—why would a man who can do anything resort to dealing blackjack?"

"That's a good question," Anne agreed. She thanked the man for his time, then hung up the line.

Both girls were looking at her expectantly. But since they had already heard Anne's side of the conversation, there was no dodging their questions.

"Dad quit his job at Tangled Web?"

"He didn't tell you?"

The girls looked at each other. Clearly they had no idea.

Anne went on, "Did you know that he worked at a casino before that?"

"He did *not*," Remi protested.

"Are you sure?" Bella said.

"I'm not sure of anything anymore," Anne confessed.

"He would have told us if he quit his job…," Bella said. Then her voice trailed away as she seemed to realize there were many things their father failed to tell them.

Remi reached into her jeans pocket and pulled out her cell phone. She hit the *talk* button.

"Mom," she said leaving a voice mail, "we're at Mrs. Gibson's. Did you know Dad quit his job at Tangled Web a week ago? Or that he worked at a casino before that? Call me back when you get a chance."

Later, Remi's eyes filled with disbelief when her mother called her back on her break. Then Remi handed the phone to Anne.

Joyce sounded tired, beyond tired. "He quit?"

"That's what his boss said."

There was a long silence. "How did you find out about the casino job?" she asked.

"His boss told me that too," Anne said.

"I can't believe he didn't tell me he quit at Tangled Web. I knew about the job at the casino—it was the source of many arguments."

"Why didn't you tell me about that job?" Anne asked.

"I didn't see that it mattered. He quit there three months ago," she confessed. "I told him he took his writing research too far, that it could get him into trouble someday. He wasn't himself when he worked there." She paused. "I was so relieved, and he did seem to change for the better for a while. I thought our marriage would return to the way it had been before, but then things started to get worse..." There was another long pause. "He seemed so paranoid, nervous. There's something else I need to tell you...and don't get mad at me."

"Mad at you?"

She went on, "I found some notes in Lucas's clothes a few weeks ago. They looked like love letters from someone whose initials were MH. I can only assume that's Marta Henshaw. I didn't have the heart to confront Lucas with them..."

"Don't jump to conclusions."

"That's easy to say, Anne, but the more I find out, the less I realize I actually knew him. I thought that he loved me but..." She let out a heavy sigh. "Have you gotten ahold of Marta?"

"I talked to her earlier today," Anne admitted, wondering where this was going.

"Anne," she said, "I saw Lucas and Marta having lunch at the Keystone Café a week and a half ago."

"Were they being inappropriate in any way? Think about it—if there was anything underhanded going on, they wouldn't be out in such a public place."

"Or that's exactly why they went there, so people would think that very thing. No one would question it if they were in public... Or may be they were rubbing my nose in it."

"Do you really think Lucas would do that to you?"

"When I first saw them, I didn't think anything of it—though I couldn't tell you why I didn't go up to them...I just don't know."

Anne ached for her, but she had no idea how to comfort her. Her only real hope was that the truth would show her she was wrong. If only she could find out what that truth was.

CHAPTER FIVE

Anne asked Joyce to bring the notes she'd found over to the house on Thursday morning. She had to admit that they did look suspicious, although there was nothing overtly romantic in their content. Simply *Meet me at Rosehill Park at 3:00*, and, *I got your message. I'll let you know…*

"With the note he left in the car…it's just more of the same," Joyce said, shaking her head.

After Joyce left, Anne pulled out her Bible and nestled in her favorite chair in the living room. Morning sunlight shone through the wavy windowpanes.

She knew that time in the Word would bring the clarity she needed. Not that God would somehow tell her where Lucas was or make the hurt the Millers faced magically go away. But spending time talking to Him, hearing from Him, reset her heart, reminded her that the One who made the universe loved her, loved those that she cared about, like the Millers. It never failed to bring her the peace she needed.

Hershey padded into the room and lay down, watching her with his big brown eyes.

She turned to the story of Zacchaeus in Luke chapter nineteen, but it was verse ten that gave her pause. "For the Son of Man came to seek and to save the lost."

"Lord," she said, her eyes still on the verse, "seek and save Lucas Miller, because he is lost right now, in a very real and tangible way."

It was a half hour until the library was due to open on Thursday, and the kids were at school. So Anne decided to make the rest of the calls she'd wanted to make to the writers in the critique group.

Douglas Pauthen was her first call. A regular patron of the library and a fellow member of Blue Hill Community Church, Douglas was also a retired army captain.

"Yes, ma'am," he said when Anne asked him if he'd heard of Lucas's disappearance. Then he added, "If he'd stuck to his own business, not meddled in other people's affairs, this wouldn't have happened."

"What do you mean?" Anne asked.

"I don't know if I ever told you this," Douglas went on. "But I knew Mr. Miller when he was younger. He served under me briefly in the military."

"He did?"

"Oh yes. But that boy didn't have discipline, couldn't take an order to save his life."

"Was he dishonorably discharged?"

The former captain cleared his throat. "Well, no. But I've seen his type. They come into the army thinking it's a cakewalk. Well, I'll tell you it's no cakewalk. We work hard! We keep our bodies and our minds sharp! You know..." Anne could tell just by his tone that he was changing subjects. "Officer Banks already called me with questions. Inferred that Lucas was involved in something illegal with all these strange occurrences going on."

Anne was surprised to hear this bit of information. "What strange occurrences?"

"The break-ins. He said that I should lock my house if I think someone is sneaking around outside. Or call the police. Now, I ask you, why would someone come around my place? It's not like I have a lot of valuables — unless they are Civil War buffs, I suppose. I do have a few firearms that might be of interest for someone like that. But of course that wouldn't have been Lucas."

"I suppose not," Anne agreed. "You said something earlier that I want to get back to — what did Lucas meddle in that caused all this?"

"Did I say that? I'm getting older, you know."

"Yes, you did." She waited a breath. "Do you know what happened to Lucas Miller, Douglas? Do you have any idea where he could have gone?"

There was a long silence. "I'm sorry, Anne, I really am," he finally said. "But I really can't say."

The rest of the phone calls were far less ambiguous and peculiar. Rita Sloan from the bank repeated over and over in her sweet high-pitched voice, "It's just not right. It's just not right."

Anne asked, "Do you think your break-in could be connected somehow to Lucas?"

"I don't see how. And I heard about Charlotte and Henry's break-in. That happened during our meeting on Monday so Lucas *couldn't* have been involved — he was with us."

"That's true," Anne conceded.

"To be honest," she went on, "I really don't know Lucas all that well other than seeing him in the bank every once in a while and of course at the writers' meetings. It was so generous of him to start that group. He's always so cordial."

Anne thanked her and hung up.

No one appeared to have seen anything unusual, no clue that the man was intending to leave his family and everyone he knew in one fell swoop. Though all agreed that Lucas hadn't been quite himself lately. He seemed nervous, anxious, they'd said. Almost as if he was afraid that something might happen... *Or he was seeing Marta Henshaw behind his wife's back*, the uncharitable thought pushed in.

Anne couldn't deny the connection of a number of occurrences. Each member of the group, except Douglas, told of a car being broken into, CDs stolen from a desk at work, people sneaking around their houses late at night. There was definitely something else going on here, and she'd give her eyeteeth to bet that they had something to do with Lucas Miller.

* * *

Ryan Slater came home with Ben after school. Ben wanted him to meet his grandparents, and since they weren't coming until the evening the boys thought it was the perfect excuse to "hang out for a while" to celebrate the last day of school.

The two boys had become inseparable since Anne and the children had moved to Blue Hill. Raised by his uncle Alex Ochs since the death of his parents in a car accident, Ryan had a lot in common with Ben—the death of parents, as well as a love of Spider-Man and soccer.

"How is your bedroom remodel coming along?" Anne asked Ryan over supper.

Ryan seemed surprised that Anne knew about it. "Uncle Alex is thinking about putting in a batting cage."

"*Inside* the house?"

He nodded.

Anne looked from him to her own two children. Ben was nodding his head, and saying, "That's sweet!"

Liddie was shaking her head in disbelief.

"How's he going to do that without windows getting broken?"

Ryan shrugged. "You know Uncle Alex—he'll make sure it's safe."

"I suppose."

Anne's in-laws arrived at seven. Anne had been in the backyard, cleaning up after Hershey, when they pulled in. Byron climbed out of the tall motor home followed by Marlene. Byron was a short man with graying hair and pale blue eyes. Marlene was petite, shorter than her husband, with pewter hair cut in a chin-length bob. Her brown eyes were the exact same shade as Liddie's.

"How was your trip?" Anne asked as she leaned to give her father-in-law a hug followed by a hug for her mother-in-law.

"It was just fine," Byron said.

"Thankfully we have that GPS," Marlene added, "or your father-in-law would've gotten lost about three times."

"She thinks!" The man's eyes twinkled.

Alex Ochs pulled up just then in his pickup. He climbed out of his car and said, "Hey, I thought I'd better come by and get Ryan out of your hair."

"He's never a bit of trouble, but I'll run and grab him for you. Before I do, though, I'd like to introduce you to my in-laws," Anne said, nodding in their direction. "Byron, Marlene, I'd like you to meet Alex Ochs. Alex, Byron and Marlene Gibson."

"We are pleased to make your acquaintance, Alex," Marlene said as Byron and Alex exchanged handshakes. "If you don't mind my asking, how is it you know Anne?" Marlene asked.

"I can't remember a time when I didn't know Anne," Alex admitted.

"Really?" Marlene's gaze shifted to her daughter-in-law.

"We went to school together," was all Anne offered. She wasn't about to tell her mother-in-law that she and Alex had dated for a few years in high school, though no doubt his name had come up here and there over the years.

"This is quite the setup you have here." Alex motioned to the enormous motor home.

"It'll be our retirement eventually," Byron said.

"For now we're taking the grandchildren on some excursions in it," Marlene added.

"Byron and Marlene are professors at Cornell University," Anne said. "Dad teaches Comparative Literature. And Mom is in the psychology department."

"That's great," Alex said.

When Anne had first met her in-laws, they seemed like such formal people, so proper in their interactions. Marlene was always cleaning her house, a perfectionist in everything she did. Byron was a bit more laid back, the kind of man she'd picture with patches on the elbow of his smoking jacket and an opinion on every subject. Anne had never felt she quite measured up to their expectations for a daughter-in-law. Yet, that had all somehow faded as she got to know them. She appreciated them, with all their little quirks, and the way they'd raised their son.

Then, once Eric died and they both became the only tie to him, a strong bond had grown. Anne felt sorry that it had happened after her husband was gone—he would have enjoyed seeing that connection when he was alive.

"So you're a friend of Anne's..." Marlene looked from one to the other.

Alex nodded. "We dated in high school before she moved off to the big city and married your son." He gave Anne a wink that caused a blush to flame up her cheeks. Why had he said that? She wanted to kick him good and hard.

Marlene didn't say anything.

Before Anne could excuse herself to fetch Ryan, all three kids came rushing down the stairs and onto the back lawn behind the library with Hershey following.

"How are my grandchildren?" Byron asked as Ben and Liddie flew to him, offering hugs and kisses. Liddie was bouncing up and down like a jumping jack.

"Did you bring me something, Grandpa?" She clapped her hands together.

"Bring you something?" His eyebrow lifted and Marlene chuckled.

"Liddie," Anne scolded.

"Don't tease the poor child, Byron!" Marlene said.

Byron climbed back into the motor home and soon emerged with a small box. Liddie quickly tore off the wrapping paper.

The five-year-old twisted her face. "What is it?"

"It's a kaleidoscope." He showed her how to look into it and give it a turn. Liddie grinned.

"It changes designs!" she oohed, still gazing into the tube.

Byron handed the other gift in his hands to Ben. Ben pulled off the wrapping paper. Inside was a stack of old Spider-Man comic books.

"Spider-Man!" Ben's eyes grew wide. "These are super old, aren't they, Grandpa?"

"They sure are," he said, giving the boy a nudge. "They were your dad's when he was your age."

Ben's eyes shot to Anne's. "Cool!" he said, awe infusing the word. "Look at these!" He held the books up for Ryan to see. His friend seemed duly impressed.

"He loves Spider-Man," Anne said.

"I found them in the attic," Marlene said to Ben, "and I knew they were meant for you."

"They're in perfect condition!" Ben was still in awe. He ran a hand across the cover. "Want to go read them?" he said to Ryan.

"Sorry, bud," Alex said to his nephew. "We need to head on home."

Ryan gave a groan, but he followed his uncle and waved good-bye to Ben as he climbed into Alex's pickup truck.

Everyone watched as Alex backed up and moved down the street. Marlene squeezed Anne's hand. "I'm so glad to be here," she said.

* * *

Marlene, Byron, and the kids headed out first thing the next morning. Anne stood in the driveway and waved good-bye as a sense of loneliness overtook her. They'd be back that night, and yet Anne wished she were going with them. She hated missing out on the memories they would make, the places they'd see together, the joy on those little faces.

Yet, she knew that today would be crazy at the library. The first day of summer reading always was.

Families lined up to enroll in the program almost from the moment she unlocked the doors for the day. Wendy and Remi came to help. They scurried about as Anne stood all day, telling children about the program, how many books they'd need to read to earn the various prizes, showing them the calendar of events and the wall of photos with the construction paper title that read *Get Caught Reading* where they could add their pictures.

When nine o'clock rolled around that night and Byron and Marlene still weren't back from their day trip with the kids, Anne mused over how strange it felt to have a quiet house to herself after her workday was done. Hershey looked at her with concern in his brown eyes. As if to say, "What happened to Liddie and Ben?"

Anne patted him on the head. "I know, boy. I miss them too."

He moved to the door and whined. Anne took him down the back stairs and watched him from the steps. He sniffed around the yard.

There had been no forward movement on figuring out what happened to Lucas Miller. She simply hadn't had time to look into it. Remi hadn't said a word about it. But Anne had seen the despair on the girl's face all day.

Learning that her father quit his job and hadn't told her must've felt terrible. Anne understood. It led to other questions.

What else hadn't they known about the man?

She couldn't begin to imagine the hurt of such secrets. It was as if they didn't even know the man they loved the most. It made them doubt everything about him.

How would Anne have felt if she'd discovered that Eric had a secret life? She shivered at the thought.

And yet… they *had* known Lucas. He was a decent man who loved his children and his wife. They hadn't imagined that. How did anyone reconcile such disparate thoughts?

But people always warred with two sides, didn't they?

Even the apostle Paul said he did the things he didn't want to do and didn't do the things he longed to do. Lucas was no different. He simply needed to turn back to what God had created him to be. Silently Anne sent a prayer heavenward, knowing that with God even the impossible was a small task.

As she turned to head back inside, she saw her in-laws' motor home turn into the driveway for the library. She let Hershey in the door and waited for them to get out.

Liddie climbed down the tall steps first.

"Did you have fun?" Anne asked.

The little girl's eyes were tired, but she nodded her head. They had spent the day at Hershey Park, in the famed city of Hershey, and at Chocolate World.

Her eyes grew round as she remembered something. "Grandpa went on the Sooperdooperlooper!"

Known for its twists and turns, the ride was one of the most well-known, spirited rides at the amusement park.

"Really, Dad?" Anne looked to Byron. "You went on the Sooperdooperlooper?"

He shrugged. "I've always liked a good roller coaster."

Anne turned to Ben. "Did you have fun too?"

The boy nodded, then said, "I'm tired. I'm going to head up to bed."

"What do you say to Grandma and Grandpa?"

He turned. "Thank you, Grandma and Grandpa Gibson."

Marlene bent to kiss him on the top of his head. Byron tousled his hair.

"See you in the morning," Marlene said. "We have another fun day planned."

The boy nodded and headed for the door.

"How about you?" Anne said to Liddie. She yawned wide and managed a sleepy good night to her grandparents.

"Want to come up for a late cup of coffee? I have decaf," Anne offered.

They followed her up the stairs. "Did you learn anything about that friend of yours?" Marlene asked. "The one who went missing?" Anne had told them about Lucas's disappearance when they'd chatted late the night before.

"No. Unfortunately," Anne said. "It was just too busy today."

When they reached the top of the stairs, Anne could hear the water running in the bathroom where the kids were brushing their teeth.

"Thank you for taking them today."

"We had as much fun as they did." Byron's eyes gleamed.

"Yes, your father-in-law was a kid in a candy shop," Marlene said. "He was pulling them from one ride to the next. It's a good thing Liddie is too short to ride most of the big rides or I would've been lonely all day." She smiled at her husband, who had taken a spot at the small kitchen table.

Anne moved to make a pot of coffee. They talked for a while about the day, and Anne could see the joy in their faces, having time with their son's children.

"So," Byron said, "you seem to like living in a small town again."

Anne paused to consider before she answered. "Don't get me wrong—there was a lot I loved about living in New York. The vibrancy of being around people, that hum of life that seems always present, not to mention the convenience of having every possible need met in a moment's notice, but there's a lot to be said for life in a small town too."

Marlene stirred creamer and sugar in her coffee, then sat back to sip.

"I enjoy always seeing people I know," Anne went on, "people who stop and chew the fat at the grocery store—though that means it's *never* a quick trip. And I can't go looking like a grub either." They laughed. "Knowing and being known has its advantages and its disadvantages." She paused and looked around the small kitchen.

It had been fully renovated when she and the kids moved in, and yet it still held the essence of Anne's great-aunt who'd lived in the place so many years before her. She was the reason Anne was here, having given this house to Anne and to the city of Blue Hill as its library.

"I like being the person in charge," Anne said, "and carrying on Aunt Edie's legacy. That means a lot to me."

"She sounds like a pretty amazing woman, from what little I knew of her," Marlene said, taking a sip of coffee.

"She was," Anne agreed.

"So what did she do for a living?"

Anne chuckled. "That's a good question. She did a little of everything, I've been discovering. She was an accomplished artist and photographer. She spent time as a travel writer..."

"She sounds like our kind of people," Byron said.

"She sure was. Living in her house is like having a part of her here."

"I think Eric would've liked raising the kids in such a setting," Marlene said, her gaze filling with memory. She took a deep draft of coffee as silence fell across them.

"I thought Dad said no dwelling," Anne reminded, good-naturedly.

She reached to pat Anne's hand. "Seeing you and the kids — it's hard not to dwell just a bit." She took another sip. "Say, do you have any recent photos of the kids? I got some new five-by-seven frames. I figured you must have school photos."

"Of course," Anne said. "I'm not totally sure where they are, but I'll dig them out during your stay."

"So..." Byron cleared his throat. "What's up with Ben? Has he been doing okay in school?"

"He's doing okay. Why? Was he acting up today?"

"No, no," Marlene said, sending her husband a scolding look. "He was just fine."

But Anne could tell something was amiss.

"He wasn't bad," Byron amended. "He just seemed quiet. And when I asked him how his school year had gone, he really clammed up."

"I'll ask him about it."

"Oh, don't please," Marlene said. "We don't want him feeling that Grandma and Grandpa tattle on him for every little thing."

"Okay," Anne said tentatively.

"So...," Byron said. "That young man who was here yesterday—are you two seeing each other?"

"Young man?" Anne asked.

"The one who was picking up his son from playing with Ben?"

"Oh, Alex?" Anne felt instantly uncomfortable. "That's his nephew. His sister and brother-in-law were killed in a car accident, so Alex is raising him."

"He said you two dated in high school," Marlene said. "What happened to that?"

"I left for college, then I met Eric and fell in love," Anne said with a shrug. "There was never any comparison between the two."

"And what about now?" Marlene asked.

Anne shook her head. "No," she insisted. "We've moved on. I've been too busy with work and the kids to think about dating."

"It has been three years," Byron said.

"Are you kidding me? I'm just..." She paused, looking them each in the eyes. "I'm not interested."

Alex was a friend. That was all.

An uncomfortable silence followed. Each sipped from their mug of coffee.

"Well." Byron looked at his watch. "I suppose we'd better hit the hay."

They excused themselves to head to bed, giving Anne a kiss on the cheeks in East Coast fashion before padding down the staircase to their home away from home.

Anne finished getting herself ready for bed, then poked her head in the kids' rooms to see if they'd gone to sleep. Liddie was snoring softly, her little mouth wide open. Anne pulled the blankets up to her chin, then kissed her on the cheek.

When she went to check on Ben, he was still awake, his bedside lamp glowing. Anne sat alongside him on his bed.

"You have fun today?" she asked.

She brushed back his bangs as he nodded.

"That doesn't sound very enthusiastic. Are you sure?"

He shrugged.

"You like spending time with Grandma and Grandpa, don't you?"

Another nod.

Clearly the boy didn't want to talk about whatever was going on. But she didn't push. She knew Ben would open up when he was ready to share what was in his heart.

"Well, you need your sleep if you're going to head out again tomorrow."

"G'night, Mom." He scooted down in his covers.

"Good night, sweetie." She moved toward the door.

"Mom?"

She turned back to him.

"I love you."

"I love you too, Ben."

As Anne climbed into bed, she thought about her father-in-law's question—was she dating Alex? The whole idea of dating was absurd. She didn't want to add the complications of a dating life to raising Ben and Liddie. Besides, how could she ever find the kind of love she'd had with Eric again in this lifetime? It had been a rare thing the first time around. To hope for it again was asking too much.

Her mind moved back to the day she had to call Byron and Marlene to tell them that their son had passed away. Marlene had answered the phone. Anne could still hear the shrill keen of a mother's loss when she finally got the words out. Then the funeral had come. Through it all, Byron and Marlene had been so kind to Anne.

Yet, Anne had felt a hesitation on their part toward her. She worried that they subconsciously blamed her for Eric's passing, for not seeing the signs of his ill health before his heart attack. Who died of a heart attack in their forties?

She lifted her face to the ceiling as the old emotions washed over her. Guilt. Grief. How could she not have seen that he had heart disease? She knew it was more likely her own sense of blame than anything Byron and Marlene put on her—they'd certainly never said a word.

But then how could they? When their son was gone and two of their grandchildren were in her care?

CHAPTER SIX

Byron and Marlene had decided to leave for their next adventure a little later on Saturday. They, as much as the kids, needed the sleep after their exhausting time at Hershey Park. They'd asked Anne to join them, but with the library open in the morning, she wouldn't be free until the afternoon. So the motor home was still parked in the driveway when Alex Ochs stopped over before the library opened.

"I can't get over that rig out there," he remarked as he came in the back door.

Anne smiled. "Byron's always wanted to travel the country."

Alex nodded, appreciation in his expression.

Her conversation with her in-laws flickered in her memory like a scene from a movie. Dating Alex? As much as she liked Alex as a friend, she certainly wasn't ready to entertain romantic notions or even date him...date anyone, for that matter.

"What can I do for you?" Anne asked, shaking the thought aside.

Ben came out of his bedroom dressed for the day. He carried the stack of Spider-Man comic books his grandparents had given him. When he saw Alex, his face scrunched up oddly.

Alex went on, "Ryan mentioned that he really likes Ben's bookcase. He's hoping I can build something similar for his room, but I can't for the life of me remember what it looks like."

"Go have a look," she said, motioning toward Ben's room as the buzzer for the intercom sounded. "Let me get that." She moved toward the intercom. "Hello."

A man's voice answered. "Is this Anne Gibson?"

"Yes."

Alex moved toward Ben's room, tousling the sleepy boy's hair as he passed him. Ben shrugged away and moved alongside his mother. "Mom," he said. Anne shushed him.

"I am Detective Bentley with the State Police," the baritone voice said. "Officer Banks mentioned that you had talked to some folks about Lucas Miller..."

"Yes, I have," Anne said hesitantly. She hoped he wasn't about to forbid her from doing any more research into Lucas's disappearance. She'd wanted to talk to Lucas's friend Mitch Bach today, perhaps Garret Jones, the last of the writers from the critique group, as well as try to get ahold of Lucas's publisher in New York. Surely Lucas would maintain contact with them.

"I was hoping I could talk to you about Miller," the man said.

"I don't understand," Anne said. "Why wouldn't Officer Banks call me?"

"You know how it is on these missing persons cases," he said. "Local enforcement has enough on their hands with the everyday stuff. They hand it off to us..."

"Um. Okay. I'll be right down."

"But, Mom!" Ben insisted when Anne released the intercom button.

"What is it?"

"Why is Alex here?"

"He's just looking at your bookcase. Is there something wrong with that?" She moved back to look him in the eyes.

He crossed his arms over his chest.

"He's not going to take anything. The most he'll do is measure it. You heard him—he wants to build one like it for Ryan. Why don't you go in and watch him if it bothers you?" She turned to head toward the stairs, then added, "Make sure your sister is up and ready. I don't want Grandma and Grandpa to have to wait for you when they want to get going."

Ben huffed and moved off toward Liddie's room. The dog padded after him.

Anne shook her head. Something was definitely up with that boy. Anne made her way down the stairs to the detective who was waiting on the back steps.

Detective Bentley was a tall man with dark good looks and a deep dimple in his chin. Dressed in plain clothes, he had an erect carriage and a presence that demanded attention. He reached to shake Anne's hand as he flashed a badge with the other.

"I'm sorry to bother you at home," the detective said. When she looked into his eyes she noted that he had one blue eye and one brown eye, something she'd seen only a couple times in her lifetime. There was a small bandage on his forehead.

"Not at all," Anne said as they moved onto the back lawn. "I'm glad to know the police haven't given up on finding Lucas."

"His disappearance is suspicious," the man admitted.

Anne agreed.

"This is a nice place you have here." He motioned to the old Victorian and the surrounding property. "You live in the library?"

"We have a private apartment upstairs," Anne said. "It was my great-aunt's house. She left it to me...Anyway, long story." She cut it short, feeling oddly self-conscious with the man.

"Officer Banks mentioned that you've been exploring some of the circumstances surrounding Mr. Miller's disappearance, so I was hoping I could ask you a few questions."

"Of course," Anne said. She motioned toward the front porch. "Would you like to sit? It's a lovely day."

The handsome man nodded and they walked around to the front porch, settling in the chairs that faced the quiet street. It was a glorious summer day. The sky was a cerulean blue without a cloud in sight, and the temperature was just right, though Anne could tell that it would be plenty warm come afternoon. She glanced toward the motor home that was parked off to the side, seeing a glimpse of movement in its depths.

"What did you say your name was?" Anne asked.

"Detective Bentley." The man's smile was white. Anne noticed the lone car in front, which she assumed was his, a new-looking black sedan with a dented front left quarter panel. Perhaps it had been involved in one too many police chases. She wondered if it was a police-issued vehicle or his own.

"You're the librarian here in town," he began. "How do you know Mr. Miller?" He pulled out a pad of paper and a pen from his shirt pocket.

"Where did you say you're from?" Anne asked.

"State College. The local branch called me in."

"Have you discovered something new in the case?" she asked.

He nodded. "Seems Mr. Miller was working with someone who might've been involved in something illegal. We're trying to determine who that person was..." He met her eyes. "I can't really divulge much more. I hope you understand."

Anne thought of the break-ins and wondered if that was what he was referring to.

He went on, "I was hoping you could help shed some light on something for me."

"Me?"

"Did you know that Mr. Miller worked at a casino outside of State College?"

Anne nodded. "I did. Just found that out."

The detective raised a dark eyebrow. "Who told you?"

"His boss at Tangled Web. His wife confirmed it."

"Lucas was going by the name Lance Martin. Did you know that as well?"

"He was? I mean, I knew about him working at a casino but beyond that..."

"When did you last see Mr. Miller?"

"The night of the disappearance. He came to our writers' meeting here at the library."

"And who was at that meeting?"

"Oh, most of the regulars, except Marta Henshaw. She didn't come that night."

He asked her to list the names of the members, which Anne did.

"Was he acting unusual? Doing anything out of the ordinary?"

"Not particularly," she said. She waited while he wrote something down.

"Can I ask what you've found out in your research?" He looked up from his writing.

Anne told the man about the notes Joyce had found, as well as her seeing Lucas and Marta at Keystone Café, and Henry and Charlotte Jordan's belief that the Millers were having marital problems. Then she mentioned the strange encounter at the gas station with Scott Milhouse, and Lucas leaving behind the prized pen.

"What time was that?" the detective said in reference to the sighting at the station.

"A little after midnight, I think."

He scribbled the information down.

"Though I don't remember if Scott actually said that or if I just assumed it, because it was shortly after that Lucas's clock stopped working." She told him about the dashboard clock.

"12:31, you say?" The man seemed to contemplate this bit of information.

"I've been trying to get ahold of Lucas's best friend Mitch Bach," Anne added, "to see if he knows anything. But he hasn't answered my calls. I thought I'd stop at his place later today, after I close up the library."

"Do you mind if I come along to talk to Mr. Bach?"

"Um…sure," Anne said, surprised at the request from a police detective.

"It sounds like you're onto something," he explained, smiling. "I know it's a little unconventional, but if we work together we might be able to solve the case. Sometimes people tend to get too quiet when they know they're speaking directly to a police officer."

"That makes sense," Anne said.

"When do you close up?"

They agreed to talk to Mitch together a little after one o'clock. Detective Bentley was just climbing into his car when Alex came around from the back of the house.

"I was wondering where you went," Alex said to Anne as he looked curiously at the newcomer. The detective gave a wave, then backed out and moved down the road.

"Who was that?"

"Detective Bentley. He's been brought in on the Lucas Miller case."

"Really?" Alex raised a brow.

"Yeah, it struck me as unusual too." Anne shrugged, not totally sure what to make of it. "But it sounded like they'd discovered some new information." She told Alex about Lucas's pseudonym and the implication that he or at least someone he was involved with was doing something illegal, though the detective hadn't gone into detail about his discoveries. Anne wondered if that someone could be Mitch Bach…or Marta Henshaw.

"I wonder if that's why Lucas left the way he did," Alex said. "Without saying a word to anyone beforehand."

"There is a certain amount of sense to that," Anne conceded. She told him about their plan to talk to Mitch Bach later in the day.

"You mind if I tag along?" Alex asked.

"The more the merrier, I suppose."

* * *

Mitch Bach's apartment was above Coffee Joe's coffee shop, which sat between the sporting goods store and the health food store on

Main Street. A side door led up a narrow staircase to the second floor abode. When Detective Bentley saw Alex with Anne his brow furrowed and Anne noted those different-colored eyes again. There was something deeply intriguing about them.

"I hope you don't mind that I brought a friend along," Anne explained, introducing the two men on the sidewalk outside the door.

The detective reached to shake hands. "You can call me Judd," he said.

"Nice to meet you," Alex said.

"And you're a friend of Anne's?"

Alex passed her a look before saying, "Yeah. A good friend."

What did he mean by that? Anne felt irritation rise.

They climbed the staircase with the detective in the lead. It was a narrow space, and the three of them were practically touching shoulders as they stood on the small landing. Detective Bentley knocked loudly on the door. They could hear sounds from the interior and then finally it creaked open. A disheveled-looking man poked his head out.

"Yeah?" Mitch Bach had light brown hair and dark eyes. His face was rumpled with sleep despite it being after one o'clock in the afternoon. "Can I help you?" he said.

"Good afternoon," the detective said. He flicked open his badge, then shoved it back into his shirt pocket beneath his dark suit coat. "We're looking into the disappearance of Lucas Miller. We were hoping you could answer a few questions."

"Disappearance of Lucas?" Mitch looked surprised, then his face shifted, as if he were about to cry. "When? Why didn't anyone tell me? I've been trying to call him..." He shook his head.

"Can we come in?" Anne said, wanting to get out of the confining space.

"Sure, sure." Mitch moved aside, allowing the three to enter.

"I had no idea," he was saying as they took seats on a torn-up couch and an equally ratty looking La-Z-Boy chair. The apartment was long and narrow, with one room leading to the next like a shotgun house Anne had once vacationed at in the Carolinas. Though this place wasn't what one would call "vacation worthy." "Rats' nest" seemed a more apt description. There were messes everywhere and an odd sickly sweet smell coming from the front of the place.

"You haven't talked to Joyce or the girls?" Anne asked.

He shook his head. "Not lately. Joyce must be devastated. When did you say he disappeared?"

"Monday," Anne supplied, telling him about the accident as well.

"How do you know the Millers?" the detective asked, pulling out that pad of paper once again.

"I went to high school with Lucas. We've been best friends forever, since before he met his wife. Man…" He ran a hand through his hair which left it standing at spiky angles. "Those two have helped me through some pretty rough days. I've bunked on their couch when my wife kicked me out, when I lost my house… They've always been there for me."

"So you and Lucas are good friends?" Anne said.

"Yeah, man, Lucas and I are pretty inseparable."

His gaze shifted to the investigator. "Don't I know you from somewhere?"

The detective lifted an eyebrow, then shook his head. "I don't think so." He wore the same suit he'd worn that morning, dark, tailored. Sharp. He had the natural good looks of a model on the cover of GQ magazine.

Mitch shook his head as if he couldn't quite get rid of the notion that he'd seen the detective before.

"It must've been someone who looked like me," Detective Bentley said.

"Yeah, man," Mitch finally said. He looked over at Anne. "You're good lookin'," he said. "I wish I'd seen you before."

Anne ignored him. His eyes were rheumy and bloodshot, and he didn't seem to be completely present. He struck Anne as a shiftless type, the kind who had no inner angst about freeloading off of friends. From what he told them, he'd spent many nights doing just that, sleeping on the Millers' couch, eating their food.

She glanced around the apartment. It was filthy. Clothes and trash were scattered about, a half-eaten pizza in a cardboard box looked cold and shriveled on the coffee table that was piled high with dirty dishes and half-full cups and mugs, not to mention beer bottles. They were scattered around the apartment like Waldos in a *Where's Waldo?* book.

His glance kept turning to the detective, his eyes shifting, his hands never quite still. He seemed nervous, as if there was something he was hiding.

"How did you and Mr. Miller meet?" the detective was asking. They seemed pretty standard questions. So why was Mitch so nervous? She wondered if that had something to do with the smell. Was he a marijuana smoker?

"Did you know that Lucas had a job at a casino?" Anne finally asked.

Mitch's eyes widened. He looked like he was deciding whether to deny knowing anything about it or fess up, then realizing it was pointless, his shoulders lowered and he nodded. "Yeah, I knew."

"Was someone working with Mr. Miller? Perhaps you?" Detective Bentley said. His eyes narrowed, boring into the poor man.

"What do you mean—working with?" Mitch was utterly flustered. "He...he had a job dealing blackjack. That's all. Nothing wrong with that." He looked at Alex then. "There wasn't anything illegal. You know Lucas—he's a good guy. He'd never get in to anything like that."

"No one said anything about any illegal activities," Anne said. "Why do you think he was?"

Mitch seemed utterly confused. "I don't *think!* No, I mean! Like I said, Lucas would never..."

"Do you have any idea where Lucas could have gone?" Anne said.

But Mitch was shaking his head. "I got nothing, honey. I still can't get over any of this."

"That's okay," Anne assured him, adding a smile that seemed to calm the anxious man. "Maybe you know why he quit his job at Tangled Web or why he didn't tell his family?"

Mitch shrugged. He reached for a glass to take a drink, then realized it was empty and set it back down. "He figured they'd get upset, is my guess. Joyce always worried about him. Nagged him for taking too many risks..."

"And what was the risk at the casino?" Alex asked.

The detective shifted, leaning forward.

"She's just a worrywart." He looked over at Alex. "You know how wives are."

"No, actually," Alex said, "I don't."

"What casino was it?" Anne asked.

He gave her the location, on the highway outside of State College.

Anne went on. "How long did Lucas work there?"

"He quit that job three months ago. Why would that have anything to do with something going on now?" he said, essentially the same thing Joyce had said.

Anne couldn't answer that question. Mitch had a point. Yet, the fact that it was a secret seemed to make it pertinent, even if she couldn't pinpoint why. She waited and finally Mitch shrugged, unable, or more likely unwilling, to offer up more information on the matter.

"Lucas wrote a note to Joyce saying he was leaving them—did he mention anything to you about having trouble in his marriage?" Anne asked.

"No," he said after a long silence, then, "They had a good marriage." His face darkened for a moment. "I'll tell you one thing, if I had a pretty wife like that, you can bet I'd never cheat on her…or leave her."

"No one said anything about Lucas cheating on her," Alex said. "Do you know something?"

Mitch shook his head vehemently. "No. Lucas wouldn't do that—I know he wouldn't."

Detective Bentley said nothing, just exchanged a look with Anne and Alex.

"I mean…" Mitch began backpedaling. "Joyce is a pretty woman. Lucas loves her. He'd be a fool."

"What do you mean she's pretty?" the detective was like a dog on a rabbit.

"She's always been pretty. In high school…I'm not saying… I'd never…Lucas was my friend."

"And?" Detective Bentley said.

"And nothing!" Mitch was shouting. He jumped to his feet. "I'm done here. You get out!" He moved to the door swiftly, flinging it open. "Just go! This is ridiculous. I don't need to be accused of something I had no part in."

"No one was accusing you, Mitch," Anne tried to soothe, but Mitch heard none of it.

The three of them were soon back on the front sidewalk.

"What do you make of it?" Alex asked the detective.

He shrugged. "Hard to say. There might've been a relationship. Or maybe it was all in Mitch's head and he acted out of jealousy. Either way, that man is hiding something."

* * *

Since the kids were still out with their grandparents, Anne stopped at the Millers before heading back home. Remi and Bella were there, buried in books and papers on the kitchen table while Joyce scurried around making a late lunch.

Anne knocked on the screen door. She could hear the sounds of a ballgame on the radio.

"Oh, hey, Anne," Joyce said, as she motioned her inside. She turned down the volume. "Old habits," she admitted. "Lucas always had a game on. What brings you out?" She wore a faded yellow apron with flour smudged across its front.

It struck Anne how ordinary their Saturday seemed. The girls studying as they always did, Joyce cooking. They carried on as if their world hadn't just fallen apart. People were amazing in that—that they could go on even when everything around them seemed to deny that possibility. She supposed she'd done the same after Eric's death, yet the miracle of it never failed to impress her. People's resilience.

"I had a talk with Mitch Bach this afternoon, and I wanted to ask you about him. She took a seat alongside Bella.

"You met Mitch?" Joyce lifted an eyebrow. "He and Lucas have been best friends since high school. It's a friendship I wish had died years ago."

"Oh?" Anne said.

Joyce nodded. "When they were younger they got in trouble together. Lucas grew up, but Mitch never outgrew that. He was part of the reason Lucas and I argued so much. I told Lucas that he needed to stop coddling Mitch. Let him face the consequences of his actions, fall on his face a few times, and maybe he'd learn."

"Consequences of what actions?"

"The man is one big headache—*every* action he makes has some sort of negative consequence. Yet, Lucas would always take him in." Her lips formed a thin line. "He was the best man in our wedding…" Joyce's eyes clouded and she glanced at her daughters. "Lucas and I had been having more and more arguments lately," she admitted in a low voice. "I blamed Mitch.

He was the one who got Lucas the job at the casino. And then…
Mitch was leading him down a wrong path."

"How so?"

Joyce sighed. "The two of them were so…secretive." She
shook her head, obviously not wanting to say more in front of
the girls.

Anne led the way outside where the two of them could talk in
private. They moved to a pair of emerald-green Adirondack chairs
that faced each other on the lush back lawn. The summer day was
warm and glorious. Blue sky was endless. The yard was beautifully
manicured with flowerbeds that flowed from one space to the
next, a river of color.

"What do you mean — they were secretive?" Anne finally said.

"Lucas would come home late. He'd smell of smoke — of
course he said it was just part of working at the casino, that people
smoked there. But Mitch would be with him and it was obvious
that he had been drinking."

"Lucas too?"

"No. Mitch for sure. Lucas was never much of a drinker,
though he had his vices."

"And when he quit the job, did that behavior end?"

Joyce seemed unsure how to answer that question. Finally, she
said honestly, "I don't know, Anne." She seemed to study a squirrel
in the distance, chattering from one of the linden trees on the edge
of the property. "What killed me was that it wasn't like Lucas. He
was always *solid*." She clenched a fist as if to prove her point.
"Where Mitch was concerned, Lucas was always the leader in that
relationship. Mitch would follow along happily with whatever

Lucas cooked up. But it was like there was a shift..." She met Anne's gaze. "I don't know what it was."

Anne wasn't sure how to ask the next question. She felt her face flush. "Has Mitch ever been...inappropriate with you?"

Joyce's brow furrowed. "You mean did he ever make a pass at me?"

Anne nodded.

"All the time. Especially if he'd been drinking. I just ignored it. We did date briefly in high school, but it only took a couple of dates for me to realize I was going out with the wrong guy. Lucas and I started going out about a year after that."

"How did Mitch take that?"

"That was a long time ago..." Joyce paused to think back. "I suppose he took it kind of hard." She sat back. "What are you suggesting?"

"Well..." Anne waited as a car passed the house, slowing down at the corner before turning out of sight. "He mentioned losing his house, being divorced, having to sleep on your couch. Has he ever acted jealous of you and Lucas, like maybe if things had worked out between the two of you he could've had Lucas's life?"

She laughed at the idea. "That's just silly."

"I know it isn't a real possibility, but do you think it's something Mitch could think?"

"I suppose..." her words trailed off. "There's no way I'd ever look at Mitch that way." She met Anne's eyes. "Do you think Mitch had something to do with Lucas's disappearance? That he did something to Lucas?"

"Is it possible?"

Joyce ran a hand through her brown hair. Anne could see the turmoil the thought sent her through. Finally, she turned back to Anne, "Yes, I suppose it is possible. In this world where everything is suddenly upside down, I guess Mitch could be that mixed up." She furrowed her brow. "But why would Lucas have written that note if Mitch…?"

Anne shook her head. "I didn't say I had it all figured out."

"Lucas trusted him," Joyce said as if trying to wrap her mind around what Anne was suggesting.

Anne understood how hard it was to admit something so painful. To not notice something happening right under her nose…It was much like not noticing that Eric was having symptoms of heart disease. A part of her had wanted to ignore that something so horrible might be going on—it was no different for Joyce.

Joyce shivered, then hugged herself. She rose to her feet. "I need a little time. She turned to walk down the quiet lane, her arms crossed in front of her as she moved.

"You go right ahead," Anne said as the sun cast amber fingers across the western sky.

When Anne went back inside, Bella was standing at the counter, filling the coffeemaker with water. "Want some coffee?" she asked.

"Decaf?"

Bella shook her head. "We're studying for the ACT. We need the caffeine."

"Then none for me." Anne smiled.

There was a long silence between the three of them, awkwardness from Anne's conversation with their mother stretching its tentacles.

"You know," Remi said, "Dad was really good at keeping secrets." Her gaze met her sister's, and Anne could see the hurt of betrayal in Bella's eyes. "It's true," Remi defended. "He loved surprising us with parties and gifts, and he wouldn't let on at all. How is this different?"

Bella seemed to think about that. "He would buy big gifts for Mom and us," she admitted as she looked to Anne. "You think his job at the casino had something to do with that?"

Anne shook her head. "I have no idea, honey." She could see the pain in the girls' faces.

The screen door's spring stretched, and Joyce came back inside. "What's up?" she said.

Anne had an idea. "Would it be okay if I looked at your bank statements from the last few months?"

Joyce hesitated a moment, then shrugged and said, "If you think it might help." She walked to the back of the house. Anne could hear closet doors open and close.

"What do you need them for?" Bella asked as she punched the button to set the coffee to brewing.

"Just a hunch," Anne said.

"But it's about finding Dad, right?"

Anne nodded. Bella smiled at her, gratitude filling the creases of her face.

Within a few minutes Joyce was back with a manila folder in her hands. She handed it to Anne. Remi plopped into her chair at the table.

Joyce pulled out a chair for Anne, and they bent over the documents together.

"Lucas handled all the bill paying and finances in our family, so I really have no idea about such things," Joyce explained.

But as Anne perused the columns of numbers, she was struck by something—there were large influxes of cash and equally large withdrawals, the same amounts almost to the penny.

"Do you know what these deposits would've been?" Anne pointed to several entries. One was for fifty thousand dollars, another for seventy-five thousand.

Joyce's mouth dropped open. "Seventy-five *thousand* dollars?" She seemed flabbergasted by the amount. "If we'd had a deposit of that size, why wouldn't I have known about it?"

"So how do you account for it? Could his royalty checks have been for that much?"

Joyce shook her head. "Not by a long shot, and he barely made anything at Tangled Web and even less at the casino before that."

"Do you have access to online banking?" Anne asked.

Joyce shook her head. "Like I said, Lucas handled all of that. I have no idea how to do that. What would that do?"

"Sometimes the online version allows you to look at the image of the check that was deposited—it could give us more clues. Like who signed that check."

"I can call the bank on Monday and try to figure it out," she said. "But even if we do figure out where the money came from, is there any way to figure out where he spent it?" Her glance took in her daughters, who looked at each other with dumbfounded expressions.

"Only if he wrote checks," Anne said, "but these look like cash withdrawals."

"You think maybe he was gambling?" Joyce voiced the thought that had edged into Anne's consciousness.

"I don't know. He certainly had access at the casino."

Anne was aware of some of the symptoms of addictive gambling—secretiveness, exchanges of money . . . the disintegration of family life, but she'd have to look it up more fully when she got home to see if the picture fit.

Joyce seemed fixated on the bank statements. "So you think he did well on a few hands of cards, deposited those winnings, then withdrew the same amount? Why would he do that? And how does this fit in with what you asked me earlier about Mitch?"

"I don't know," Anne said. "There isn't evidence that he'd pawned anything of value, is there?" Anne knew that was another symptom of gambling.

Joyce shrugged. "Not that I know of. Not even his pen collection. And he has some pretty pricey pens." Anne asked if she could see them, and Joyce led her into their bedroom.

Every room in the house was expertly decorated, using a palette of soft browns and taupes that gave the home an upscale feel even though it fit more into a mid-level price range. Anne guessed that was Joyce's doing.

Joyce opened a bureau that held the collection of over fifty gold-plated rollerball and fountain pens. Most were Waterman pens with a few Pelikan and Montblanc pens as well.

"You don't think he sold any?" Anne asked.

"No. He loved his pens. I know they're all here."

"But he didn't take them with him either," Anne said, meeting her gaze, the intent of her comment clear.

Joyce closed the bureau. "I don't know anything, Anne." Anne could hear the edge of tears in the woman's voice. "Nothing adds up. Nothing!"

Something about that comment jarred a memory for Anne. "You know, he did make some comments at that last writers' meeting…"

"About what?" Joyce said.

"Missing you when he was gone. He talked about you all with such tenderness that night…"

"This isn't helping me, Anne." Joyce's tears had turned to bitterness. "It isn't helping me at all."

* * *

When Anne got home, she let Hershey out, then made herself a sandwich and set up her laptop on the dining room table. Once it turned on, she looked up the symptoms of addictive gambling on the Web site for the Mayo Clinic. She read the article through several times, yet she didn't get a strong sense that it had been the life Lucas had come to. Perhaps he'd gotten thrills from taking big gambling risks, but she didn't recall him even talking about gambling. He didn't brag about past gambling experiences. Nor had he seemed depressed or complained of feelings of guilt. Had he borrowed money or resorted to stealing to gamble? That might account for the large deposits and withdrawals. He'd certainly kept those a secret from Joyce.

That much was undeniable.

CHAPTER SEVEN

S unday, Anne and the kids took Eric's parents to Blue Hill Community Church. Friends gathered around the minute they walked in, wanting to meet them and shake hands. Even Coraline Watson, Mildred's nosy neighbor, rushed over to say hello.

Reverend Tom and his wife, Maggie, invited Anne's family to join them for lunch after the service, so they gathered at the Keystone Café on Main Street.

The restaurant was a hopping little place, tucked in one of the historic downtown buildings. The decor was pure charm with checked white-and-salmon floors and whitewashed brick walls. The food was sophisticated and delicious—offering both Italian fare, as well as grilled sandwiches that rivaled any Anne had ever had in New York.

Byron and Marlene studied the menu, while Liddie and Ben colored the kids' menus. Anne already knew that she wanted the pastrami on rye.

Reverend Tom lifted his gaze across the long table. "You've been enjoying your time in Blue Hill?" he asked Anne's in-laws.

"We sure have been," Marlene said, her glance taking in Anne. "Though we miss having Anne with us during the week."

"Anne's a busy girl," Maggie Sloan said, sending a wink Anne's way. "I don't know what this town would do without her."

"We've noticed that," Byron said, chuckling. "It's a good thing she isn't interested in getting remarried. She'd never find the time with all she has to do at the library."

"Byron!" his wife scolded. She sent Anne an apologetic look, but the comment had already hit its mark.

Was that what her mother- and father-in-law thought? That she was keeping busy so she wouldn't have to face the idea of marrying again? Anne pushed the unsettling thought aside.

"He's just kidding," Marlene said.

"I'll get him back," Anne deflected, adding a wink.

Yet, the comment still hurt.

* * *

On Monday, Anne spoke to Garret Jones, the last of the writers from the critique group. But he offered nothing new, just that his house, too, had a possible break-in. Then she'd called Lucas's publisher in New York. The woman had seemed deeply disturbed to learn of Lucas's disappearance and promised to call if she heard anything.

Joyce called Anne right after the bank opened. "I was able to get into the online statement," she said.

Anne waited for her to go on.

"The signature on the checks was *Vincent Barrio*." She paused as if that name might mean something to Anne.

"Who's that?"

"I have no idea."

"Are you on the site right now?" Anne asked.

"Yeah."

"Can you see if Lucas wrote a check for gas that night?"

There was a long silence while Joyce looked. Anne thought about her conversation with Scott Milhouse, the late-night encounter, and the pen Lucas had left behind.

"I'm not seeing anything," Joyce finally said. "I'd think it would've cleared by now."

"Well, keep an eye out for it and let me know if it turns up."

"Why would Scott lie about Lucas writing a check?"

"We don't know that he lied. He might not have deposited the check yet." She paused before she added, "There are explanations we don't always understand for why people do things."

* * *

Detective Bentley stopped by the library just before lunch. Dressed more casually than the last time she'd seen him, he wore a lightweight pale blue crew neck sweater that set off his different-colored eyes. When he cleared his throat, Anne realized she'd been caught staring.

Can I help you?" she said.

The detective smiled and said, "You'd mentioned Marta Henshaw last time. I was wondering if we could head over there to talk to her today."

Anne studied him, surprised that he would ask for her help.

"When we talked to Mitch, I saw that you have a way with people…" He shrugged. It's your call. I don't want you to feel uncomfortable."

Realizing she had learned much about Marta's behavior since the last time they'd spoken, she said, "You know, that's a great idea."

She twisted in her chair to look at the clock on the wall behind the checkout desk. "I'm about to take my lunch break anyway. Want to wait a few minutes?"

"Sounds great."

She moved to the back of the library to tell Betty Bultman she was heading out. She got her purse, checked in the mirror to make sure she didn't have anything in her teeth, gave her hair a quick brushing, and then met him in the front again.

"Ready?"

The detective straightened and they headed out.

Anne had only been to Marta's apartment once before, when she'd returned a cell phone Marta had forgotten at a writers' meeting.

Marta was a tall, thin woman with high cheekbones and striking green eyes. Anne had always thought she looked like a fashion model. She seemed surprised when Anne and Detective Bentley arrived at her door. "Who are you?" she asked him.

He pulled out his badge and gave his name. She studied it for a long moment, then undid the chain and invited them in to the sparsely decorated apartment.

"I told you everything I know about Lucas when we talked before," Marta said to Anne.

There were no paintings or art on the walls. The tan sheer panels that covered the windows looked like they'd come with the place. They were closed against the bright June day. The only thing in the tiny space that offered any kind of color was the couch—a bright-red sectional that looked like it had come straight from the set of the *Dick Van Dyke Show.*

Anne didn't know the woman well. Yet, Marta seemed uneasy, looking from her to Detective Bentley, to the closed windows as if she was expecting someone. Anne wondered if she was looking for Lucas. She glanced around the small apartment. There was nothing there that suggested a man's presence—no wallet or keys, no man's dress shoes shoved in a corner.

"I don't know what more to tell you," Marta was saying to Anne, "I just couldn't make the writers' meeting after a busy day at work."

"Do you mind?" Anne motioned toward the sectional, asking if they could be seated.

"Of course." She turned to the detective. "So…is it *Detective* Bentley?" Anne and the detective sat on the red couch, and Marta on a wooden chair across from them.

"Yes." He crossed his legs and sat back.

"What department do you work for?"

"I'm in from State College."

"*Hmm.*" She seemed to be staring the man down.

"I wanted to ask you some more about the pages you edited for Lucas," Anne said.

"What about them?" Her attention shifted.

"I was looking through his manuscript and I noticed some…*codes*, for lack of a better word."

"What kind of codes?" Detective Bentley leaned forward as he turned to Anne. "You didn't mention this before, Anne."

Anne's gaze remained on Marta. "They were combinations of letters and numbers." She pulled out one of the pages she'd stuffed into her purse when she'd first discovered the code and handed it to Marta. The code read: VT224OML.

Marta bent to study the page, but Anne hadn't missed the unease that took over her body when she'd first glimpsed it.

"Can I see that?" the detective reached for the page.

Marta handed it to him, then she looked at Anne. "I have no idea what that means," she said. She immediately glanced away. Anne would bet her eyeteeth the woman was lying. But why? What could the code mean?

"What exactly do you do for a living?" Anne asked her, wanting to get a better gauge of the woman. "I can't remember."

"I'm a photographer."

The detective handed the sheet back to Anne. "Were there more of those?" he asked Anne. She nodded, though she didn't say how many.

"Does the name Vincent Barrio mean anything to you?" Anne asked Marta.

Marta's face immediately turned a deep shade of red. "Where did you get that name?"

"Do you know who it is?"

"No," she insisted. "I really need to get going." Marta stood up. She glanced at the modern-looking clock on the end table. "I have an appointment I'm late for."

Anne thought to ask Marta about meeting with Lucas at the Keystone Café, but she could see that nothing would come of that now.

"Of course," Anne said, rising and tugging her purse up onto her shoulder.

Detective Bentley rose to standing too. His eyes were narrowed, taking her in. "Are you sure you've told us everything, ma'am?"

"Yes, I've told you all I know," she insisted. "Now, if you'll excuse me." She moved quickly to the door.

Anne felt as if they'd just been kicked out.

The drive back was excruciatingly quiet. They both knew that Marta was hiding something, but what? Finally, Detective Bentley broke the silence, "She knows what that code means."

Anne simply nodded.

He turned and looked Anne in the eyes. "Can I see the other sheets?"

"Of course." When they returned to the library, she unlocked the back door and invited him up. Hershey looked at the man and immediately sat.

"Since when are you well behaved?" Anne asked the dog, chuckling at his prompt obedience.

"I have that effect on animals," the detective said. He scratched the dog under the chin and Hershey leaned into it. "That too!" He laughed.

Anne went into her bedroom and pulled out the pages that had the code on them. Returning, she handed them to the detective. He bent his head the study them. "Can I keep these?"

"Of course." She shrugged. She'd made copies when she'd first discovered them so she had several sets to spare.

"I better get back to work," she apologized.

He tipped his head then headed down the back steps to his car.

For the rest of the day Anne couldn't get their conversation out of her head. Something was definitely going on with Marta— but what? Once she locked up for the night, she decided to drop in on Marta alone to finish their conversation, but as soon as she reached the apartment door she knew something wasn't right.

It was ajar and the lower corner looked like it had been kicked in. Anne knocked and the door swung open.

"Marta?" Anne called as she went in.

No one was there. The place looked like it had been ransacked. The beautiful red sectional that Anne had sat on earlier in the day had been slit open so that stuffing foamed out of it like popcorn overflowing from its bowl. Every cushion and panel had been shredded. The end table's drawer lay on the floor upside down, its contents spilled there. Anne called for Marta as worry filled her throat.

She moved into the bedroom. The bed was the same as the couch, ripped open, the sheets and bedding on the floor in a tangle. There was no clothing in the closet or in the dresser.

Had Marta discovered the carnage and fled town? Or had she been home when this occurred?

Reaching into her purse for her phone, Anne tried to call Marta on her cell. There was no answer. She quickly hung up, unsure what to do. She tried Detective Bentley, but he too didn't answer, so she called Officer Banks's direct number instead.

"Michael," she said to her old friend before she told him of her discovery. "She's nowhere around. The door was obviously kicked in." Anne told herself to take a deep breath as she parted the tan curtains to look outside. Perhaps the person who had done this was still watching the place.

"See if you can find the apartment manager," Michael said before he hung up. "I'll be right over."

Anne quickly made her way to the first floor where Apartment 1 was located. Her cell phone rang. It was Detective Bentley, but when she told him that Michael was on his way he said, "He has it covered then. I'll connect with Michael later and see what he thinks about it. No sense in both of us heading out."

Anne hung up as she reached the manager's place. A sign on the door read *Manager* and gave office hours. Anne knocked and waited, taking a couple deep breaths as she stood in the dimly lit hall.

A short balding man answered the door. "What can I do for ya?" he said.

Anne introduced herself then said, "One of your tenants has been vandalized, upstairs."

"Which one?" he asked, immediately reaching for the set of master keys he kept just inside the door.

"Marta Henshaw. I didn't see any sign of her there. I've called the police." He followed her back to Marta's apartment.

The heavy keys on his hip jangled as he walked.

"Did she tell you she was moving out?"

"Not a word." He kicked at some papers scattered on the hardwood floor.

"Was she a good renter?"

He shrugged. "Until this," he said. "She always paid her rent early, cash only. Never wrote a check. Kept the place spotless... She did bring a man to her place a lot." The description he gave seemed too similar to Lucas. "And they'd act all shifty like. Like they didn't want anyone to see him coming and going."

* * *

After Anne and Michael left Marta's, she headed to the grocery store to pick up a few items to make herself a quick supper. Then she'd see if she could dig out those photos Marlene had requested of the kids. She needed some sort of distraction. The realization that something might've happened to Marta too seemed too difficult to take in. She'd told Officer Banks about her belief that Marta was somehow tied to the Lucas Miller disappearance. He'd promised to talk to Joyce about it.

Anne wondered how that was going. Would Joyce take Marta's departure as another nail in her marriage's coffin?

As Anne pulled into the grocery store parking lot, the phone rang. It was Alex Ochs.

"Hey, Anne," he said in his deep voice. "I heard that Marta Henshaw's place was trashed."

"Oh?" Anne said.

"Are you okay?"

"I'm fine," Anne assured. "Just fine."

"I was wondering if you could meet me at the library."

"You mean *now?*"

"I've been thinking about Lucas and what could've happened…"

"Of course. I'll be there as soon as I finish getting some groceries.

Alex was already at the library when Anne got there. He paced the front porch, then gave a wave and moved down the stairs toward her waiting car.

"Are you okay?" he repeated as she got out.

"I'm fine." Anne unlocked the front door and they moved into the darkened library. She turned on the lights in the front room, and they sat down on the small couches in the periodicals section.

"What exactly happened?" Alex asked.

She told him about her first meeting with the woman that day, with Detective Bentley, how Marta had acted suspiciously especially when she saw the detective, then finding the apartment barren, obviously broken into, the second time she'd gone.

"Was there any sign of a struggle?" he asked.

"Other than the kicked-in door?" She shook her head. "No. It was a mess, but my guess is someone broke in while she was out. She discovered it and took off."

"Could Lucas have done it?"

"Lucas?" Anne paused to consider. "I'm not seeing it. But…maybe. She certainly was nervous, looking toward the window as if she expected someone. There's no doubt that the two of them have some sort of relationship beyond our little writers' group."

Alex nodded. "What could possibly cause her to flee town as if she were running for her very life?"

"The apartment manager didn't seem to know all that much about her."

He shook his head, then leaned his broad arms on his knees in a pose of thoughtfulness, his knuckles just touching his lips.

"We need to find out what the connection is between those two," he finally said.

"And the connection to Mitch—what were he and Lucas doing at that casino? Was it just work, research for a book?"

"Or something else," he agreed.

She told him about what Joyce had said about seeing Lucas and Marta together at the Keystone Café, then she mentioned the bank statements showing large exchanges of money and the name Vincent Barrio on the signature line. "Did Joyce show those to Officer Banks?" Alex asked.

"I'm not sure," Anne admitted, but I did tell Detective Bentley. She ran a hand through her hair and looked him in the eyes.

Alex had been a dear friend for as long as she could remember. Having him nearby was like warm cider on a cold day. Anne shifted away, uncomfortable with the sudden thought.

"What is it?" he said

She cleared her throat, trying to recall what they'd been talking about. "Vincent Barrio," she said awkwardly. "Marta really reacted when I asked her who that was."

"Sounds like someone to look into," he suggested.

"Definitely."

CHAPTER EIGHT

After Alex left, Anne went upstairs to her apartment, dumped her groceries on the kitchen counter, and found her house slippers in her bedroom. Then she flipped open her laptop on the kitchen table and typed in "Vincent Barrio."

There were a couple links bearing that name, a Facebook page for some boy in France, several Vincent del Barrios, or St. Vincent *in* Barrio, San Diego, but nothing that fit what she was looking for. She clicked on the next page, and then the next. The links were growing less and less relevant.

But there was a link on page three that caught Anne's eye, an old newspaper article from the *Philadelphia Inquirer* dated December 2, 1991. Anne opened it.

The title read, Vincent Barrio Commended for Bravery in the Line of Duty.

Anne's eyes scanned the page.

Officer Vincent Barrio of Willow Grove, Pennsylvania, deserves the gratitude of the city of Philadelphia for his bravery and genius detective skills. The five-year veteran was instrumental in tracking down and apprehending a man believed to be behind several bank robberies in the Philadelphia area — in Hatboro, Willow Grove, and Roslyn.

The only catch?

The thief was Barrio's superior officer at the Willow Grove P.D.

"Things didn't add up," the humble sounding man told this reporter. *"He was always the first one on every scene. And then I started noticing things — the ritzy house that he lives in. His wife wore fancy jewels. I knew he only made 50K or so. Something was definitely wrong."*

It didn't take long for the rookie officer to put two and two together and realize his own captain was the culprit.

The article went on to detail how the officer had gone about catching his fellow officer in the act.

Anne sat back staring at the fuzzy image on the screen of a dark-haired, Italian-looking man with a thick mustache and piercing brown eyes.

Vincent Barrio was a police officer? Anne hadn't been prepared for that. It had been years since the incident—1991. She did the math in her head. Was Vincent Barrio still an officer of the law?

If it was the same man, why would a police officer be writing checks to Lucas Miller? And more, what was Marta Henshaw's connection to him? Had he become like his former captain, turning to the dark side, as it were? Or was it something else?

Finally, realizing she'd found all the answers she was going to find here, she closed her laptop and moved to gather the school photos for Marlene.

It was so quiet without the kids at home. She let Hershey out back, then, when he was done, she meandered to the closet where she was pretty sure she'd tucked the photos. Her thoughts wandered.

Why had she been so affected by Alex when she'd seen him downstairs? Then there was Detective Bentley with his dark good looks, those interesting different-colored eyes...She'd felt attracted to him too, she had to admit.

She shook her head, unwilling that her thoughts should travel that path. He was a good-looking man, that was all. She'd hardly be alive if she didn't notice.

Boxes of old and new photographs filled the small closet. Anne pulled out the one that held the kids' latest school photos. An envelope fluttered to the floor.

Anne bent to pick it up—it was a letter addressed to Aunt Edie. Her flowery script graced the front with the words *Answered February 12, 1971*. Anne touched where pen had met paper. There was something about seeing the tangible reminder that the woman she'd adored as a child had been here, in this house. It made her presence real, not imagined. Not forgotten.

She glanced at the return address. Senator Richard Duffy from the great state of Pennsylvania. The date on the postmark was January 1971.

Why would a senator have written to Aunt Edie?

Anne's curiosity grew as she slipped the yellowed paper from the envelope. The letterhead certainly looked official.

Dear Edie Summers,

Thank you for your concerns about the upcoming vote on whether or not to make the Pennsylvania State Lottery legal.

The letter went on to talk about the proposal including the supposed benefits to senior citizens that were to be integral to the new program designated to come up for a vote later that year, 1971.

It concluded with these words that Anne found deeply interesting:

Your insights into this matter give me much to think on. I would like to encourage you to consider a run for the Senate yourself. Rarely have I seen your level of foresight and wisdom among my peers. The voice of someone like you in high office would be most welcome. You offer a level-headed approach with keen insight. We're looking for more women to enter political office. If you are interested, give me a call and we can talk in depth about building support and creating the kind of platform needed to win that seat.

Anne took the letter and photographs to the kitchen, where she made herself a sandwich. She sat to eat it at the table. The man wanted Aunt Edie to run for political office? She'd never heard any such story before. If it was true....

Anne read the letter through again. What an honor it had been for someone of such influence to recognize her great-aunt's brilliance.

That was so like Aunt Edie, to research a matter and contact her representatives with her concerns. She always seemed to know that her voice mattered, that she needed to speak up, let herself be heard. That challenged Anne. So often she let issues slide by without saying a word. How different the world would be if people like Aunt Edie, people who cared about where the world was going, spoke up to try to make a difference for the better.

Hershey padded to her side and sat on the tile floor looking up at her. She petted him on the head, then he twisted in several circles before settling for a nap.

She glanced over the letter again. Had anything ever come of it? There was so much she'd discovered about Aunt Edie since moving into this house—secret rooms, secret engagements. Perhaps her great-aunt had indeed considered running for the office and Anne had never known. She tucked the letter in with the photos she set aside to give Byron and Marlene. She'd ask Mildred about it the next time she saw her.

Who knew—maybe Aunt Edie had spent weekends in Hyannis Port with the Kennedys.

* * *

Anne felt on edge all evening. Finding Marta's apartment trashed and missing… The scene kept replaying through Anne's mind. And with the empty house and the kids and Byron and Marlene not due to come home till later, she suddenly felt the need for company.

She dialed Wendy first, but Wendy was out of town at a soccer match with her kids. She tried Mildred. No answer there. She tried Grace Hawkins, the editor from the paper, but Grace was out working a story.

Finally, she dialed Alex. "Ryan's at my folks' house tonight. I'll be right over."

Within ten minutes he was pushing the buzzer on her intercom. "Come on up," Anne said, buzzing him in.

She handed him a cup of coffee. "Thanks," she said, feeling suddenly shy. She was grateful that he'd come, yet that awkwardness she'd felt earlier moved back in.

"Ryan came home talking about Marta," he said. "It's all over town."

Anne made a groaning sound.

Apparently thirteen-year-old Jed Banks overheard his father talking about the incident, and he promptly peddled the news among their friends.

"I think I found out who Vincent Barrio is," Anne said. She led the way into the living room, where she took a seat on the couch while Alex settled in the adjoining stuffed chair. "Or at least who Vincent was in 1991."

Alex took a drink of his black coffee, waiting for her to go on.

"He was a rookie police officer who was commended for discovering that his boss, a police captain, had been robbing banks in several Philadelphia suburbs."

Alex let out a low whistle. "And that was the name of the person who signed those deposits of Lucas's?"

Anne nodded.

"Why would a cop from Philly send money to a writer from Blue Hill?"

Sounds of footsteps filled the staircase ending their conversation. Anne and Alex turned their heads as a tired-looking Byron rounded the corner with Liddie right behind him. Her freckled nose had been kissed by sunshine, and she was grinning from ear to ear.

"I got to milk a cow, Mommy." She was practically bouncing up and down. "Have you ever done it? It feels so weird!"

"How fun," Anne said, laughing. She gave her daughter a quick squeeze.

Marlene came in then, followed by Ben. The boy straightened when he saw Alex. Anne watched him, wondering why he was acting so oddly around the man who had been a good friend since they'd moved to Blue Hill.

"I'm sorry it's so late," Byron said. "I had no idea Amish country was so far away!" He wore a blue polo shirt with plaid shorts. Sunglasses rested on the top of his head.

"I told him to Google the drive before we left," his wife chided. Byron only smiled at her and shrugged.

"We had fun even if it was a long day, didn't we, kids?"

Liddie grinned up at her grandpa, but Ben excused himself to head to his bedroom.

"I'm tired," he said to his mother.

"That's okay, buddy." Marlene tousled his hair as he passed her. Then she looked at Anne, mouthing, "He's tired."

The boy went to find his dog, then Anne heard his bedroom door shutting.

"He really did have a good day," Marlene assured. "Just too long."

"I'm sure," Anne agreed.

Alex had risen to his feet.

"It's good to see you again," Marlene said.

Alex reached to shake hands, adding a bright smile. "Likewise." Then he looked to Anne. "I'll talk to you later, okay?"

"Of course." Anne walked him to the door that led to the stairs. "I'll give you a call so we can unravel this thing."

He waved good-bye and moved downstairs.

"He seems like such a nice man," Marlene said, meaning heavy in her words.

"He's just a friend," Anne said, moving past her to where her father-in-law was reclining in the living room.

"You know, honey," Byron said, even though his eyes were closed. "It'd be okay if he was more than a friend."

"Alex is *just* a friend!" Anne didn't mean to blurt that out so forcefully, but she couldn't help herself.

Byron sat up and Liddie raised her head and looked at her mother. She seemed confused. "What's wrong, Mommy?"

Anne moved to her and soothed, "Nothing, honey. Mommy just overreacted." She sent a meaningful look to each of her in-laws and then said to Liddie, "Why don't you go get ready for bed, huh? It's getting pretty late."

"Okay," she agreed. "I had a lot of fun today," she added to her grandparents, hugging and kissing each in turn before she moved toward her bedroom.

"I'm sorry," Anne said when the little girl was out of earshot. "I guess I'm tired too."

"It's perfectly okay, Anne," Byron assured. He patted the seat next to him on the couch.

Anne took the seat next to him. She told them about her day, searching for any clue about where Lucas Miller had gone—her conversation with Mitch Bach the day before and then Marta Henshaw's disappearance today.

"That's serious business." Byron's brow furrowed. "Are you sure you aren't in any danger?"

"The police are involved," Anne assured, telling them about Officer Banks and Detective Bentley. "I'm looking into it as a personal favor to Remi and Bella—those two girls have become like family."

"Well, speaking of family," Marlene said, "we are loving having this time with the kids."

"Oh, before I forget," Anne said. She went into the kitchen and brought back the school photos she'd pulled out for them, handing them to Marlene when she returned.

"These are lovely!" Marlene oohed over the shots. "That Liddie!" She pointed at the girl's photo—her hair was in pigtails that stuck off the side of her head, and she wore a lopsided smirk.

"I decided not to do retakes," Anne said, "because that shot caught the real Liddie."

"These are just perfect," Marlene said, handing the photos to her husband.

"We've missed being grandparents to Ben and Liddie...," Byron said as he looked at the pictures.

Anne heard the unfinished part—*since Eric passed.*

She hadn't meant to keep Liddie and Ben from Eric's folks. She loved them and valued their place in her children's lives. Yet, had she put off inviting them because of this very thing? Their presence brought everything back. The good and the hard. The joy of who Eric had been, the man she had loved so deeply, as well as the pain of losing him.

Marlene noticed the expression on Anne's face. "Oh, he didn't mean anything by that." She sent her husband a scolding look, but Anne shook her head.

"No, he's right. I want you to be involved in Liddie and Ben's lives. They need you. I wasn't trying to...I mean—"

"It's okay, Anne." It wasn't until her mother-in-law laid a hand on her arm that Anne realized she had become tense, defensive. Marlene's eyes met hers. "You're doing a fine job with the children," she said with the utmost kindness in her voice.

It was Anne's undoing.

She burst into tears. A torrent that shook her thin frame. She'd tried so hard to be so brave, to be the mother Liddie and Ben needed, to be a professional at work, to just keep going. But these two saw her like no one else. They understood her grief, her pain. She cried as she hadn't cried in three years.

Marlene moved next to her and held her, not rushing her, just patting her back.

"Are you all right?" she said when Anne's tears subsided.

Anne laughed. "I think so." She swiped at her face with the backs of her hands. Marlene handed her a tissue. Then Anne inhaled and looked into those eyes that were so much like Liddie's.

"You carry a heavy weight on those shoulders," Marlene said. "It has to be hard, all alone."

* * *

Once Byron and Marlene said good night and headed downstairs to their motor home, Anne felt better, more in control of herself.

She went to check on Ben. At first she thought he was asleep. But then he lifted a sleepy head.

"I didn't mean to wake you," she said.

"It's okay," Ben said, scooting up in the bed and flicking on the bedside light. Anne sat next to him. His eyes were rimmed in red, tired looking.

"What's wrong, honey? Is it something to do with Grandma and Grandpa?"

He shook his head.

"Then what is it—"

"Is Alex your boyfriend?" he interrupted.

Anne was stunned. "No! Why do you ask that?"

At first Ben didn't want to answer, so Anne waited. She knew he'd spit it out eventually. Finally, he said with a sigh, "Because Grandma and Grandpa talked about you someday meeting someone else and getting remarried."

She smoothed his troubled brow. "I have no intention of marrying Alex or any other man anytime soon," she told him. "Alex is just a friend. You know that."

Ben seemed to be holding his breath, finally allowing his eyes to meet hers.

"I'd tell you if he was something more," Anne assured. "Okay?"

He nodded.

"Don't you like Alex?" she asked.

"He's nice and all, I guess. Just not like... *that*." His face twisted into a look of disgust. "He's Ryan's... well..."

"I understand." She pulled the covers up under his chin. "You have nothing to fear." She smiled at him. "Really."

Yet, when she climbed into her own bed she wondered if that was really true. Did Ben have nothing to fear? Did she? Was she ready to love again?

Her right hand moved to her wedding rings, twisting them around her finger. Liddie asked if she'd always wear them. What was wrong with wearing them?

She could still see the glow of love in Eric's eyes when he gave them to her. She had fallen hard for him, and that realization had shown her that what she'd felt for Alex in high school was puppy love. An infatuation compared to the deep sense of connection she felt with Eric. And yet, was she blocking herself from ever finding love again?

Yes, she missed Eric. But she wasn't dead yet. Could there possibly be room in her heart to try? She sighed and pictured Ben, devastated by the idea that she could be more than friends with Alex.

She didn't want to put her children through the heartache of relationships that started and failed. She knew how hard that could be on them, how it introduced a certain instability into their tenuous lives. Wondering if this man would become their stepfather or if he'd be gone the next week. No, she didn't want that.

She'd rather live alone than put her children through that.

* * *

"Eric, what are you doing here?" Anne said. She knew distantly that she was dreaming, yet to see him flooded her with joy. They were in the library. Shafts of sunlight flooded the old Victorian. They were alone and Eric was sitting in a chair in the corner of the Nonfiction Room.

He didn't seem to hear her. She moved toward him. The air was thick, hard to move through. "Eric," she repeated, and he lifted his face as she moved over to him. His smile was bright, and when she looked him in the eyes she realized that his eyes were different colors, one blue and one brown. That wasn't right. She started to say something about it, ask him what had happened, but then she felt an urgency to ask him to come upstairs to see the children. "They'll be so glad to see you. They've grown so much, Eric." She reached for his hand, but then something was wrong. He looked at her with the most puzzled expression as his body transformed into Lucas Miller.

Anne felt the loss instantly. She wanted Eric—where had he gone? She shook Lucas saying, "Where's Eric? I want Eric!"

Then Remi and Bella were there. "Have you seen Dad?" Remi was asking.

Anne turned to tell her that Lucas was right there. But by then he'd left the library. Anne could see him hiding in the bushes along Mulberry Street behind their house.

Anne was shouting to him, "Go inside! Your family misses you!" Then the leaves of the bush shifted into sheets of paper that burst into flames. Remi and Bella came out, crying. They were begging Anne to help them. "Anne, you've got to help us!" Remi was shaking her.

Finally, Anne awoke in a sweat. She clutched a hand to her chest as the images faded from her memory, but the loss she'd felt in the dream clung to her—both her own and the Millers'. Closing her eyes, she sent up a prayer asking God to ease the pain she'd felt so sharply. It had all seemed so real—Eric, Lucas, the flames.

She lay there for several long minutes as the images replayed. She would never get back to sleep. Finally, she reached for Lucas's manuscript that was still on the nightstand in her room and turned on the light.

Joyce's words echoed, *"Maybe it'll give you a clue."*

Anne soon was engrossed in the story—one of intrigue. The main character worked as a Butler—though why would that word be capitalized? Lucas was usually a stickler for such things, yet every time the word was used it was capitalized. The Butler worked in an extravagant estate at the turn of the century.

The story seemed a bit disjointed. Like Anne's dream, it shifted in and out of reality, and she was confused. She'd read Lucas's stories before, and they usually had a lovely sense of rhythm, a pace that moved the reader along naturally. But the Butler kept doing things that Anne didn't quite understand — his motivations felt wooden, unnatural, and other characters who weren't part of the scene would suddenly start talking. In one scene the Butler drove a white van to Baylor University to cater a meal for his Boss — the man who met him at the back door to the reception hall was dressed in a Bear costume.

While it made sense in an Alice in Wonderland sort of way, for Lucas it was odd. It wasn't how he wrote. And there were other similar scenes that left her scratching her head — Panthers and Longhorn Bulls eating at the same table. Was there some symbolism she was missing that would make sense of it all?

At a ball he was approached by several guests of the Manor asking what time it was. The question seemed insignificant. Why would they ask this? The Butler glanced at the grandfather clock near the Wall…12:31. The *W* in Wall was capitalized, Anne noted. That too seemed weird.

Then it struck her — 12:31. That was the same time that was on the dashboard clock of Lucas's car. What were the odds that the times would be exact? She'd assumed it was the time of the crash, but could it have been something else?

She sat up in bed as her mind began to make connections. In the manuscript there had been characters Victor Babbit and Justus Brandt. Did those names mean anything?

Or was she just grasping at straws?

Sighing, she closed the manuscript and padded to the living room, the pages still tucked in her hand. It was dark out, very early. She could see her in-laws' darkened motor home through the old Victorian's windows.

Reaching for a pad of paper and a pen, she sat to write. She worked best when she put her thoughts on paper.

First, Lucas had taken a job at a casino, supposedly as part of his research for his book. There were big deposits and withdrawals of cash from their checking account—the name "Vincent Barrio" on the signature line of the cashier's checks. Anne put a question mark beside the man's name. If he was the same man as the one in the article he was a police officer, or at least a former police officer, but what was his connection to Lucas? And how did Marta Henshaw know him?

Anne picked up the manuscript, glancing through it. There was nothing in it about a casino. Had he lied to Joyce about his reasons for taking the job, or was there another manuscript where he would have used that research? The Mayo Clinic piece about men with gambling problems said that they often resorted to lying in order to keep at it.

Where did Marta Henshaw fit into all this, and where had she disappeared to? Had the two of them run off together? Or had something sinister happened to the woman? Had their interview prompted the disappearance? And what did the odd code mean? What caused the car accident? There hadn't been foul weather that night. Had Mitch Bach played some part in all of this? Had Lucas been hurt? Was he even still alive?

Anne tapped the pen on her chin as she read through what she'd written down. So far she had more questions than answers.

And then there was Scott Milhouse. What role did he play in all this? She wrote in big letters, *Check to Fowler's.*

* * *

Joyce called Anne before Anne got out of bed.

"I couldn't sleep last night," Joyce confessed, "I had this dream."

"Really?" Anne said.

"I was looking for Lucas…"

A chill ran down Anne's spine. "I had a dream that I was looking for Lucas too."

"Okay, that's weird."

Anne told Joyce about her dream, Eric shifting into Lucas, him hiding in the bushes, the leaves becoming sheets of paper that burst into flames.

"What do you think it means?" Joyce said.

"I'm not sure," Anne confessed, "but I did get up and make a list. I wanted to ask you about that check that Lucas was supposed to have written to Fowler's."

Joyce was silent for a long moment. Finally, she said, "Well, when I got up I went searching on the bank's Web site. I looked through all the statements. Then I found the checkbook. Lucas didn't even take it with him—it's here."

Anne felt a rock sink to the pit of her stomach. It looked as though Scott Milhouse had lied.

CHAPTER NINE

A nne headed downstairs to the library to work. Her kids were still in bed, resting up from their day in Amish country. She had yet to see Byron and Marlene stir from their motor home.

The library was quiet. Dust motes floated in the early morning sunshine that filled the majestic interior with its polished woods, rich carpets, and beautiful photography. Anne moved about her daily routine, turning on lights, starting the computers, emptying the library's return bin, straightening the file of summer reading logs that seemed to always fall into disarray by day's end.

By the time she finally unlocked the doors for the day, her curiosity was getting the better of her. So she ran an Internet search for "Scott Milhouse." She'd known Shaun Milhouse in high school, but they were never close, and she didn't know much at all about his brother.

When the computer finally brought back its results Anne was stunned by what she discovered—a laundry list of past crimes including theft, burglary, drug charges...

Had he stolen the pen?

Clicking on the link for eBay, she looked up the Waterman's value. The site listed several similar pens for an asking price of well over five hundred dollars.

Just then Anne heard the front door open. Remi came in, looking disheveled. Dark circles ringed the girls' eyes.

"Are you okay, honey?" Anne asked.

The girl nodded, but Anne could see that she was far from okay.

"What are you looking up?" Remi asked as she moved behind the desk and began to check in the books that were in the bin under the desktop.

"I thought I'd look up the value of that Waterman pen of your dad's. The one Scott Milhouse had."

But Remi didn't seem interested in Scott Milhouse. Clearly she'd heard the news about Marta's disappearance. "If he was planning on leaving us for her, why wouldn't he have packed up all his stuff and gotten an apartment in town? So at least Bella and I could see him once in a while?"

"You're adding two and two and getting five," Anne said. "There's no proof that that's what happened."

"No?" Remi insisted. "But it is true that he left us. He left me and Bella just as much as he left mom. And with all these rumors about that Henshaw woman…" She shook her head.

Anne patted her on the shoulder. "I know it's hard."

"Do you think he had a gambling problem?" Remi asked as her eyes filled with tears. "That's what people are saying—that he went over the deep end, gambling and…" Her words trailed off.

Was that what Lucas's connection to Vincent Barrio was all about? Was Barrio some sort of loan shark?

* * *

Wendy stopped in around noon. Anne had heard Byron and Marlene head out with the kids a couple hours before, so she knew she'd be alone again during lunch. Remi was helping out at the library.

Wendy set a stack of books on the checkout desk. "I adore this new author," she said.

"You read all of these in the last week?" Anne reached for the pile.

Wendy shrugged. "And your point?"

Anne chuckled. "Actually, I was hoping to see you. I'm wondering if you could come with me to talk to Scott Milhouse at Fowler's."

"Sure…," she said, a question heavy in her tone.

Anne explained her discoveries about the man then told her that Remi had offered to cover for her so she could to talk to the mechanic.

"No time like the present," Wendy said, tugging her big leather purse up onto her shoulder.

So the two climbed into Anne's silver Impala and meandered through the quiet summer streets of Blue Hill. They passed the city pool where children splashed in afternoon fun and town hall where Mayor Bultman was climbing into his car. He waved at Anne and Wendy, then moved off down the street.

The car repair shop looked empty when they first arrived. Anne rang the bell on the counter, its hollow sound bouncing off the dingy concrete walls. Anne strained her neck to see if anyone was in the back. She couldn't see anyone.

They were just ready to turn around and head back when footsteps sounded from where the mechanics worked on cars.

"I told you already," Scott said before he even reached the front desk, "I don't know anything about what happened to Lucas Miller." His eyes narrowed as he glanced at Wendy.

"You lied to Anne," Wendy said, not afraid to get in the man's space. "Lucas Miller didn't write a check. Did you know that pen was worth over five hundred dollars? We know about your police record. Do you want to be arrested for stealing again?"

Scott's face fell. He looked to Anne as if she would rescue him. "I didn't steal that pen. I promise you I didn't. Lucas left it on the counter."

He was so earnest that Anne believed him.

"Why would Lucas leave an expensive pen lying around?" Anne said.

She studied Scott, noted that his body language was open, not closed off. He leaned toward her and looked her in the eye when he spoke.

"I don't know," he said. "He just left it. That's all." He paused, as if weighing whether to say more. Finally, he went on, "Lucas wasn't thinking straight that night."

"You mean he'd been drinking?" Anne asked.

Scott shook his head. "No. He wasn't drunk. He'd been hurt. He came in to Fowler's late. It must've been after his car accident. I didn't know about the accident till later, when I saw it in the paper. After I talked to you."

"Why didn't you call me when you realized that? You could've set the record straight."

He fidgeted with the stub of a pencil he picked up off the counter. "Lucas asked me not to say anything. He said people he loved would get hurt."

Anne and Wendy exchanged worried looks.

Scott went on, "I'd been up late working on my truck—I didn't lie about that. My Dodge Dakota needed some new shocks on the front end. Anyway, Lucas had a cut on his forehead when he came in." Scott pointed to his forehead, above his right eye. "I asked him what happened. But he wouldn't say anything about where it came from, just that he was afraid that someone would find him. He kept looking out the front window, ducking down."

"Did he say why?" Anne asked.

Scott shook his head. "Like I said, he made me promise not to say anything to anyone, especially the authorities. Said he just needed to use my phone, that he didn't have his cell phone. He must've lost it in the accident," Scott added, shaking his head.

"Who did he call?" Anne asked.

"Someone named Marta."

"And did Marta come?"

"I couldn't tell you. I just saw him get into a 1960s VW Westfalia van."

The only thing was, Anne knew Marta drove a light green Ford Focus.

* * *

After their talk with Scott, Anne and Wendy headed to the impound lot where Lucas's car had been towed after the accident. Anne knew it was highly unlikely she'd find anything new there, especially since the police had been over the vehicle with a fine-tooth comb, but she had a hunch that she couldn't ignore. She thought to call Detective Bentley or Officer Banks to see if they knew anything in that regard, then she decided against it. It was one thing for her to share information with them—she knew it wouldn't go the other way.

The lot was out of town, just off the highway to Deshler, Pennsylvania. The man who ran the place wore a tattered flannel shirt and he smelled of motor oil. His orange ball cap read *Dungey*. Anne had no idea what that referred to. When she asked about the vehicle, he immediately knew which one she meant.

"Sure thing," he said. He moved from the trailer/office and led the way to the crumpled Honda Accord. Vehicles filled the fenced-in area. Some were new looking, but others like Lucas's were victims of horrible accidents, their windshields gone or shattered, hoods dented in, roofs caved.

Anne and Wendy followed the man's quick pace. "You're the second ones to ask to look through this car in as many days," he said offhandedly.

"Oh?" Anne said. "Who else was looking?"

Dungey shrugged. "Just a guy. He said he was a police officer. No one from around here, that I know anyway."

Anne wondered if he meant Detective Bentley.

The sight of the car was instantly sobering—the front end completely smashed in and a dent in the rear bumper as well. Had she noticed that the first time she'd seen the car? Anne and Wendy stood back from it at first, like visitors at a wake, not wanting to approach the macabre sight yet unable to stay away. Finally, when the man gave them leave and ambled back toward the office, Anne dared open the driver's side door. She could see that the passenger's side door was wedged shut since that side of the vehicle had been crushed by its impact with the tree.

Wendy moved to the back, climbing in to search the depths of the seats. "What exactly are we looking for?" she said as she shoved her hand between the cushions.

"I'm not sure," Anne said. She bent her head to look where the glove box had been, now opened onto the front seat. Nothing there but the car's manual and an insurance card and registration. She lifted the rubber mats. Nothing. Then she looked under the driver's seat. Nothing there. As she sat up the shifting afternoon light caught a reflection between the passenger seat and the console, wedged deep. Anne reached her hand carefully into the tight space and pulled out a cell phone.

Anne pushed the *end* button and the screen lit up, going through its startup gyrations.

"I don't see anything—" Wendy came around the car, but she stopped talking when she saw that Anne had found Lucas's phone.

"How did the police miss that?" she asked, coming alongside Anne and staring at the screen.

Anne shrugged.

Finally, it finished loading. Anne clicked on *history*—no incoming or outgoing calls. But there were several text messages, all to M. H. Anne could only assume the initials referred to Marta Henshaw.

The first, an incoming message, read, *Meet at the usual place?*

Lucas's reply, *Yes, but later. Someone is watching us.*

What did that mean? Did "someone" mean Joyce? And he used "us." Anne's heart sank. Surely he didn't mean it the way it looked.

They stopped at the police station to drop Lucas's phone off with Michael Banks. She also told him about the new information Scott Milhouse had revealed, and then they returned to the library. Wendy took over for Remi at the front desk. They didn't dare talk about what they'd discovered at the impound lot. But Anne knew the teenager could tell that something was up.

"What did Scott say?" she asked.

"He saw your dad that night." Anne couldn't lie to her. "He said Lucas just left the pen behind."

"Was it before or after the accident?"

"After."

Remi nodded, thinking. "Did he have any idea where Dad might've gone?"

"No, honey," Anne said. "No idea. But it's good. It means your dad wasn't hurt in the accident."

"But why wouldn't he have come home after that? I don't get it." Her brow furrowed. She turned back to her work, obviously not wanting to talk about it anymore.

Remi didn't stay long after that. She needed time alone, she said, to sort things out. How could she go to college next year? How could she plan anything? Without her dad there to see it? To help her?

Anne sighed as she realized the same could be said of her own children. Their father wouldn't be there to see them through the big events of their lives—the school plays, the graduations, the weddings...

That was different though. Ben and Liddie knew their father would never return. Lucas Miller could well come home and resume his life. Couldn't he? Or had too much happened for even that?

"What's up with you?" Wendy said when she wheeled the book cart back to the main desk. Anne's friend never seemed to miss a thing.

"Just feeling sorry for myself," Anne confessed.

"You?" Wendy almost laughed, then she seemed to think better of it and took the chair next to Anne. "Anne, you've had it hard. You've lost your husband. You're trying to raise two little kids all alone. Have you *ever* just wallowed?" She lifted an eyebrow. "Go ahead and feel sorry for yourself. I would!"

That made Anne smile.

Then she shook her head. "I think I'm pinning too much on finding Lucas Miller," Anne confessed.

"What do you mean?"

"Deep down I'm hoping that if I can bring that family back together it'll somehow solve my own loneliness from losing Eric."

"That makes no sense at all." Wendy said it without a hint of teasing. Anne knew she was right—it didn't make sense. Yet, it was how she felt. She thought of her dream and of Joyce having a similar dream the same night. There was a reason for that. She knew it deep down. She was meant to bring this family back together.

"I know," Anne finally said. "And I know it's wrong—nothing will bring Eric back."

"What's prompting all this?" Wendy met her gaze with her no-nonsense manner.

"Having my in-laws here...the way Ben's been acting..."

"How's Ben been acting?"

"Moody. He asked if Alex was my boyfriend last night. You should've seen his face."

"*Is* Alex your boyfriend?"

"No!" Anne said.

Wendy held up her hands as if she were calming a wild mare. "It wouldn't be the end of the world, you know. Alex is a pretty decent guy."

"I know he is…" She shook her head. "He's a great guy. But I'm just not…"

"Ready?"

Their gazes met.

"Will I ever be ready?" she said honestly.

"You are still young. You have a whole life ahead of you. Do you think Eric would want you to live it alone, with just some memory of him as your only companion?"

Anne felt hot tears burn the backs of her eyes. She managed to hold them in.

"He loved you," Wendy went on. "And he knew that you loved him. That wouldn't be diminished if God brought another man into your life."

"But Ben…if you'd heard him last night. He's very opposed to the idea. I don't want to be one of those women who brings men in and out of their children's lives."

"And a nine-year-old is going to determine your whole future?"

"But he and Liddie would have to live with anyone I married. A *stepdad*…" She shook her head at the word. "I just…"

"Just promise me one thing," Wendy said. "Don't limit God. He can open doors. He can help little boys and little girls understand when their mommy is lonely."

"Do you think that's *all* this is? Loneliness?"

"Honey, we're all lonely." Wendy reached a hand across Anne's shoulders and gave her a side hug. "You wouldn't be betraying Eric, I promise."

* * *

It had been over a week since the last writers' meeting. Anne had called all the members to meet at the library that night so they could talk about Marta Henshaw's disappearance. Everyone seemed subdued—Mildred, Wendy, Douglas Pauthen, Garrett Jones, Rita Sloan, and Charlotte and Henry Jordan—a somber procession of writers. Once they'd all taken their seats, Anne stood.

"I hope you don't mind if I take a few minutes?" she said to Douglas.

Though Lucas had been the leader of the group, directing who would read when, offering advice, and taking questions, she'd asked Douglas to step into Lucas's shoes. The retired army captain, a business leader in the community, knew how to take charge.

"That's fine by me," Douglas said. He crossed his arms over his chest. Anne knew the man didn't have a high opinion of Lucas, though in all fairness, his command of the man had been years earlier, when Lucas was a mere eighteen years old. Yet, some people were like that. They pigeonholed others, then left them there in that hole, in their minds, for as long as they knew them. Was she that way? she wondered. Or did she allow herself to forgive, to see people as new, changing, growing? She hoped so.

"I know I talked to most of you privately about the night that Lucas Miller disappeared. But I wanted to bring you all together because Marta Henshaw has turned up missing as well—"

Knowing heads nodded around the room. People murmured with their neighbor.

"I wanted to see if any of you have any idea where Marta could have gone, if the two might be connected."

The room went quiet. Heads shook in disbelief.

"I don't know Marta all that well," Rita said. "Other than our meetings here…"

The rest seemed to agree. It seemed no one knew much of anything about Marta other than that she hadn't lived in Blue Hill long, a year at the most.

"What exactly does she do for a living?" Anne asked.

"She's a photographer," said Rita. The thirty-something bank manager squinted and waited on Anne for an answer.

"Really?" Charlotte Jordan said. She crossed her tanned arms and leaned toward her husband. "Didn't she say once that she worked in law enforcement?"

"I thought so too," he answered as a couple other heads nodded.

"She was good with a gun," Douglas added.

Every head turned to him.

"I saw her at the shooting range once," he said. He turned toward Anne. "She carried a Glock 19. I saw the butt of it sticking out of her purse a couple times."

"A gun?" Anne said.

Why would a young woman living in Blue Hill need a gun?

CHAPTER TEN

The meeting dispersed early, so Byron built a small campfire in the portable fire ring they'd brought for the backyard, and Marlene got supplies for s'mores. The kids were thrilled to roast marshmallows and make their sweet treats, while Hershey jumped at sparks that came his way.

Anne watched their happy faces in the glow of the campfire's light. Ben was talking quietly to his grandfather about the day, laughing at his dog and patting him on the head. Liddie was stuffing her face with the graham crackers, chocolate, and marshmallows.

Yet, Anne couldn't get what Douglas Pauthen said out of her head—Marta carried a gun. What exactly had the woman gotten into? If she was in law enforcement, what was she doing in Blue Hill? And what did Lucas Miller have to do with that?

Anne sighed and decided to put the mystery aside for tonight. She'd simply enjoy some time with her family.

"Grandma," Liddie said, "where are we going to go next?"

"Aren't you tired, honey?" Marlene said, handing her a napkin.

"Nuh-uh," she said.

"Use words," Anne said.

"I mean *no*," Liddie corrected. "I like going out in the motor home and seeing new places every day. I'm having fun!" She grinned.

"Actually." Byron turned from placing more wood on the fire and took his folding chair. "We were wondering, now that you've finished the sign-up for the summer reading program, if you and the kids could get away for a few days, come on a camping excursion with us. We were thinking of heading into Philadelphia to take in the historical sites there. We could take a road trip over most of next week—maybe even head toward Washington, DC. It would allow us to really get out and explore this country of ours."

"That sounds wonderful," Anne admitted. Anne saw the way Ben perked up.

"Like we could really go camping?" he said.

"Sure could," Byron said. "Maybe go hiking, explore the Pennsylvania countryside."

"How about fishing?" Ben added, excitement in his tone. "Could we go fishing?"

"*Ew*, fishing!" Liddie said. "I don't want to touch no worms or slimy fishes!"

"I don't want to touch *any* worms or slimy fish," Anne corrected.

"You either?" Liddie said.

"I'm sure we could fit some fishing in," Byron promised, sending a wink to his grandson.

"I'll ask my regulars if they can fill in for me," Anne said. The kids immediately erupted in whoops of joys.

"Really, Mom?" Ben said, his eyes alight.

Anne nodded. "I said I'll ask. But I think between Wendy and Betty and the Miller girls we might be able to swing a few days."

Eventually the kids ambled off to bed. Anne, Byron, and Marlene reclined around the dying embers.

"Thank you for all of this," Anne said. "It's been so good to see you…"

"We're loving it." Marlene touched Anne's hand that held a warm cup of tea.

"It's good for them to get out and experience things they don't normally do," Anne said. She looked forward to time alone with her family, yet guilt pulled at her. She hadn't felt this way before Eric's passing, hadn't been overwhelmed by the need to work.

"If you can't come, you can't…," Byron said. He sent her a smile that said he understood.

"No," Anne assured. "I can. I just might need a day or two to get things organized at the library."

"To be honest," Byron said. "A day of rest would be just what this old man needs!"

"The kids are wearing you out, are they?" Anne gave him a wry smile.

"We could head out first thing Thursday and go through the weekend," Anne offered, hoping that Betty Bultman or Wendy would be willing to fill in for her. "Maybe I could take Monday and Tuesday too."

"That would be wonderful," Marlene said.

"Ben would like that. Don't you think?" Anne said.

"He would," Byron said.

Anne nodded, adding, "He hasn't been himself lately."

"He's just fine," Marlene said. Yet, her words didn't alleviate Anne's fears. Marlene must've seen the way her brow furrowed because she disappeared into the depths of the motor home in search of something before she reemerged with a letter in her hands.

"I wasn't sure about giving you this before, but now I can see that you need to read it." She handed the letter to Anne. Eric's precise printing covered the page. He never did like cursive. The image caught Anne by surprise—a letter she'd never seen from Eric to his parents.

"I found it when I was going through some papers," Marlene said, her gaze on the page in Anne's hand.

"What does it say?" Anne clutched it to her chest.

"It's about you. But read it in private," Marlene said. "He worried about you...He loved you."

* * *

When Anne finally trudged upstairs to get ready for bed, it was almost ten thirty. The light was still on in Ben's room.

"Hey, bud," she said when she poked her head in the door.

Ben lifted his face from his book. His eyes were so serious. He was becoming a young man. She could see it starting in him, even at age nine—that sense of responsibility, of wanting to take charge, to protect those he loved.

"This is becoming a habit," Anne said, moving into the bedroom. "You need your sleep."

"Sorry," he said. He closed the book and set it on his nightstand, then scooted down under the blankets.

Anne took her place alongside him. She touched his cheek, then smoothed the bedding with one hand.

"Are you excited to go camping?"

Ben nodded vigorously. "And fishing, like we use to with Dad..."

"I'm looking forward to it too." She smiled into his eyes.

Sudden hot tears streaked his cheeks.

"What's wrong, honey?" Anne said. She reached to touch his face, but he moved away from her hand. "You miss Daddy?"

Ben nodded.

"You can tell me about it, you know."

Anne could see the struggle in his face, the desire to pour his heart out, to trust, at war with something she couldn't name. Finally, he pushed farther down in the blankets, pulling them up to his chin. She studied him for a long moment. She knew there was no point in pushing him, he'd just dig in deeper. He was like Eric in that.

Finally, she said, "You'll feel better tomorrow, once you've had some rest."

His brow furrowed and he turned his back to her.

By the time Anne reached her own bedroom, she felt like crying. So much for doing a good job of raising their kids. What was troubling him? Ben wasn't even talking to her.

She closed her eyes as she sank onto her bed, a prayer rising from the pit of her stomach. "Lord, I feel so lost," she admitted. "What can I do with that boy to make him understand, to get through to him? What's troubling him? I'm trying to do my best, be the kind of parent he needs, but to be honest I have no idea what that looks like. I have enough guilt, leaving the library so suddenly…"

Wasn't that how it always was with adults? The thought intruded of its own accord. Obligation. Duty. The need to provide. She knew those weren't the only things that mattered in life. Her children needed so much more than her provision for their basic needs. *Man shall not live on bread alone.* The verse from Matthew 4:4 flashed in her mind.

"I know that's true, Lord," Anne said. "Help me find the balance that I need."

She stood back up to get ready for bed, realizing that the letter her mother-in-law had given her was in the pocket of her lightweight jacket.

Anne pulled it out. It was so strange to see Eric's handwriting so long after his death, a letter she'd never seen before. She noted the perfectly straight lines, so orderly, so like Eric. She could see him bent over the page, pen in hand, carefully crafting every word.

Dear Mom and Dad, it began. His warm voice held those words lovingly as he spoke them in her mind.

> *I'm so sorry it's been so long since I've last written. In this day of e-mail and Internet, I think I've forgotten how to write a real letter. But I know how much you treasure them, Mom, so here is my attempt.*

He talked about the usual day-to-day fodder, Ben starting preschool and Anne doing well in her pregnancy, though of course he didn't know yet that the baby would be Liddie. It had been a sweet time of anticipation in their marriage, already knowing the joy that children brought to their union, and wondering who this new little person would be.

It was the second page that caught Anne off guard.

I already love this new baby, even though he or she hasn't been born yet. How can that be? To love a total stranger like that? And yet I do. Anne is absolutely glowing with joy. Her pregnancy has gone well — no health problems of any kind, for which I am thankful.

Which brings me, in roundabout fashion, to something that has been troubling me. I haven't breathed a word of it to Anne, and I ask that you not say anything either. I don't want to worry her, especially in her condition, but I've been having weird "episodes" lately. That's the only word that really describes them. I feel faint and if I don't lie down I fear I'll pass out. My lips and extremities turn a bluish color when it's happening. I've talked to my doctor about it and he wants to run a series of tests, but then I wonder if I'm just imagining it. I hate to go to all that bother.

The thought of something happening to me — that scares me. And not for my sake. I love the Lord and there is no place I'd rather be than with Him. You know that's true. My deepest joy is to think of being in that place where Paul said, "To live is Christ, to die is gain." I truly relate to that and that's in big part thanks to you and the way you raised me, to love God more than anything. No, my fear is for Anne and the kids. How would she carry on without me? I've hidden this all from her of course.

As Anne read the words tears filled her eyes, one after the next, rolling down her cheeks in a flow so that she could barely read. She swiped them away and read on.

I don't want to worry her, but I felt someone needed to know. And who better than my parents? I do have a will. Anne and I wrote it when Ben was born, although we did that just because it seemed the thing to do, not because we ever thought something could happen to one of us.

But I need you to promise that you'll help take care of Anne and the kids if, God forbid, anything should happen to me. Watch out for her. Help her find happiness again. If she meets another man, encourage her to remarry. I know her — she would be stubborn about that! And she thinks I'm stubborn. I don't want her to be alone, to struggle in raising our children as a single mother. Perhaps I'm being morose, so forgive me. I'm not trying to worry you and I'm not even sure why I feel so compelled to write this. But now that I have, I'm glad. I know that you love Anne like a daughter — that makes me happy. Because you have each other. I suppose that's what family is all about.

Your loving son,
Eric

Tears stained the paper, causing the words to smear. Anne clutched the pages to her chest as sobs came in violent hiccups. His love for her was so palpable on the page. How she yearned for him. "I don't want another man like you," she whispered into the night. "I want you, Eric. I just want *you*."

* * *

The next day, Byron and Marlene got the kids out of bed a little before the library opened to "plan their next adventure," Byron said with a wink to Anne.

He pulled out his laptop computer as Liddie and Ben climbed next to him onto the couch, still in their pajamas, with bowls of cereal in their hands. They looked sleepy yet content. Marlene brought Anne a cup of coffee, but Anne waved it off saying she needed to head downstairs to open up the library soon.

Still, something held her in place.

"We have to start in Philadelphia, I think," Byron said. "See the Liberty Bell and Independence Hall. Then we could head to other historical sites. Look here—Wikipedia says there are sixty-seven national historic landmarks. So we have our pick of places to see."

"We could head to Washington, DC, on Friday," Marlene put in. "Do a quick tour of the highlights there, or is that trying to do too much?"

"We can go fishing, can't we, Grandpa?" Ben said.

"We sure could. The Potomac is right there," Byron assured Ben. "You do know who crossed the Potomac, don't you?"

"That was the Delaware," Marlene corrected. "Washington crossed the Delaware."

Byron gave his wife an aggravated look. "Anyway," Byron went on, ignoring Marlene, "we'll fish there. It'll be fun."

When Anne had called Wendy and Betty earlier that morning to ask about taking time off, both ladies had been gracious in insisting that they could cover the days with ease. She was grateful for their help.

She turned to descend the big Victorian's steps into the library.

Soon the place was crawling with patrons. Children were lined up at the checkout desk to sign up for the reading time that was due to start any minute. All of the computers were assigned in the Reference Room upstairs. Anne closed her eyes and lifted a quick prayer for help, then went to work. She was glad the Miller twins were coming in later.

She could hear the phone ringing in the back room so she excused herself, despite the impatient looks people tossed her way, and moved to answer the call.

It was Michael Banks. "Anne, I'm glad to catch you," he said. His tone sounded sympathetic, almost apologetic. "I just talked to Joyce Miller. She asked me to call you too." She waited for him to go on. "We've decided to close the active search for Lucas Miller."

"What?" Anne was stunned. Hadn't Detective Bentley just been running down leads with her? "What about Marta Henshaw's disappearance?"

"No one's reported her missing. It isn't illegal for folks to up and move in a hurry, even with the vandalism in her apartment." He paused. "Besides, there's no proof the two are related, other than that they knew each other, a few allegations. But we need concrete evidence to keep a case open, and we simply don't have that. Not in either case, to be honest."

Anne turned to face the window in her tiny office. Piles of books and papers reached toward the ceiling, yet outside the day was bright. Birds flitted into the thick lilac hedge along the back of the property.

"If anything comes to light," Michael added, "of course we'll open it back up. But at this point all we have is a car accident and a man leaving his family. When he decided to leave that note telling his wife that he was leaving her...Well, that tied our hands, Anne. It just did. Even Joyce said it was his handwriting."

She knew he was right, but still it was hard to see the officials drop the case. It seemed so final. So foreboding. Would they ever know what happened to the husband and father?

"There will be an article in the *Gazette* about our decision. I talked to Grace Hawkins yesterday. It'll be online today and in the print version next week."

"Okay," Anne said absently.

"If we'd found any leads on the car crash, anything..."

"You don't have to apologize," Anne said. "I understand."

She could hear Michael clear his throat even over the phone. "Joyce didn't want you to be surprised if you heard it somewhere else first. Me either."

"Is it okay if I keep looking into it?"

"You're free to do whatever you like."

"I'm not ready to quit yet." She paused, not sure she fully understood what was driving her. Yet, she couldn't deny that she felt compelled.

"You know, Anne, it doesn't seem right to me either. If you need anything, any help, give me a call. I mean, within reason." He laughed good-naturedly. "I can't give out proprietary information, but you know what I mean. There is a lot I can do, even in my off hours..." His words trailed off.

"I appreciate that," Anne said. "If I discover anything new I'll let you know."

"Sounds like a deal," he said. "You never can tell."

After she hung up, Anne looked up the online article he'd mentioned about closing the case. The article recapped the investigation, the police finding nothing of consequence, and thus the closing of it. Citizens were encouraged to continue to offer any clues that might reopen the case for the hurting family. There was a photo of Joyce and the girls at the scene of the accident—Lucas's car wrapped around that giant oak tree. Lucas's family had looked devastated. As she bent to study the photo closer she realized Detective Bentley was in the shot. He was looking under the car.

She didn't know he'd been at the scene that day, though there had been a lot of people there. And of course she hadn't yet met him. Why wouldn't he have mentioned it? Had he already been brought in on the case that first day? That seemed odd, didn't it? To bring in a specialist before the local officers even had a chance to track down any leads? Especially when the case didn't seem to merit anything beyond a cursory examination—at least as far as the law was concerned... With a jolt, Anne realized she needed to get back to all the library patrons waiting on her.

Around ten, Remi and Bella showed up at the library. Anne could see by the expressions on their faces that they were devastated that the police were dropping the investigation.

"You can't give up hope," Anne said as she touched Bella's arm.

"But if they aren't looking for Dad, how will we ever find him?" She tugged her curly light brown hair away from her face and slumped into the chair next to Anne.

"I told Officer Banks that I'm going to keep on looking," Anne assured them.

"Really?" Remi said. She remained on the other side of the desk, her hands folded in front of her. "You aren't going to just give up too?"

"Of course not," Anne assured. "The police have their hands tied, but we don't. Once I get back from this camping trip we'll keep running down leads and figure out what happened. We need to find that VW van that Scott Milhouse said picked up your dad. How is your mother doing with all of this?"

Bella said, "She says she's fine, but if she doesn't have to work she doesn't get out of bed at all. She's anxious, upset about every little thing. You should have heard her go off because I didn't clean up supper dishes last night…" She shook her head. "It's just not like her."

Anne's heart ached for Joyce. She understood such responses — she'd had many days like that right after Eric died, not wanting to go on, not wanting to face the difficulty of life alone.

"Tell her that I'm not giving up yet, will you?" She looked each of the girls in the eyes. "You can't give up either. And we'll pray about it…together. God knows where your father is — He just needs to direct us there."

* * *

Wendy brought the mail in around ten thirty. She plopped it onto Anne's desk in her office. But Anne was so busy moving from one task to the next that she didn't notice the letter amid all the junk mail till almost three o'clock when her body told her it was time for a coffee break.

There was no return address and it was all typed, no handwriting.

"When did this come?" Anne asked as she moved toward the checkout desk, noting that the letter had been posted just the day before and marked *One Day Mail* with a New York cancellation stamp.

Wendy paused from checking out some books and looked at her. "This morning," she said simply and returned to her task. A middle-aged gentleman thanked her and then left.

Anne tore the envelope open. Inside was a plain sheet of paper with only six words in the same typeface as the envelope and several photographs of street signs and houses that Anne didn't recognize. She stared at the note in disbelief.

"What is it?" Wendy said, looking over her shoulder to see what it said.

"Who sent it?" Anne glanced at the envelope again. No return address.

Then she stared at the page, trying to comprehend why someone would send it. And to her. But the words were clear. Someone didn't want her looking into the Lucas Miller matter.

It read, *Some dead are better left buried.*

CHAPTER ELEVEN

Anne was unsettled by the note, although she managed to maintain her composure in front of the library's patrons and especially in front of Bella and Remi who were busy upstairs in the Children's Room, supervising a craft project for the summer reading kids. Anne was glad at least for that. She didn't want them seeing the note.

Clearly somebody didn't like her digging. But who? And what was the significance of the photos? Who knew she was looking into finding Lucas Miller, and what did they have to lose if she found him? She reached for her phone to call Detective Bentley, too late realizing that the police were off the case. Though maybe this threat—was it a threat?—would be enough to reopen the case. She let it ring.

"Anne," he answered right away, "I was hoping you'd call. Have you found out anything new about the connection between Marta Henshaw and Lucas? I've been looking into it, and…" He went on, but Anne was puzzled. He sounded like he had no knowledge that the police had withdrawn from the case.

"Did Officer Banks tell you that the police were pulling out of the case?" she asked.

"Oh…" He hedged. But it was obvious that the man was surprised. "I guess Michael did leave me a message here on my phone. I just hadn't gotten around to listening to it."

Anne wasn't buying it. He should've known long before Anne did. "Who exactly are you?"

"What do you mean?" he said. Then the line went dead.

She immediately called Michael Banks.

"Michael," she said, "what's Judd Bentley's role in the Lucas Miller case?"

"Judd who?" the officer said.

"The special agent you brought in to investigate…"

"Anne, there was no special agent assigned to the case."

Dread filled Anne. "Then just who is Detective Judd Bentley?"

"Are you telling me someone approached you posing as a police officer wanting to investigate the Lucas Miller case?"

"Yes."

How could she have been so gullible? *He was handsome*, the answer mocked her. She knew the police were limited in what they could share with civilians—why hadn't she questioned it more? She'd known, on some level. Yet, she'd ignored that sense. Just how much information had she given the imposter?

"Can you give me a description of the man?" Michael was saying.

She gave him the basics, especially noting those different colored eyes. They would be critical in finding him.

"Michael, there's more," she said. "I got a letter from New York that I think you're going to want to see."

"What does it say?"

She read the six words to him as the note shook in her hands. "I think it's a threat."

"I'll be right there," he said, hanging up.

While Officer Banks was on his way to the library Anne tried to call Judd Bentley again. The line went to voice mail several times. He was avoiding her.

Glancing around the library, a sense of dread overcame her. Suddenly Anne felt as if she were being watched. Fear rose in her throat. What exactly was the man capable of?

When Officer Banks arrived, Anne could see the worry on his face as he read the note in the privacy of her small office.

"Do you think Judd sent it?" Anne said.

"No idea. When was the last time you saw this Judd Bentley?"

Anne thought back. "Before Marta disappeared." That sinking feeling deepened. "He was with me that morning when I went to see her."

"You didn't mention it," Michael said.

"I assumed you knew."

"Just how much did you tell this Judd Bentley?"

"Oh, Michael!" Anne gasped. "I told him everything about Lucas." Her eyes grew wide. "I gave him those codes from Lucas's manuscript…He knows about Vincent Barrio…" Anne shook her head. "Who could he be? And what could he possibly have to do with this?"

"I don't know. But this, combined with Marta Henshaw disappearing…" He shook his head. "Was there anything else you can think of—you mentioned his eyes. Did you see his car?"

"Yes, I did," Anne said, as she described the sedan with the dented front panel.

"Did that damage look recent? Was there grass or debris on it?"

Anne paused to consider. "Yes, actually. There was grass under the front bumper. I remember because I wondered if he'd been in a police chase in it. And, you know...he had a bandage on his forehead when I first met him."

"Did you ask him where he got the cut?"

"No..." Suddenly the tumblers were clicking into place. "Lucas's accident—do you think he had something to do with it? He was in that first photo Grace took at the accident site, in the background..."

"Well, there has to be a reason he wanted to know what you were finding out about Lucas."

"Do you think he could be the reason Lucas left town in the first place?"

Chills ran down her spine at the thought.

"It's entirely possible."

After Officer Banks left with promises to call her once he looked into the matter and to be on the lookout for Judd Bentley, Anne called Mildred Farley and asked if she could come by. Wendy and the Miller girls had gone home for the night. Anne was ready to close up the library for the day anyway, and she needed the older woman's wisdom to know how to cope with the mess she'd made. Byron and Marlene had taken the kids out for a bit of shopping, promising to bring takeout and ice cream home when they returned. Anne was glad they weren't there right then.

Mildred had been like a second mother to Anne since she'd moved to Blue Hill. She knew how to tell Anne the truth even when it hurt, and she did it in a way that made a person listen rather than bristle with defensiveness. Mildred personified wisdom with grace.

Anne finished locking up for the day while Mildred looked at the note. Then they went to the third-story apartment where Hershey waited patiently. He tilted his head at Anne as if he understood the turmoil that boiled inside her. They sat in front of the sunny window in her living room.

"Detective Bentley was fake," Anne said. "I fell for his spiel completely." She told Mildred about the first time she'd met the supposed officer, how charming he'd been. What a fool she'd been.

Mildred's gray brows drew together as she studied Anne. "And Officer Banks said that this Judd Bentley had nothing to do with the police investigation?"

"Nothing."

"Oh dear," Mildred said. "What exactly have we gotten ourselves into?"

Anne smiled at her phrasing. "I feel so duped," she confessed. She thought of her attraction to the man, and the word *stupid* came to mind. "I need advice for what to do now. I hope I haven't put Lucas in harm's way."

"First," the older woman said, "you need to stop beating yourself up. Being trusting isn't something to be ashamed of. That's a good thing." She patted Anne's hand. "And it wouldn't hurt to talk to the good Lord about it."

So right there in the quiet of her apartment, with a chocolate Labrador retriever looking on, they bowed their heads as Mildred offered up a prayer asking God for help. She finished with, "And help Anne not to think she did anything wrong here. We've got enough to feel guilty about in our lives. You aren't one to beat us up, Lord, so help Anne not to do the same. Amen."

They lifted their heads and Anne smiled at her friend.

"There has to be a good reason for the things that have happened," Mildred reasoned. "So we simply need to think this all through. "Why would the good Lord put all this in your hands? And what was that Judd character after?" She paused, allowing Anne to draw her own conclusions.

"Okay." Anne nodded. She knew the older woman was right, that the Lord had placed these things in her care for a reason. She thought about her dream. She wouldn't allow the person who wrote that note, Judd Bentley or whoever he was, to intimidate her.

"The Lord is still in control," Mildred said.

She made everything sound so easy. Yet, Anne had to admit she felt better, even though nothing had been resolved.

"I forgot," Anne added, getting to her feet. "Wait here." She went to the kitchen to retrieve the letter she'd found from Senator Duffy. She handed it to Mildred.

The older woman studied the yellowed envelope for a long moment. "What is this exactly?" Her eyes shifted back to Anne.

"I was hoping you could tell me."

She pulled out the page and began to read, her lips moving ever so slightly. As her eyes scanned the page Anne saw recognition grow.

"Oh yes," she murmured. A hand lifted to cover her mouth. Then she said, "I remember this. This is a letter from Senator

Richard Duffy to Edie." She looked back at the envelope. "Must've been the early seventies."

Anne nodded that it was.

"Your aunt Edie lobbied against the state lotto becoming law. She was quite a thing, that aunt of yours." Mildred laughed. "She knocked on every door for several counties trying to get people to call their lawmakers. And she wrote letters. I'm pretty sure she wrote to every sitting legislator in the state! She knew the dangers of legalized gambling, and she was bound and determined to keep it from affecting the state of Pennsylvania."

"And what was the outcome?"

"Well, you can probably guess that—the law passed anyway." She shook her head. "Every time she ran across a study that showed the link between the rise in crime and gambling, she clipped it out and sent it to her lawmakers. She never did fully give up on that cause—hated seeing the heartbreak it brought to families."

"But he encouraged her to run for office," Anne said. "Did she ever consider doing that?"

"I know she was flattered, and there was a time she considered running for a state office to help defeat it."

"Aunt Edie?"

Mildred nodded. "Oh yes. But once the law passed and she saw all the programs the state set into motion for its senior citizens with the proceeds, she kind of gave it up. Not that she ever appreciated gambling, mind you. She still believed a gambling habit often led to bad things, and she was vehement about it till her passing."

Mildred placed the yellowed letter on the end table between them. "Edie realized she was a one-issue candidate. She didn't have the heart to keep fighting so she never did take up the gauntlet. She said the battle was the Lord's — if He wanted a thing done He'd do it with or without her help."

Anne thought about what she'd said. The outcome of Anne's present dilemma *was* the Lord's. And yet she'd taken so much of that upon herself, and not just the outcome of her investigation, but of her in-laws' visit with the kids. How Ben and Liddie would grow without a father. The outcome of her very life.

As Mildred said farewell, sounds of Liddie, Ben, Byron, and Marlene returning filled the stairs.

"Are you all packed for our trip?" Ben asked before Anne could even greet them. Liddie was carrying boxes of Chinese takeout while Marlene had a gallon of mint chocolate chip ice cream.

"I'll do it in a few minutes," Anne said, noting the smudges on his cheeks. She reached for a tissue and handed it to him to wipe his face. "How much can a girl need for a six-day trip?"

Liddie pointed to the heaping stack of luggage she and Ben had set aside and said, "A whole lotta stuff, honey," in her sassy voice.

Byron burst out laughing. "Where does she get that stuff?"

Marlene held a hand over her smiling face.

The phone buzzed to life and Anne moved to answer it. "Gibsons."

"Anne?" Joyce Miller's voice filled the line. Her anxious tone immediately set Anne on edge.

"What's wrong?"

"Are the girls with you?"

"No... They left for home right after the library closed at five."

"Well, they aren't here. I just got home from work, and there's no sign of them. I'm worried."

"Don't go assuming the worst," Anne cautioned. Yet, her own sense of worry was in overdrive. Her thoughts rushed to Judd Bentley and the threatening note she'd received. She forced herself to take a deep breath. The girls had probably just stopped at a friend's house and forgotten the time. Anne glanced at the clock. It had been three hours since she'd seen the girls leave the library.

"I've called all their friends," Joyce went on. "I've tried their cell phones, but their phones are here at the house. They never leave their phones behind!" Her voice rose in volume and intensity. Anne glanced at her family who were watching her, fear on their faces.

"There has to be a logical explanation. Have you called the police?"

"Not yet. I just..." Her voice cracked as tears overwhelmed her. "With Lucas gone... this just can't be happening. It can't be!"

"I'll be right over," Anne said, then she hung up. "It's Remi and Bella. They seem to be missing, too," she said to Byron and Marlene.

"Their mother needs you right now," Marlene assured. "We've got everything covered here." Her gaze took in the children. "Just go. We'll be fine."

Anne gave her a grateful look. She reached for her purse to head to the Millers' when the phone rang again. Michael Banks was calling her back. "I don't have anything on a Judd Bentley," he said without preamble, referring to the police database that listed past arrests and convictions.

"Michael," Anne said, getting his attention. "I just got off the phone with Joyce Miller. Her girls never came home from work after the library closed today. I'm heading over there right now."

"Oh man," Michael said, clearly as shocked as she felt. "She suspects foul play?"

"She knows something isn't right."

"I'll meet you there."

* * *

Joyce met them at the door. Her face was streaked with mascara and her eyes were puffy and red.

Michael pulled out his notepad as they took seats at the kitchen table. "Any idea where they could've gone?"

"Michael, I've looked everywhere," Joyce said. "I don't know where else to look."

His brow wrinkled. "With the note Anne got…"

"Note?" Joyce said. Anne hadn't had a chance to tell her about it.

Anne pulled it from her purse and slid it across the table to Joyce. "Some dead are better left buried?" Joyce repeated its lone line. "What does that mean—that Anne's investigation caused this?"

"There's more," Anne admitted in a low voice. "The man I thought was an officer, Detective Bentley?"

Joyce nodded. "You told me about him."

"He was *impersonating* an officer."

"We have no idea who he was or what he was trying to do," Michael added.

"So," Joyce was adding all this new information up, "this stranger used Anne to get to my daughters? Is that what you think?"

Anne felt herself grow pale at the possibility.

"We don't know anything for sure," Michael assured in that calm voice of his. "But you can be sure the police will be on this, Joyce. If there was any foul play..."

"Like you did for Lucas?" she accused.

But Michael didn't seem offended. He merely let the comment pass.

"We need to question some people—your neighbors for starters," he said. "If Remi's and Bella's phones are here it seems reasonable that they came home after work."

"Okay." Joyce rose to her feet, though Anne could see that she was struggling to hold herself together. "Let's do it."

* * *

"Oh, a couple of men picked them up," the fifty-something woman across the street said when they knocked on her door and explained the situation.

"Picked them up?" Joyce spun to look behind her at the street, though it had been hours since the incident.

"Do you know who it was?" Anne said in a calm tone, hoping her demeanor would put Joyce more at ease.

The man who stood behind the housewife at the door wore a mechanic's jumpsuit, its badge read *Rudy*. He shrugged and said,

"They were waiting out front when I pulled in after work. Seemed odd to me so I asked them what was up. They said some police officer had called telling them they knew where their dad was. I saw them get into a van. I had no idea anything was amiss…"

Joyce groaned and Anne placed a comforting hand on her back.

Rudy scratched his chin. "One was quite tall, dark hair, good looking, I guess. He had a suit coat on. The other one stayed in the car so I didn't see much of him."

It had to be Judd Bentley.

Officer Banks moved into the house to get a full description from the couple as Anne begged God to keep the girls safe. As she was praying silently, her phone rang, displaying an unknown phone number.

"Anne Gibson?" the deep, husky voice said. Was it Bentley? She couldn't be sure.

"Anne?" she could hear Remi's and Bella's voices in the background.

"*Shh!*" the man hissed. "We have the Miller girls."

"Where are you?" Anne demanded.

"You've got this backward, sweetheart. You're listening to *me* here."

"Okay."

"Bring us Lucas Miller. And no cops."

"I have no idea where Lucas is!"

"That's your tough luck, then, isn't it? 'Cause I think you know a lot more than you're saying."

Panic filled her throat. "What are you going to do?"

"Don't you worry about that. You just bring us Lucas Miller. We'll call you." He hung up.

For a long moment Anne just looked at her phone. Had that really just happened? Then she realized Joyce was staring at her, or rather through her. She was clearly in shock.

"My girls have been kidnapped," she finally said. "We don't know what those men are capable of…" Her voice trailed off, unwilling to speak the unthinkable.

"You're going to have to lay low," Officer Banks said when Anne and Joyce told him about the call. "We'll station some men outside your place, some wiretaps and surveillance." He turned to Joyce as if asking her permission. She nodded.

"You've got to find Lucas," Anne said.

"We'll do our best," he promised.

But would their best be good enough?

Chapter Twelve

It was eleven o'clock by the time Anne drove home. The Blue Hill police had set up post at Joyce's house, with FBI reinforcements on their way now that they knew this was a kidnapping. They urged both women to get some rest so they'd have the strength to face whatever the next days would bring. Joyce reluctantly went to her bedroom, though Anne doubted she'd be able to rest at all, then she headed home. She knew it was late, but she called Alex anyway. She needed to hear his strong voice.

"Anne?" his sleepy voice answered. "What's up?"

"I need your help," she confessed, wishing he were here at her side rather than across town.

"What's going on?"

She closed her eyes. A tear slipped down her cheek.

"What is it?" the concern in his voice undid her. Her tale came out in bits and pieces, the threatening note, Detective Bentley's deception, Remi and Bella's disappearance, the call she'd received…

It was Alex's calming voice that pulled her back.

"You need to call the police," he said.

"The police are already set up at Joyce's place."

There was a long silence over the line as Alex thought.

"You don't understand—they want *me* to bring them Lucas. We have to find him, and *now*, or who knows what will happen to Remi and Bella!"

* * *

"Does this mean we aren't going on vacation?" Liddie said the next morning as Anne, Byron, and Marlene sat at the kitchen table discussing that very thing. The little girl looked rumpled. Her pajamas were twisted oddly around her small torso and her hair was matted at the back of her head. Ben had taken Hershey outside for his morning duties.

Marlene patted her lap and Liddie plopped into it, allowing her grandmother to cuddle her. "Your mom is the best person to help the Millers," she said to Liddie.

"I suppose," Liddie conceded. "But it isn't fair!"

"No it isn't," Anne agreed.

"But you have to help," Byron said before he turned to Liddie. "Remi and Bella are in real danger. Your mom is needed here."

"I know."

Just then Ben and Hershey came up the stairs. "Who needs Mom?" His face darkened in understanding almost instantly. "You're ditching us again?"

"Not ditching," Anne corrected, though the pain of his accusation still hurt. "It's my fault that those girls were taken. If I hadn't been fooled by Detective Bentley—"

"You don't know that," Marlene said gently. "That man had evil intentions from the start, regardless of any information you gave him. Someone like that can't be stopped."

"Still, I feel responsible."

"I know you do," Marlene said.

Ben crossed his arms over his chest, clearly having none of this.

"Why don't we just stay here then?" he said.

"I think you'd be safer if you left with Grandma and Grandpa for a few days," Anne said. "We've already seen what that man is capable of. Who knows what else he might be planning."

"But *you* aren't safe," he argued.

"I'll be as safe as I can be," she promised. "But, honey, you have to understand—I can't just go on vacation while some monsters are holding Remi and Bella hostage."

She could see that he understood. He didn't like it. But he did understand.

"Fine." He moved to the hallway and lifted his suitcase to haul it down to the motor home.

Anne exchanged a look with her in-laws.

"He'll come around," Byron said. "He's just disappointed."

"I am too."

* * *

The family headed out without Anne a few hours later. Anne watched the lumbering motor home turn out of view as she stood on the library's sprawling front porch. Oh, how she wished she could go with them. She'd called Joyce and Officer Banks earlier. Michael had told her the police were tracking down leads, but the kidnappers' warning echoed in her memory—it was her job to bring Lucas in, without police. If things got too complicated, she'd call Michael. But she had to at least dig in and find out what she could.

Wendy pulled up in her red SUV and gave Anne a little wave before climbing out. Anne had called her this morning to update her on all that had happened and her decision not to head out with her family after all, though she would still need her friend's help at the library.

"I just remembered!" she said.

"What are we talking about?" Anne lifted a teasing eyebrow. Wendy did have a tendency to jump into things without explanation.

"Lucas was on the computers a few days before his disappearance."

"Okay…" Anne wasn't sure where this was leading.

"Maybe his history is still stored on them. I hadn't thought of it till now…We need to see!"

A smile grew on Anne's face. She led the way into the darkened library with Wendy following.

She opened the computer log and found the time that Lucas had been online, then led the way upstairs to the room that held the library's computers. Anne moved to computer number two and turned it on, motioning for Wendy to take the seat next to her, which she did.

"You know how to navigate all this better than I do," Wendy said.

Once the computer was up and running, Anne clicked on the link that revealed the computer's history. It had been ten days since he'd been on, so Anne had to scroll back quite a ways to find the right day that would've been Lucas's history. He'd gone to a couple social media pages, and a Wikipedia page on the history of the Catskill Mountains, Anne presumed as part of his research for his book since that was where his story was set. But the site that caught her attention was www.howtodisappear.com.

Surprised, she looked at Wendy. "Lookee there."

Wendy's mouth opened in an *O*.

"It's far too coincidental to be research for a book," Anne said. The site linked to a full course taught by a former FBI agent on recommendations for how to vanish from one's former life and take on a new identity in another town. Anne scanned the pages, noting a list of suggestions for preparing the perpetrator's family for the event, including purposely starting arguments with loved ones to make the disappearance "more believable in retrospect."

Hadn't Joyce said their arguments of late hadn't been typical, that she knew Lucas loved her and his daughters, that she thought it was a passing phase?

But what about Marta Henshaw? No one seemed to know what she and Lucas were doing together. Helping each other write their books—that possibility had gone out the window a long time ago.

If only I hadn't given Bentley those codes.

"You have something here, Wendy," Anne finally said.

Anne had to get back on the trail of finding Lucas Miller, and fast. Her first order of business, another chat with Mitch Bach, Lucas's best friend.

* * *

She knocked on the door to his upstairs apartment half an hour later. The hallway was so grimy she half expected a rat to run across her shoes.

"Who's there?" a sleepy voice said through the door. Was the man ever fully awake?

"It's Anne Gibson. I need to ask you some more questions about Lucas Miller."

The door cracked open.

"You alone this time?" he asked.

"I am."

He nodded, then let her in. "I remembered who your friend was," he said. "The guy with the weird eyes."

He led the way into the apartment and slouched onto the ratty-looking couch. Anne took a wooden chair across from him, pushing aside the dirty clothes that were draped across it.

"Really?" Anne said.

"His name was Jeremiah Briggs," Mitch said. "He worked at the casino with Lucas. Didn't recognize him with the nice duds on."

"What happened at the casino?" Anne asked when she met his gaze again. She saw the slight twitch of his cheek. She waited. "Was that where you met Marta Henshaw?"

"It was." His voice was so quiet she almost missed his words.

"What was the nature of her friendship with Lucas?"

Mitch shrugged. "Hard to say. Seemed mostly business."

"You mean as writers?"

"No." He didn't want to meet her eyes. "They both liked to place bets."

"You mean on games at the casino?"

He nodded. But then he seemed at war with himself. "On other things too."

At first Anne was stumped. "You mean like on ball games, that kind of thing?" Anne remembered the radio being on at the Millers' when she'd gone to see them, and Joyce's comment that Lucas always had a game on.

Mitch's eyes refused to look up. Then finally, reluctantly he said, "Yes, he was giving Marta some kind of information."

"Did he use some sort of code?" Anne asked, pulling one of the manuscript sheets from her purse to show it to Mitch.

He studied the script with bleary eyes before finally saying, "Yeah. *VT224OML* means Vermont two to four over Mass Lowell."

"So they're betting odds."

Mitch nodded and handed the sheet back.

"Is that why Lucas quit his job there?"

Again a shrug. "He didn't say. His wife wasn't happy with him. And he just seemed...scared."

"Scared...why? Did that have something to do with why he disappeared?"

"He stopped going there three months ago."

"Are you sure? Joyce said you two still went out after he quit his job," Anne said, "that you'd come home late together smelling of smoke."

"I don't know what his extracurricular activities were," Mitch said. "Maybe he was doing something illegal, maybe not."

"Come on, Mitch. You want me to believe that?" Anne said, but she had one more question she needed to ask. "Was Lucas planning on disappearing? I mean days before he left?"

Mitch shrugged. Anne could see he was done answering questions.

And the truth was, she could guess what had been going on. If Lucas was gambling and owed money to some loan shark...that would surely follow him wherever he went.

A solid motive to disappear if ever there was one.

* * *

"I'm telling you, Lucas was doing something illegal," Anne told Alex when she stopped by his place right after seeing Mitch. She needed to process what she'd just learned about Lucas. "Betting on games," she added.

"So why would he need to take those odds to Marta? Was she gambling too, or what?"

"I don't know. Maybe he was working for a bookie... delivering information to him through her," she guessed. "I have to go to the casino and find out."

Alex barked a laugh. "Are you kidding me? You can't just go digging for potentially dangerous information alone, Anne."

"I'll be fine."

"You're not going to that casino alone," he repeated. "If what Mitch said is true, there's no telling what you'll be walking into."

She sent him a look that was really more of a dare.

"Really, Anne?" He finally relented. "Why do you have to be so stubborn?"

She hated to admit it, but she enjoyed riling the man. It was something she'd done since they were kids and it never grew old.

"So you're coming along?" she said.

Alex practically growled at her. "Let me grab my keys."

* * *

The casino was just off the highway outside State College, Pennsylvania. It was a bit of a drive from Blue Hill, and by the time they got there it was almost noon. The sky was a deep blue, warm and cloudless.

The tires of Alex's truck crunched on the gravel parking lot as they pulled in. There were only a handful of cars there and the concrete building was run-down. Anne shivered even though the day was quite warm.

"You okay?" Alex asked.

"I'm fine."

They made their way inside, where slot machines stood in long rows like brightly lit headstones. The rancid smoky air filled Anne's nostrils, stinging her eyes and causing them to water. Several men lifted rheumy eyes their way before glancing back at the mind-numbing machines.

They moved toward the center of the outdated building that looked like a scene from some late-eighties mafia movie. The carpet was avocado-green shag. Anne hadn't seen anything like it since she was a kid. She half expected the people inside to be wearing bell bottoms and have their hair styled in groovy braids.

"Hello?" Anne said when they stopped alongside a green felt-covered table where several men sat playing a card game. Anne wasn't familiar with the protocol in such places.

A man was there, dealing cards. He stood a good six feet tall and wore a mustache that drooped from the corners of his mouth making him look sad.

"Can I help you with something?" he said. His voice was a deep bass, and when he looked at her, he tilted his head down as if he were looking over the top of his glasses. Only he didn't wear glasses.

Anne gave him a smile, hoping it would boost her lagging confidence. He wasn't fazed. "Yes," Anne said. She exchanged a look with Alex, who was scoping out the place. His eyes moved from one patron to the next, before he nodded at her. "I'm hoping you can help me find someone."

"Okay." He waited for her to go on.

"Lucas Miller?"

Anne wasn't sure if the man had any idea who Lucas was or not. Finally, she decided to try the name Judd Bentley had said he'd used.

"Lance Martin?" she amended.

The card dealer's face turned dark red, and he told the men who'd been playing cards at his table that he was closing up. When they were gone, he leaned close and hissed the words at her face. "I don't know what you're trying to do. But you can't just come in here slinging that name around—do you understand me? You're going to get yourself in trouble. Big trouble."

Alex moved into the circle, placing his arm around Anne's back. "Maybe we should just go," he said calmly to Anne.

"No," she insisted. She looked back at the tall, burly man. "What exactly did Lucas do here? I mean, Lance?"

"He was a blackjack dealer." The man glanced around the room, as if to see if he was being watched. "Why do you need to know?"

"He disappeared, and his two daughters have been kidnapped."

The man cursed under his breath, then he said, "Why didn't anyone tell us?"

Without a word he started walking. He moved toward a back door.

Anne and Alex followed. "Are you sure this is smart?" Alex whispered in Anne's ear.

"If he kills us, you can blame me," she whispered back. The brilliance of the afternoon sun flooded in when he opened the heavy metal door. It closed with a clang behind them.

"What are you doing here?" he turned on them and said, anger in his tone. "Why aren't the police looking into this? The FBI?"

"Trust me," Anne said, "the officials are looking into this. But, you see, the kidnappers told me to bring Lucas in. If I don't…"

The man ran a hand through his graying hair. "This isn't going to be easy—I doubt that the man wants to be found." He shook his head, his lips pursed. "It's hard to explain…without putting you in even more danger. You don't know…"

"Well, do you know Judd Bentley—Jeremiah Briggs?"

"Oh yes. I know Jeremiah. But you have to understand, that man is a cog in a much bigger wheel."

"What does that mean?"

"It means you're touching on the tip of the iceberg here, honey."

"So many clichés," Anne said. "But no answers. Can we be more original?" Anne's frustration rose. She felt Alex's hand on her upper arm. She glanced at him, saw the caution in his gaze.

"Listen, I'm not trying to upset anyone," Anne calmed her voice. "If you could just give me the name of anyone who can help me..." She paused. "His wife is going crazy with worry."

The man's face softened just a fraction. He sighed. "I can't guarantee you'll get anywhere with him, but you could try Ramon Sanchez."

Anne glanced at Alex, a smile growing on her face.

"The only thing is," the man added, "if you want to talk to him, he's in prison."

Chapter Thirteen

Y ou almost got yourself killed just now. There is no way I'm
letting you walk into a federal penitentiary," Alex complained
as they made their way back to Blue Hill. Given the waning day,
they would have to wait at least until the next day before heading
to the penitentiary in Allenwood, Pennsylvania, a two-and-a-half-
hour drive from Blue Hill. "Aren't you afraid of anything?"

"I'm afraid of a lot of things," Anne said in a quiet voice. "But,
what can happen in a maximum security facility with guards
around every corner?"

Alex sighed, followed by a long silence. "Plenty," he finally
said. "With you around — plenty can happen."

Anne smiled at him. She saw the way the corner of his eyes
crinkled up as his gaze stayed on the road.

"I'll be fine," she assured.

"Of course you will, because I'm coming with you."

* * *

After making a phone call or two, they decided to leave at 8:00 AM
on Friday since that was the soonest the Allenwood Penitentiary
allowed visitors.

Wendy and Betty had volunteered to cover things at the
library while Anne and Alex headed there.

Alex was quiet as they made their way east. The sunrise was glorious — shades of salmon, peach, and lavender combining in an artist's palette across the sky. She'd talked on the phone to the kids the previous night. Liddie had gone on and on about seeing "that cracked bell," as she'd dubbed the Liberty Bell. But Ben had been subdued. He barely said a word to her, just said he was okay and handed the phone off to his grandmother. Marlene had said he was fine, not to worry. But guilt edged forward. Anne wondered if she would ever be able to do enough, be enough to make him happy?

"Is there something you need to talk about?" Alex said.

Anne lifted her eyes to his, surprised by the question. She wasn't in the mood to pour her heart out, not with everything that was going on. Yet, she knew that if anyone would understand her guilt about the Millers' kidnapping, as well as her fears about her son it would be Alex. Surely he had similar worries raising Ryan alone, without a mother's perspective.

"Come on, Anne. I know you. Something's up."

"Kids," was all she said.

"They doing okay on their expedition?"

"I guess so."

Alex sighed. "Anne, I *know* you. Out with it."

"Why didn't you ever marry?" She could sense his body stiffen the moment the words left her lips, and immediately she regretted asking. It was a topic they hadn't spoken of since she'd moved back to Blue Hill. It had seemed too touchy to approach, and yet Anne wondered why. They were friends — so why couldn't they talk about it? She knew she'd hurt him all those years ago when she'd left for college and had found Eric. Had Alex pined for her? Wished she'd made a different choice, to come back to him and the plans they'd once had all those years before in high school?

There'd been no comparison, though. Not for her.

She turned to study Alex's handsome profile. She hadn't paid attention to how the years had marked his face with smile lines around his eyes and mouth. His hair was still thick, not balding as other men his age were, but there was a bit of gray along his temples. When had that happened?

Alex cleared his throat. "I, uh…wow, Anne. I didn't expect that."

"You don't have to answer if you don't want to. I'm sorry. I didn't mean to—"

"No. It's okay," he said. "There were others…after you, I mean. In college I had a girlfriend."

"You did?"

"Liz Mielke. I even bought her a ring. But I never gave it to her."

"Why?"

"You know the expression 'out of sight, out of mind.' She left on an internship…and well, once I was out of sight she found someone else. That seems to keep happening to me." There was an awkward silence, then he added, "Things just kind of fell apart."

"I'm sorry."

"Don't be. If it was meant to be it would've lasted." His gaze landed on hers. "Like you and Eric."

There was another long silence.

"So was that really what was bothering you? Why I stayed single all these years?" he asked.

Anne smiled at him. "No. I'm worried about Ben. He's been such a pill lately. He won't talk to me, won't open up. I think if Eric were here it'd be easier. I worry that raising him without a father will hurt him somehow." She paused. "Do you worry about Ryan that way? Raising him without a mother?"

"Of course I do," he admitted. "But I can't change it. Neither can you. Unless God puts a husband in your path, this is the task you've been given. God will help you with it, you know. He's not going to leave you alone."

Such practical wisdom. "Thank you for that," she said. "I guess I forgot. You know us mothers—we look for excuses to worry."

They passed through the city of Allenwood and made their way toward the federal penitentiary outside of town. The exterior of the building looked more like something she'd have expected at a national park than a prison, its green roof giving it an outdoorsy sensibility.

They told the guard at the outer gate their intentions and were eventually led into a dingy room where they waited after having handed over all of their valuables—cell phone, keys, purse—to the swarthy-looking man at the front desk.

The place felt so cold. Anne rubbed her hands on her upper arms. Alex took a seat in one of the vinyl-covered, padded chairs at the table in the room's center.

"Are we crazy to be here?" Anne asked.

Alex shrugged. "I guess we'll find out."

The metal door echoed as Ramon Sanchez was brought in flanked by two guards. Ramon was a short, wide-set man with a Spanish accent and piercing black eyes. His hair was slicked back from his pockmarked face. He took the chair opposite Alex and Anne and studied them with suspicious eyes.

"Who are you?" he said, his glance flicking to the guard who remained in the corner of the room, his thick arms crossed in front of him.

Anne took the lead. "We're looking for Lucas Miller. You'd know him as Lance Martin. We were told you might have some idea where he is."

Alex held up the photo they'd brought of Lucas, as well as the shots that had arrived with the threatening note. Ramon reached for them and studied the shots, then closed his eyes and blew out a breath.

"Why should I help you find him, the...?" He didn't finish the sentence. "Does he owe you money?"

"No," Anne said. "Does he owe you?"

"He owes lots of people. And not just money either."

"What was he doing at that casino?" Anne said.

Ramon shook his head. "If you don't know..."

"Why are you here? In prison?" Anne said.

The man let out a laugh and leaned toward them, handing back the photo. "Let's just say when the boss needed a scapegoat I was the easiest target."

"Who's the boss?" Anne said. She met the man's gaze. He winked at her, but she narrowed her eyes, refusing to let him intimidate her.

"You don't have any idea what you're getting yourself into, lady." He shook his head. "Why would you want to get ahold of such a lowlife anyway?"

"We just need to," Anne insisted. "This man's family is looking for him. If you have any idea..."

Ramon let out a single barking laugh. "Now that's irony. His wife is looking for him. Well, pity. My family's waiting for me too, but they aren't going to get me. Why should his?"

"Are you saying he has something to do with why you're in prison?" Anne said.

"He has everything to do with why I'm here!" he shouted, rising to his feet. The guard was instantly next to him, grabbing him.

Ramon blew out a breath, his thick brows furrowing as the guard shoved him back into his chair.

"We're sorry to upset you," Anne said sincerely. "Truly." She waited a long moment. Finally, the man looked her in the eyes. So much pain in his gaze. "We didn't come here to bring up difficult memories for you."

The man didn't seem to know how to handle that. He blew out a heavy breath.

"Do you know Marta Henshaw?" She pulled out a photo of Marta that she showed to him.

He nodded. "Lance's girlfriend."

"Is that what she was to him?" Alex said.

Ramon merely shrugged. "Looked like it to me. They would meet after he got off of work. She had a place in Lock Haven. I know 'cause I followed him there one night."

He seemed to be testing Anne with this bit of information, as if he wanted to see if it would scare her to know he'd followed someone else. Anne looked him in the eyes. "And what about Jeremiah Briggs?" She'd almost said Judd Bentley. "Where does he fit into this?"

"You know Jeremiah?" He lifted a brow. "Jeremiah and I have a lot in common. An awful lot."

When they'd had all they could take of the man's ramblings, Anne and Alex finally said farewell and left.

"He was talking in circles," Alex said, frustration in his voice.

"But he made a lot of sense."

Alex turned his attention from driving for a moment to glance at her. "What do you mean?"

"Lucas and Marta were in some sort of an illegal gambling ring—booking, according to Mitch Bach. Ramon and Judd—Jeremiah—were both working for the same man. Someone high up."

"And what was Lucas's role? Marta's?"

"That I'm not sure of yet."

Anne and Alex drove straight to Lock Haven. Anne pulled out her smartphone and typed in "Henshaw," hoping there was someone in the town with that last name. There were three addresses that came up. The first house was in a modest neighborhood with streets that curved from one to the next and names ending in Circle or Lane. Anne made her way to the front of the brick home. She was met by a woman in hair curlers and a housedress.

"I'm sorry to bother you," Anne began.

The woman lifted a thinly plucked brow.

"We are looking for a woman named Marta Henshaw, or someone who knows her." She held up the photo they'd showed Ramon.

"Sorry, honey." She shook her head and shut the door.

The second house was no different.

But it was what was in the driveway of the third house, the home of Irving and Emmaline Henshaw, that made Anne sit up straight when they reached the address—a Westfalia VW van, the same kind of vehicle that Scott Milhouse had said picked Lucas up the night of his accident. It was hard to mistake the hippie-style camper van.

The house behind it was small but in immaculate condition. Perfectly trimmed evergreen hedges lined up beneath the large picture window that smiled at the front of the house with a metal awning bearing the letter *H*.

"This is a shot in the dark," Anne admitted as she got out of Alex's truck.

"At least it's something." He followed her to the front door that rose from the lawn by a few brick steps.

She pressed the doorbell and could hear its distinctive *ding-dong* inside followed by the yipping of a dog.

A shadow moved across the picture window and the door creaked open. "Can I help you?" an elderly gentleman said. He held the dog, a miniature dachshund, in his arms. The man Anne assumed to be Irving wore a mustard-colored cardigan that reminded her of something Mr. Rogers would wear, and his straight smile lent itself to the image.

"Good morning," Anne said. The grandfather clock on the wall behind him read 12:05. She introduced herself and then Alex, then asked if he was related to Marta Henshaw.

"She's my daughter," he said tentatively. "How do you know her?"

"We live in Blue Hill," Anne said. "She's in the writers' group that we attend."

His face took on a smile as if what she'd just told him made them long-lost relatives.

He said, "You two don't need to be standing out here all day. Why don't you come on in?" He took a step back for them to enter.

When Anne's eyes adjusted from the bright day, she could see that the house was just as meticulous inside as it was outside. The furniture was lined up to face a tube-style television set in the corner, and a short table in front of the large picture window was covered in Christmas cactuses and geraniums that released their particular scent into the air.

The man set the dog down and it immediately began to sniff at Anne's and Alex's ankles. Alex patted it on the head and the dog sat.

"Do you know where Marta is?" Anne said.

"Has something happened to her?"

"I don't think so," Anne said, not wanting to upset the man and unsure if she should tell him that his daughter might be involved in dangerous activities. "We need to find Marta is all. Do you know where she is?" she repeated the question she'd asked earlier.

Irving reached to pick up the dog and patted its head. "We haven't seen Marta in several weeks," he admitted. "But she calls home regularly." He called out for his wife to come into the living room. "Is she in trouble?" His wrinkled brow furrowed.

"We don't know," Anne admitted. "I went to see her on Monday after work and discovered that she'd left town in a hurry. It looked pretty obvious that someone had been looking for something there—her place was ransacked."

A cloud seemed to enter the man's gaze.

A petite woman with white hair bustled into the living room but stopped short. "I didn't know we had company, Irving." Her dark eyes were lively. She looked from her husband to Anne and Alex.

"These are friends of Marta's—Anne and Alex. They're looking for her. Anne here says someone broke into Marta's place on Monday."

"Marta called just last night," she said, wiping her hands on the dish towel in her hands. "She didn't say anything about a break-in."

"Last night," Anne repeated, relieved to know the woman was all right. "Do you know where she called from?"

"Not specifically," Emmaline said. "She was on the road, she said. Her work takes her all over the place."

"What exactly does she do for a living?"

"She's a freelance photographer. Works for several popular magazines," Irving supplied. "They send her to different places around the world. That kind of thing." He was obviously proud of her accomplishments.

"Did she sound okay when she called?" Anne asked Emmaline. The woman took a wooden captain's chair near the door.

"She did. Should we be concerned?" She exchanged a worried look with her husband.

"No. I don't think so," Anne said. "I mean if she sounded good…" She pulled out the photos she'd received with the note and showed them to Irving first. He studied them with a twisted expression for a long moment before handing them back. "Do these hold any sort of significance for you?"

"No, ma'am," he said.

Next she pulled out the shot of Lucas and showed it to Irving. "Does this man look familiar to you?"

"That's Lucas," he said right away. "I gave him a ride a couple weeks ago. Marta called me to go get him. He was having car trouble so Marta called me to give him a lift."

"Was it just car trouble? Did he look injured in any way?"

The man paused to think. He ran a hand across his clean shaven cheek. "I guess he did have a cut on his forehead."

"Did you see his car?" Alex asked.

Irving shook his head. "I picked him up at a car repair shop, so I assumed it was inside."

"Did Lucas say anything about being in an accident that night?"

His eyes widened. "Not a word. Is this man in trouble?"

"Yes," Anne said simply. She glanced at Alex. "Where did you take him?"

"The bus station in Deshler."

"Do you know where he was going after that?"

"No."

"Did Marta tell you how she knew him?" Anne leaned forward. The elderly gentleman pursed his lips.

"Just that they were friends."

"What exactly," Emmaline put in, "do you think is going on here? What were they involved in?"

Anne wasn't sure how to answer that.

"We aren't sure," she confessed. "Lucas has been missing for almost two weeks—his family has no idea where he is. And his daughters have been kidnapped."

Emmaline gasped, a hand across her mouth.

"Kidnapped?" That clearly troubled the man.

"And you think our Marta had something to do with that?" Emmaline said.

"She is the one he called for a ride," Anne said.

"Well, she didn't come with me when I picked him up," Irving said. "I was just doing her friend a favor. That's all she told me."

"Do you think he was doing something illegal?" Emmaline asked, her brow furrowed in motherly concern.

But Irving was shaking his head. "No. We know our daughter. Marta's a good girl. If there's anything I know about my daughter, it's that."

Irving tried to call Marta several times while they were still there, but she didn't pick up. He left a message telling her she needed to call him back as soon as possible.

"I'll keep trying," he promised. Anne checked the number he was dialing to make sure she had the right one for Marta and said her thanks before she and Alex moved back to the car.

"What do you think of it all?" Alex said when they were back on the road. "Either they really do know their daughter or they don't. Maybe she's been telling the truth."

"Alex, she knew where Lucas went—she's been lying to all of us."

"I assume our next stop is the bus station in Deshler?" Alex asked.

"You assume right," Anne replied.

He turned the car onto the Interstate and pointed the car toward Deshler.

The bus station was attached to a truck stop off the highway on the edge of town. It was a little after four o'clock by the time they got there from Lock Haven. Anne called Wendy at the library to see how things were going and to make sure it would be okay that they got back a bit later than they'd originally planned.

"So he saw Lucas?" Wendy asked of Irving Henshaw.

"The night that he disappeared, yes," Anne said.

"That's good!" the excitement in her voice was undeniable. "Did he say where Lucas went?"

"That's why we need to head to Deshler—Lucas took a bus from there."

"Stay however long you need to. I'll close up here in just a little bit."

But when they got to the station, no one seemed to know a thing about Lucas. The woman who worked at the Greyhound desk, a tall thin woman who smelled strongly of cigarette smoke, clicked on the keys of her computer. Her skin was dark and leathery looking. "I'm not seeing anyone by that name in the system."

"How about Lance Martin?" Anne said.

The woman lifted an eyebrow, but she didn't look up as she clicked on the keyboard.

"You say it was twelve days ago?" She mentioned the date that it would have been.

"Yes."

She clicked around for a few more minutes before looking back up at Anne and Alex. "I'm sorry, but I'm still not finding anyone by that name who would've bought a ticket here."

"Can I look at the screen?" Anne asked. She motioned toward the laptop.

The woman turned the thin computer to face Anne. She scanned the names of those who'd purchased tickets that night and the next day. None of the names looked familiar.

CHAPTER FOURTEEN

I s it possible he hitchhiked or caught another ride from there?"
Alex asked as they drove back to Blue Hill.

"Of course it is."

They'd shown Lucas's photo around the restaurant, especially among the staff. But no one seemed to have any idea who Lucas was nor where he'd gone that night.

Anne was more discouraged than ever. She dialed Marta's number again. It went straight to voice mail so Anne left a message.

"Marta," she said. "I talked to your folks today...I need to get ahold of you. This is really important—Lucas's daughters have been kidnapped. I know that your dad gave Lucas a ride to the Deshler bus station. Please"—she was begging—"please call me back."

When she glanced at the screen of her cell phone as she hung up, she realized that she'd missed a phone call from her father-in-law.

Hitting the *talk* button, she waited for the line to connect. Liddie's voice bounced across the line. "Hey, Mommy!"

Anne instantly missed her. "How's my baby?"

"We're having fun!" she said. "We're in Washington!"

"Wow," Anne said. "Tell me what you've seen."

"Um...there was this big man sitting in a chair."

"A man in a chair?"

"He wasn't real."

"Oh, was it a statue?"

"Yeah! That's the ticket!"

The child certainly had a way of picking up expressions wherever she went.

"So you're at the Lincoln Memorial?"

"That's the place! I asked Grandpa if I could climb up on the big man's lap, but he said no."

Anne chuckled.

"Is Grandpa there?"

She could hear Liddie talking to her grandparents and Ben's voice in the background. Finally, Byron came on the line.

"Hi, Anne," he said.

"She didn't actually try to climb up on Honest Abe's lap, did she?"

"Oh yes, she did," he said. "We've got to keep a close eye on that one." Byron laughed. "Pretty sure she gets that from your side. We're enjoying DC. Heading to the Washington Monument right now."

"I wish I were there," Anne said.

* * *

After Anne got home, she invited Wendy, Alex, and Mildred to come over so they could brainstorm the case. Ryan was at a friend's house, so Alex was free, as was Mildred, but Wendy had taken off for some sporting event with her family. Anne checked in with Michael and Joyce to see if there were any new developments there and to tell them of her discoveries. Anne could hear the defeat in Joyce's voice. "Why don't you join us too?" she said. "We need your insight."

Joyce finally agreed, saying she'd be over in a half hour. Yet, Anne couldn't help but feel that she had given up hope. Lucas had left her and now her daughters were gone for good. She probably thought Marta had joined him wherever he'd gone. But there were too many problems with everything else in the story for Anne to believe that. No one would have taken Lucas's daughters if that were the case. But the thing that finally convinced Anne was — she'd known Lucas. He was an honest, honorable man.

No doubt Joyce had felt that same way. At one time.

Maybe Anne was being foolish. Maybe Lucas was just a good liar. A gambler who'd wasted his money on bad bets, had taken one too many loans from the wrong guy...But something deep within said that wasn't so. He loved his family. It had been so evident in the way he spoke about them that night. Men like that didn't just leave. Not of their own free will, not without some extenuating circumstance pushing them out the door.

Figuring out what those circumstances were...that was the hard part.

Alex grilled burgers while Mildred set out buns, coleslaw, pickles, and chips. Joyce was setting the picnic table behind the house. She seemed anxious, then hovered near as Anne flipped the burgers. "So no one saw him at the bus station?" she asked again as if she still couldn't believe Anne had uncovered a new lead. "Unfortunately, no."

"But he was *there*. Marta's dad took him there, and he said Lucas wasn't hurt or anything."

"Not badly anyway. Marta's dad did say he had a cut on his forehead, just as Scott Milhouse said."

"Somebody had to have seen him. You just have to find that person."

"That's true." Anne closed the lid of the grill and met Joyce's eyes.

"You were so close," Joyce said.

"And we aren't giving up." Anne placed a hand on the petite woman's shoulder.

Anne lifted the lid of the grill, sending a wave of heat across the three of them. It smelled of goodness. Joyce handed Anne the platter, then they all joined Alex at the table. Mildred said the prayer.

"Thank you all for coming," Anne said, her gaze taking each of them in as they reached for chips and ketchup. "I thought it would do us good to brainstorm a little." She looked at Joyce. "Try to figure out what we're missing in this search for Lucas."

She told them what she and Alex had discovered that day—Ramon Sanchez's inference that Lucas was involved in illegal gambling at the casino and his connection to Marta, though she was careful to leave out his mention of Marta being Lucas's girlfriend. Then she mentioned that Marta Henshaw's father had picked him up at Fowler's Auto Repair that night, thinking he was simply giving a lift to a friend of Marta's. He'd taken Lucas to the bus station in Deshler. She didn't miss the anguish that stole across

Joyce's eyes. She was being so brave. Still holding onto hope in such dire circumstances.

Anne took a bite of her burger. "Let's start at the beginning — lay out all the facts that we know so far and see if we can piece them together."

Anne read through the clues she'd already written out — Lucas's job at the casino, quitting it three months ago. That he'd kept the job a secret from his daughters. Then she mentioned the deposits from Vincent Barrio, the police officer from Philadelphia.

"Did Lucas ever say who Vincent Barrio was?" Anne pointed to the sheet.

Joyce shook her head.

"If he was writing checks to Lucas, is it safe to guess that Lucas was working for him?" Alex said.

"Like a police officer turned gambling bookie?" Anne said. She gave her head a shake. "How does that work with the withdrawals, then?"

"Maybe loan shark?" Alex offered.

"Perhaps." Anne nodded, writing down the possibility.

"We know that Lucas and Mitch Bach had been gambling in Lucas's off hours," Joyce said.

"Betting on ball games," Anne said. She made a note to look into the legalities of that issue. It was something she knew little about. Why was some gambling legal while other gambling was still illegal?

"And though Mitch claimed that Lucas gambled a lot, Lucas didn't fit the profile of addictive gamblers that I looked up," she added.

"We had an argument that night," Joyce added.

"But that could have been intentional on his part. A setup for the 'cover' described in that class on how to disappear which Lucas was taking—starting arguments so you wouldn't suspect anything after he left, and thus wouldn't go looking for him."

"He did leave a note saying he was leaving his family," Mildred reminded.

"But why would he leave it in his car?" Anne asked. "That's the part that doesn't make sense—if you're leaving your family, you leave a note at the house, on the refrigerator, not in the car you're supposedly taking with you. And why sneak out at all, and not just leave in broad daylight? There would have been no reason to make it so secretive."

"Unless he decided to leave that night," Alex added. "After the writers' meeting. If something prompted his departure, something sudden."

"You might have something there!" Anne said, sensing they were onto something new.

"And he left that pen with Scott," Joyce said. "Not to mention leaving his whole expensive pen collection."

"Perhaps he was trying to send a message to you," Anne suggested. "He didn't take his clothing or any of his stuff. That's a huge clue."

Mildred lifted her face. "So something prompted him to take off when he did."

Anne was already thinking it, just waiting for someone else to voice what was on her mind.

Alex was the one who did. "Judd Bentley," he said.

"Posing as a police officer." Anne nodded her head. She still felt the betrayal of that. So gullible.

She felt Alex's comforting hand on her shoulder.

"But if they worked for the same man, why would Lucas be running from Jeremiah?" Joyce said.

"You're assuming they worked for the same man," Anne said.

"If they didn't both work for Vincent Barrio, who did they work for?"

"Who do you think wrote the threatening note telling me to leave the case alone?"

Everyone seemed to pause on that one. "Who would have the most to lose if you found him?"

"And who knew that you were looking?" Mildred added.

"Lucas?" Anne said.

"But how would he know that you were looking?" Joyce said. "If he caught a ride out of Deshler he's not anywhere nearby..."

"What about Marta Henshaw?" Alex said.

"She certainly knew I was looking, and considering her own hasty departure it would seem she had something to lose."

She pulled out the photographs she'd found at Marta's apartment from her purse and studied them. One photo was a shot of a green street sign with the words *Butler Street*. Another was a man's hand—he had thick knuckles and he held tight to a stogie cigar. Each seemed obscure, abstract. So how did they connect?

She made a note to call the apartment manager to see what he had done with Marta's things.

"Maybe it was something at the casino," Mildred said. "You said that both Mitch and Ramon placed her there. So she played some role there."

"She lied to us about knowing where Lucas went," Alex said.

She pushed the pen against the top of the picnic table. "If only she'd call me back."

"Well, they were both in our writers' group," Mildred said.

"Yes, and the manuscript pages they were passing held codes—gambling odds for whoever Lucas worked for."

"Her disappearance right after you talked to her is deeply concerning," Mildred said.

"Except that her parents talked to her," Anne reminded. "We can be fairly sure that she isn't hurt or in danger."

"Have you tried to call her again since we talked to her folks?" Alex asked Anne.

"I did. It goes to voice mail. She's avoiding me. But why?"

Then there was Judd Bentley...Jeremiah Briggs—Anne traced his name on her sheet, thickening the lines, making it bolder. She glanced to the lilacs that lined the expansive backyard. Since she'd found out about his duplicity she'd felt watched, played.

She shuddered and rubbed her hands together.

"We have much to think about here," Anne said.

"It looks to me like you've already thought a lot through," Mildred lifted the list and studied it.

Anne said, "Except for where he is now and why he's running from Jeremiah Briggs."

Once they'd cleaned up from supper and everyone had gone their separate ways, Anne climbed the staircase to her apartment.

She called the apartment manager who informed her that they'd donated all of Marta's things to a thrift store in Deshler. Anne thanked him and hung up.

She wished she could call the kidnappers, talk to the girls. Were they okay? Where were they? Why hadn't they called back yet?

Hershey stared at her as if he too were deeply lonely. The house was simply too quiet. Too still.

When had that become part of who she was? That need to always have noise, motion? Had it come with losing Eric? Running from the pain, filling her life with busyness?

She paused with the thought. Was that what she'd been doing all this time? Running? Hiding from issues that she didn't want to face?

"Oh, Lord, help me face the quiet," she murmured sincerely. "It's in the quiet that I can hear You," she added. "And I need to hear from You."

Finding a spot on the couch, she sat and closed her eyes. The house settled around her in creaks and groans. Late afternoon sunshine cast pumpkin and neon shades around the old walls, illuminating the curtains in their hues.

It had been so long since she'd simply allowed God to talk to her, to comfort that deep place in her heart where loneliness hid. "I'm so tired of being lonely," she murmured.

"You're never alone," His spirit whispered to her heart. "I promised."

The verse from Deuteronomy 31 came to her, *"He will never leave you nor forsake you."*

"I know that's true, Lord. I do." He was there, in that quiet house. He was always there, even in her busyness. She'd simply failed to look for Him, to recognize when His tender hand was reaching out to her.

"I'm sorry, Father." They were the only words she needed to utter. With the confession came a subtle sense of peace. There wasn't resolution for her problems—she still had no clue where Lucas Miller was. She couldn't solve her own problems with Ben or melt her fears about the future. But that calm was there, quiet yet undeniable.

God was holding her hand and it was enough. After all, He'd made the universe. He could certainly handle her troubles.

"Thank You" fell from her lips then.

The moment passed and yet it lingered, like a beautiful perfume. She sensed God's nearness. Oh, that she could always sense it.

Anne reached for her laptop computer and booted it up. Once it had gone through its startup she clicked on the search bar at the bottom, typing in "Judd Bentley" as well as "Jeremiah Briggs." There were scant mentions of either name—and most seemed to be other people, photos that looked nothing like the man with two different-colored eyes. Finally, she dialed Michael Banks on his personal line.

"This is Michael," he said on the second ring.

"Michael. Anne," she said.

"You haven't learned anything since high school, you know," he said, scolding her for visiting a federal penitentiary without first checking with him. "Didn't anyone ever tell you it isn't safe to visit convicted felons?"

"Hey, he gave me some important information!" Anne protested. "Besides, Alex came along."

"Ah…Alex," he said.

"What does that mean?" she said, feeling irritated at her old high school friend.

"Nothing."

"Fine!" Why did she suddenly feel as if they were seventeen again? "Judd Bentley—Jeremiah Briggs—is part of a much bigger operation," she began, repeating some of what she'd told him in her earlier call.

The line grew quiet for a moment before he said, "Maybe I'll have better luck looking him up by the name Briggs."

When she hung up she glanced at the clock. It was eight o'clock.

Anne typed in "illegal gambling." She wanted to understand what constituted legal gambling versus illegal gambling since Ramon had implied that Lucas had been involved with that element.

The main difference, one site said, was that legal gambling was regulated, and taxed, by the State. Dealers went through background checks and were approved before being allowed to work. Gambling without those strictures, where someone took a cut of the wager, was always illegal.

Within a few minutes, Michael called her back. "I've run his name through the system—both names. Seems you didn't have his real name after all. It's Jared Bigaouette. He's been arrested several times, on gambling charges, booking, that kind of thing…"

"Organized crime."

"Yeah."

"Do you think he's the top guy?" Anne said.

There was a long pause. "You mean whoever Lucas is running from?" he said.

"Can you look up Vincent Barrio? It was the name on those deposits Joyce found."

Michael paused again. "You need to be really careful here, Anne. I know I was teasing you about visiting the man in the pen, but this is serious stuff. Don't go wandering into situations unaware. Do you understand me? Call me if you see him. We'll get officers to you within minutes."

"I understand."

Organized crime. That phrase stuck with Anne. Judd Bentley… Jeremiah Briggs…Jared Bigaouette—whatever his name was!— was involved with organized crime. And she'd thought he was cute. She shook the thought off, recognizing it for the needless condemnation that it was.

So what did Jared's connections mean for Lucas? Somehow he'd gotten involved. Just what had he done? And how deeply was he entwined? Irving Henshaw had said Marta was a good girl, that she would never do anything illegal. Was that true or was it the wishful thinking of a father blinded by love?

What about Lucas? Was he as blameless?

* * *

Anne lay in bed the next morning, knowing she needed to get up and get ready for the day yet not wanting to. She glanced at the clock—6:15. It was already later than when she usually got up.

Her cell phone rang. Anne glanced at the display—it was Joyce Miller.

"Sorry to call so early."

"I'm awake." She sat up in bed. "What's up?"

"I was looking at our checking account online last night, and there was a deposit into our joint checking account from a bank in Wilkes-Barre."

"Lucas?"

"I can't imagine who else it could be."

"Did you look at the check image?"

"Yeah, it's from a place called Homer's Coffee Shop, signed by none other than Homer himself."

"When did he make the deposit?"

"Yesterday." Anne heard the hesitation in Joyce's voice.

"What is it?"

"It's just…I thought he'd left us. That he didn't care…"

"But he put some money in your account," Anne finished for her. "He's looking out for you. Giving you something to live on."

She could hear the inhale of breath on the other end. "Yeah," she said. "I was just ready to…" She let her words fall away. "Anyway, I thought you'd want to know."

"Would you like to come with me to try to find him?"

"I would."

* * *

"Don't you think he would've known that we would see the deposit and come looking for him?" Joyce said shortly after Anne picked her up to head to Wilkes-Barre.

She hoped that was true. Yet, she also knew that if the man wanted to come home he could at any time.

"Maybe," Anne said. "It's a definite opportunity. I wonder what prompted it."

There was a long silence then. Anne glanced at Joyce. "What are you thinking?"

Joyce stared out the windshield. "I don't know anything," she said simply. "But I'm learning to trust God."

"That's a pretty good thing."

She nodded. "It's hard, but I was reading my Bible last night, and God promised time and time again to be with His people. I hope He's with the girls right now."

Homer's Coffee Shop was a step back in time, the first floor of a two-story house with green awnings over the upstairs windows and glass blocks to let in light on the first floor. Chrome stools with vinyl seats lined a long wood-grain Formica counter and booths of green vinyl brought back images of sitcoms from years gone by. A sign near the ceiling read, *There's no place like HOMER'S.*

A waitress passed them in a hurry, saying over her shoulder, "I'll be right back."

Anne strained to get a glance of Lucas. Was he working as a short-order cook in back? As a bus boy?

Anne didn't see him. Finally, a balding man with a rim of white hair along the back of his head moved toward them. The smile on his face and his outstretched hand told Anne instantly that this was the restaurant's namesake.

"Homer," he introduced, shaking hands with each of them, a huge grin on his face. "Would you like a booth or a table?" He reached for two menus from the checkout counter by the front door.

"We were hoping to talk to you actually," Anne said. Another group came in then and the waitress returned to seat them. She looked at Anne and Joyce, obviously wondering why her boss wasn't seating them, but Homer motioned for Anne and Joyce to follow him toward the back.

When they were in a hall away from the hubbub of the restaurant, he turned toward them. "What's this all about?"

"We're looking for someone. We have reason to think he might be working here," Anne said. She handed him the photo of Lucas that she'd been carrying around.

"Lucas Miller," he said immediately. "He worked here."

"Worked?" Anne asked. "As in no longer?"

"He was a decent cook. He worked here as recently as two days ago but he came in for his check then said he was done. Took off without a word. Quite frankly I'm worried about him." He scratched the top of his bald head. "He was a nice guy. Didn't talk a whole lot, kept to himself." He looked at Joyce. "He seemed distracted, like something was going on beneath the surface that he didn't want to tell anyone about. Hang on a minute." He lifted a finger as if he'd remembered something. Then he left for a minute, disappearing into an office that held a cluttered mess just off the hallway. "You look familiar," Homer said to Joyce.

"I'm Lucas's wife."

"That's what I was wondering." He held up a family photo of the Millers.

She reached for it. "We had this taken on vacation in Ocean City, New Jersey," she said. "It was taken two years ago. I loved that picture of us—we're all so happy. Lucas used to keep it in his wallet."

"You said he left a couple days ago?" Anne asked the man.

"Yes he did. But he left that behind." He motioned toward the photo. "A man doesn't just leave something like that behind. He used to look at it all the time…"

"Did anyone call the authorities?" Anne asked.

Homer shrugged. "And say what? That he quit his job? That isn't a crime."

"Do you know where he lives, if he has any friends or acquaintances in the area?"

"I'm sorry, I don't. There was another guy looking for him though…"

"Oh? When was that?" Anne said.

"Yesterday. Said his name was Charles something or other."

"What did he look like?" Sudden fear rose up in Anne. She hoped it wasn't Judd.

But the description didn't fit Judd. Homer said he was older, heavyset, balding.

"You don't recall his last name at all?" Anne asked.

He shook his head. "I think it started with an *M* and that it made me think of that Charles Dickens book…the Christmas one?"

"*A Christmas Carol?*" Anne and Joyce said in unison.

"Yeah, yeah. That's the one."

"Marley?" Anne asked.

The man snapped his fingers. "That's the name—Charles Marley. He didn't say why he wanted to find Lucas, just that he'd been looking for him for a while."

Anne and Joyce left disheartened. Their hopes had been so high. It was like watching a balloon deflate, flailing on the wind, unable to catch it, unable to stop it.

"Don't forget," Anne said once they were back in the car. "We aren't that far behind him."

CHAPTER FIFTEEN

They were only two days behind where Lucas had been. They knew he was alive! Not only that, but he was well enough to work. Had he made the deposit then because he'd known he wouldn't be there if and when someone came looking for him? Or because he knew Charles Marley—whoever that was—was looking for him and he wanted his family to find him first? Why couldn't he just phone home?

She sighed as she folded a towel and placed it on the pile of clean laundry.

When Anne had dropped Joyce at home she'd seemed even more dejected, though she put on a brave face, tried to pep talk herself into believing that they would still find Lucas and her daughters. But perhaps it wasn't meant to be.

Homer had said Lucas seemed nervous, watching, waiting when he'd come in to say he was done working there. Had something happened to force him to leave? Did he know about the girls' abduction? Or had Judd found him already? Could that be why Judd hadn't called her since that first call after they'd disappeared? Maybe this Charles fellow worked with him? She thought of Michael Banks's warning to be careful.

She knew organized crime wasn't something to trifle with. It was a terrifying thought. Yet, she couldn't make sense of it.

She ran through the conversation with Homer. Charles Marley. Who was that? C.M. Suddenly something clicked. She'd read those initials before. Then she realized J.B. — Judd Bentley, Jeremiah Briggs, Jared Bigaouette. She'd seen those initials too.

Her breathing quickened. They were characters in Lucas's manuscript! She moved to her bedside table and lifted the thick tome to page through it. She hadn't read the whole thing, hadn't seen its full relevance, other than the codes, but now she did.

Her eyes scanned the pages, looking. Vincent Barrio — the name on the checks. Same initials as Victor Babbit in Lucas's story — the man who was L.M.'s boss. The man that Lucas was working for. Lucas was living out the plot of his own book. He was Larry Mahoney! Working as an impromptu spy for Vincent Barrio.

She kept paging through till she found another character named Justus Brandt — Judd Bentley or Jeremiah Briggs. He worked for a man named Cash Montenegro — Charles Marley. The man who'd come looking for Lucas at the restaurant. Marta Henshaw, dubbed Mandi Hinckley in the story was working with Lucas Miller — Larry Mahoney — to bring the big guy down.

Like a lock finding all the right tumblers, everything fit. The manuscript had been the key all along — it was Lucas's way of communicating with Marta and passing that information on to Vincent Barrio. Yet, Lucas never had the chance to deliver his manuscript on that last day, because Marta Henshaw didn't show up at the writers' meeting.

Lucas was no gambling addict. He had none of the symptoms, hadn't ruined his life the way most addicts did. Was he being paid to do it—by the FBI? She couldn't be sure. It could always be a rival boss. Someone who felt Charles Marley was eating into his territory.

How had Lucas gotten involved in this racket? Anne still had no idea. Had he always worked undercover? Without his family knowing? Or was it all a part of his writing research as he'd claimed?

She wouldn't know that till she found him and brought him and his girls home. And how was she going to do that? Given Homer's description of him, he was still thinking of his family. Missing them.

But how could Anne find him without endangering him more? There was no guarantee that the girls hadn't already been hurt. Was she merely leading this Charles Marley fellow or Judd Bentley to Lucas's front door? She sighed, realizing how impossible it was.

No doubt Judd or Charles Marley was trying to make sure all his tracks were covered, trying to determine just how much Lucas had found out about whatever they were doing. Who else might know?

Then it hit her—all the strange happenings at the homes of the other writers in the critique group. Maybe whoever Judd worked for thought the other writers were in on what Lucas and Marta were doing. Or they hadn't known it was Marta working with him and they were trying to narrow it down.

A chilling thought struck—had Judd thought *she* had been the one working with Lucas? At least until they had interviewed Marta.

She scanned through the pages, noting the capitalized words that had caught her attention the first time she'd glanced through the book—Wall, Butler. Each time those words were used they were capitalized even though they weren't proper nouns. Lucas was usually meticulous when it came to such things.

On a hunch, Anne headed to her computer and typed in "1231 Wall Street, Butler, Pennsylvania." Combining the time on the dashboard clock with the words in the manuscript.

When the results popped up, she sat back. There on the screen was a listing for a Charles Marley at that address. Anne's heart kicked into high gear.

Was this the man who was looking for Lucas, the one he wrote about in his book?

She searched for his name, clicking on sites that revealed any arrests or past crimes.

The list was long, all having to do with organized crime—tax evasion, drug charges, then gambling and booking crimes. Anne sat back as a feeling of dread came over her. No, this man wasn't some punk kid. He was someone to be very, very afraid of.

* * *

"I don't think this is very smart," Alex said as he and Anne made their way to 1231 Wall Street the next morning.

"I'm not going to do anything stupid," Anne said. "Just drive past, see what we can see. That's all."

"So why not call the police?"

"We can…just in a little bit. I have a hunch. Just trust me, okay?" Anne glanced at Alex, though he didn't respond. He felt protective of her—she'd seen it on many occasions. It touched her. Yet, what should she do about it? Did it mean he felt more for her than mere friendship or was it simply the way men were with single women? She turned slightly to stare out the side window of his pickup as they passed farm fields.

She'd called Byron and Marlene to see how they were doing. They were spending the day exploring Washington, DC.

Yet, Anne couldn't help but feel guilty for missing out on the family time. Liddie's words concerning Remi and Bella came back to her. "Their kind of needing is just for a little while." How was it her daughter could give her such grace when she couldn't give it to herself? Anne drew in a deep breath, allowing herself to sit back in the seat. Alex had insisted on driving and she was glad for it—she didn't need to be concentrating on the road right now.

Her mind floated across the fields from Lucas and Marta to Liddie and Ben...to Eric. What would he do if he were in her shoes? She exhaled with a sigh. She had to stop doing that. Thoughts of Eric often took this wistful path, never found the home she longed for—a different reality than the one she lived every day of her life.

"Still thinking about the kids?" Alex said.

Anne shook her head. "No. Eric," was all she said.

"You loved him."

"Of course I did."

"Nothing wrong with that. So what brought on the sigh?"

"Ben...my in-laws." She laughed, then added, "Me."

Alex waited, not saying a word.

"Ben is worried that I'm going to start dating again. He's directed some of that fear at you."

"Me? Why?"

"I don't know. You're a man. He knows we went out in high school…" She thought of the letter from Eric. How he'd wanted her to go on, to live happily without him. Had she done that? In her heart she knew the answer — not fully.

"But you and I aren't…"

"I know. My in-laws have been pushing me to consider opening myself up. Well, not pushing…*encouraging*."

"They must know you well."

"What does that mean?"

"Anne, it's no secret that you're closed off to dating. You're closed off to even *thinking* about dating again."

"I am not."

He pointed to the wedding and engagement rings on her left hand. "That says it all right there. Any man who sees that sees a big *stop* sign." He shrugged. "I'm not trying to hurt your feelings here, but you're sending a message whether you know it or not. You've blocked out every possible man who might look your way."

She grew quiet, thoughtful. She hadn't meant to close herself off from the possibility of loving again. Not consciously anyway. Yet, she knew he was right.

"Even if I did start dating again, what man wants to take on two kids?"

"A decent man," he said simply. "You'd be surprised."

She studied him for a long moment.

"I do want to live again," she finally admitted. "I do. But it's scary. Finding someone who would love Ben and Liddie…love me. I've felt like that's impossible. Eric was so…" She exhaled through her nose. "Perfect."

"I guarantee you the man wasn't perfect," Alex said. "You don't need perfect anyway—you need God's best. You're underestimating His ability to bring that."

Anne's gaze turned back to the stunning scenery. Pennsylvania was a beautiful place.

"When did you get so smart?"

He chuckled. "It's a recent development."

"I know that's what Eric wanted for me—to find love again," she admitted. "He told his folks as much."

"So what's holding you back?"

Anne shrugged.

"Me."

CHAPTER SIXTEEN

Alex drove past the expensive-looking home, turning at the end of the block and parking so they could watch it. The home matched, almost exactly, the description in Lucas's novel — a white, majestic looking home with tall Grecian pillars, a high porch that spanned the front of the whole house, green shrubs in perfect formation.

"I don't think this is a good idea," Alex said for the dozenth time. "We could sit here waiting all day for nothing. Maybe no one is even home."

"We can go to the door, if you like," Anne suggested. "If someone answers, I will say I am taking a survey for the local library…something like that. I won't go in. I just want to go up to the door."

Anne climbed out of the truck and started for the door. She heard Alex's door shut a moment later, then he caught up with her. She heard his groan.

"All right, you win," he conceded as he rang the doorbell. "But stay right next to me. We don't know what we're dealing with here."

A maid answered the door. She wore a black-and-white uniform that looked rather dowdy.

"Can I help you?" she said in a Spanish accent.

"We are looking for Charles Marley," Anne said, glancing behind the woman. The immense foyer was spotless, black-and-white checked tile and a staircase that swept to the second floor.

"Can I ask who's calling?"

"I'm Anne Gibson and this is Alex Ochs. We just have a few questions for him."

The woman crossed her arms over her chest and raised an eyebrow.

Anne could see that this wasn't going to go anywhere.

"About Lucas Miller," Anne blurted.

"Wait here," she instructed, then shut the door in their faces as she retreated.

"Are you kidding me?" Alex scolded Anne. "We were going to pretend to be taking a survey...? Does that ring a bell?"

The maid returned, saying, "I'm sorry. Charles isn't here."

"Is his wife home?" Anne persisted.

The woman let out a *harrumph*, then shut the door again to disappear into the house's depths.

"Now's our chance," Alex said. "Let's get out of here." He grabbed Anne's hand to tug her down the street, but another woman came to the door. She was a pretty, trim blonde, in her early thirties. Anne wondered how old Charles was. Hadn't Homer said he was older than Judd? Perhaps this was a daughter rather than a wife.

"Can I help you?" she said, her imperious tone betraying her condescension.

"We were hoping we could talk to Charles. Are you his wife?" Anne said.

"I am."

"And what's your name?"

She ignored the question.

"He isn't here. What did you need him for? My maid said something about Lucas Miller…"

"Do you know Lucas?" Anne said, sensing recognition in the way she spoke his name.

"Not personally. He works for my husband."

"He does?" Anne cleared her throat. "And what does he do for your husband?"

Anne could hear the nervous breath Alex let out at that.

"My husband owns a string of casinos. Lucas is one of his blackjack dealers."

"Your husband is that familiar with his employees?" Anne said. "I mean, a blackjack dealer? I'm surprised. Besides, I thought Lucas quit his job at the casino three months ago."

She shook her head, obviously not willing to say more.

"Listen," she went on. "I'm not sure when Charles will be back. Who did you say you were again?"

Anne exchanged a look with Alex, telling him with her eyes that they needed to scram, and quick. "Sorry," Anne said, then they turned to leave.

Anne heard the door shut behind them as they made their way down the walkway. Anne could hear a man's voice in the house. Shouting. Though the words were indistinct she knew the voice belonged to Charles, and he wasn't happy that his wife had said anything about Lucas Miller to them.

They moved into a run and didn't stop till they were safely in the truck and on the road home.

"We could have gotten ourselves killed!" Alex complained.

"Oh, it wasn't all that bad," Anne said. Though she was relieved to be away from the tense situation.

"She obviously knew who Lucas was," Anne added. "And it sounded to me like it was a surprise to her that he was no longer working for her husband."

"Yeah, but how many wives keep close tabs on their husband's employees?"

"With that logic she wouldn't have even known who Lucas was though. No." Anne shook her head. "That wife has met Lucas. I'd bet money they've had him into their home."

Alex gave her a sideways glance. "Now who's placing bets?"

He glanced behind them as they merged into traffic. "And we just put a big target on our backs."

"I realize that," Anne said. "I had every intention of doing just that. How else are we going to get Bella and Remi back?"

Within fifteen minutes Anne's phone rang. An unknown number. She exchanged a glance with Alex before answering. Her heart hammered in her chest.

"This is Anne," she answered.

"I don't know what kind of game you're playing," Judd Bentley's voice surged through the line. "But you're going to get these girls killed if you pull another stunt like that."

"What stunt?"

"Don't play dumb. You visited Marley—that's not going to get you anywhere."

"It got you to call me," she said. "And it confirmed a hunch."

"You underestimate us. Trust me—if the police show up at Marley's place, it won't go well for you."

Anne knew the man was dead serious. A shiver traced her spine. What had she done? She could hear crying in the background.

"Let me talk to the girls—I need to know that they're okay. That you haven't hurt them. Or you'll never see Lucas Miller. I'll make sure of that." She was playing hardball, she knew. But she needed to assure herself and Joyce that Bella and Remi were okay.

A moment later Remi's scared voice said, "Mrs. Gibson, have you found my dad?"

How Anne wished she could tell her yes, that Lucas was in the car with her. "I'm sorry, honey. I'm looking for him. Are you and Bella doing okay? Are they mistreating you?"

"We're okay," she said.

Then Bentley was back on the line. "You've heard enough," he sneered. "Here's the deal—you get me Miller by sunset on Monday night or you'll find out the hard way that we are not to be trifled with."

"Where should I meet you?"

Bentley laughed. "I'll call you."

Then the line went dead.

Anne stared at her phone, then placed her face in her hands. She closed her eyes. Tomorrow night. How in the world would she have Lucas at her side in a single day?

* * *

As soon as Anne gathered her wits she called Officer Banks.

She didn't want to admit what she'd done that morning, going to Charles's home, yet Michael needed to know everything if he was to be fully prepared.

Finally, she told him.

There was a long silence.

"Michael?" she said.

"Anne." He didn't need to say anything else. Then, "What matters right now is being on our guard, doing what they say until we can figure out where the girls are. I'll put surveillance on Marley, but we won't move in till we know Bella and Remi are safe. How far out are you?"

"Another hour and a half."

"And are you being followed?"

"Followed?" She glanced in her rearview mirror. Suddenly every car on the road was a potential stalker. A dark-colored sedan pulled up on her tail. Her heart rate sped up, but then it turned on its blinker and passed her. Anne let out a sigh.

"You've got to be careful," Michael said.

"I will."

When Anne hung up, a horrible guilt filled her. She'd been so sure approaching Marley would help them, draw the man out, show him that they knew who he was, what he was up to. But he wasn't one to be cowed. She should've known that. And now the Miller girls were in even greater danger.

She'd awakened a sleeping giant.

* * *

Anne couldn't seem to stop pacing. She moved from one window to the next, one room to the next.

The FBI was on full alert in the kitchen of Joyce's modest house. She knew there were several officers moving through the sleepy Blue Hill neighborhood too, watching for any sign of Marley and Bentley.

What did they think they'd accomplish there? She wondered, though she didn't voice it to them. They needed to be tracking down Lucas Miller.

The agent was a young man with flaming red hair and a thick, equally red beard. He'd introduced himself as Agent Josh Reinhold. Josh seemed an awfully young-sounding name for someone assigned the task of rescuing Joyce's family from organized crime.

Anne shook the thought and moved to the next window. Were they being watched? Was Bentley hiding in the bushes fully aware that she'd disobeyed direct orders not to call the police?

This wasn't helping anyone, especially Joyce.

Alex and Mildred were there. They sat at the dining room table talking in low voices. She knew they were being careful not to upset Joyce, their furtive glances moving to her every few minutes. The woman was in shock. She sat, staring into space for the most part. Answering questions when asked in a monotone voice.

"It's going to be okay," Alex said to Joyce as Anne passed. She could see that he was just as worried as she was about the frail woman. His face was pinched, his jaw tense.

Anne sat in one of the chairs.

Mildred placed a comforting hand on Joyce's back.

"They're doing everything they can," the older woman assured.

"I hate this waiting. I want to *do* something!" Joyce uttered.

Finally, a bit of emotion. It was a step forward. Alex got up to pour her a cup of coffee. It smelled bitter from sitting on the burner too long. She drank it anyway, closing her eyes.

"Stop beating yourself up," Mildred leaned toward Anne and whispered.

"How can I not?"

"Simple." The woman's gaze was direct yet kind. "You just don't."

They sat that way for quite a while, a wake without a corpse. One person getting up to move around while others spoke quietly.

She had to think about Lucas, where he was. How to find him!

"Joyce," she finally said, motioning for the woman to join her at the table. Mildred and Alex lifted their faces. Anne pulled out her laptop and started it up.

"We found where Lucas had worked through your bank statements," she began. "I have another idea. Can we check your credit card statements? See if there were any charges on those?"

"Oh yes," Joyce said. Anne moved the laptop in front of Joyce who typed in the address. "I set all that up right after Lucas left so I could pay them online."

They watched as the site loaded, then Joyce put in her username and password. Finally, the statement popped up.

Joyce scrolled down. "Nothing on this one," she murmured, typing in the next address. The buttons on the keyboard clicked, the only sound in the quiet house. Everyone was waiting, hoping.

Joyce sucked in a breath. "How did you know?" she said.

"What does it say?" Anne leaned in to read the statement. Joyce pointed at the charge.

"He charged gas in Deshler yesterday." She told her the name of the station. "Yesterday!"

So close by!

Anne was instantly on her feet. "We need to go talk to them, see if anyone remembers seeing him."

But Agent Reinhold was right there. He held up a hand of caution. "We'll look into it for you," he reminded.

He called his superior officer while Anne watched, her frustration rising. When he closed his phone he said, "Someone's on their way."

More waiting. More hand wringing.

When the agent's phone rang again over an hour later everyone jumped. Agent Reinhold held up a hand and answered. "Okay," he said. "I'll let them know." Then he hung up.

Anne looked at him expectantly. "It was a dead end." He shrugged. "No one there remembered seeing him."

An hour later the phone rang again, this time Anne's cell phone. An unknown number. Anne sent the agent a look and he motioned for her to answer it.

"This is Anne," she said.

"You called the cops," the low voice said. "Bentley told you no cops!"

"I'm sorry." Anne knew she needed to calm the man down.

"What am I supposed to do with you?" he went on. "We tell you no cops and who are the first people you call?"

Josh motioned for her to keep the call going as he triangulated its location.

"What do you want me to do?" Anne said. Sweat beads broke out on her forehead.

"You better tell those cops to go home." He clearly still wanted Lucas alive, and he knew that chance would disappear if anything happened to Bella and Remi.

"Okay…and how do I know that Joyce's daughters are still alive?"

He put Bella on the phone. "Mrs. Gibson?"

Anne's heart broke at the sound of Bella's voice. But now Joyce was standing right in front of Anne. She was straining to hear her baby through the line.

"Tell Mom we're okay," she said.

A man she assumed to be Marley was back before Anne could respond. "Ditch the cops," he said. "Last chance." Then he hung up.

Every eye in the room was on her.

"You have to leave," Joyce said to the agent, turning immediately. "This was all a big mistake."

The agent's face furrowed in confusion.

"If you stay, there's no telling what those men will do to my girls. I was wrong to let you come!"

The agent shook his head. "It won't go well if you kick us out."

"You don't understand—we don't have a choice here!" She was vehement. "You have to leave. Call off your men."

"You can't do this alone. More than just your family will get hurt."

Joyce's face flushed red. "I don't know how they figured out that you were here, but they did. That can only mean that they have ways to know what you're doing." She turned to look at Anne, Alex, and Mildred.

"There's no choice here," she repeated. "The police have to go."

CHAPTER SEVENTEEN

After several calls to his superiors, Josh packed up his equipment and left.

"What now?" Anne said to Alex.

She could see that discouragement pushed at Joyce like a bully in a school yard.

"Think," Mildred said. "There has to be a way." She was the one pacing now.

It was late afternoon. Joyce's girls had been gone for four days already. It was a lifetime.

"I need to try Marta again," Anne finally said. She exchanged a glance with Joyce who was nodding, although Anne knew it likely hurt her to admit it. She dialed Marta's cell. It rang several times before Marta's perky voice came on the line.

"Leave a message," it said.

"Marta, I need to get ahold of you. It's very important. I can't stress that enough." She was afraid to say more over the open airwaves.

She hung up, closing her eyes as a prayer rose from the depths of her soul. "Lord, let her call me. Let her know where Lucas is."

"We should see if Irving has heard from her," Alex suggested.

"Good idea," Anne said. Alex gave her a look but said nothing as she punched in the number for the elderly man.

He answered after a few rings.

"Mr. Henshaw, do you remember me?" Anne said, adding her name.

"Of course I do. You and that nice Alex fellow came for a visit a few days ago."

"I'm still trying to get ahold of Marta."

"We haven't been able to get ahold of her either," he admitted. Worry filled the old man's voice. "You don't think she's in trouble, do you?"

"When was the last time you heard from her?"

"It's been several days. She hasn't called since we saw you. It's not like her — normally when she sees that I tried to call... well, she always calls me back right away."

"Well, you just keep trying her cell. And call me if she gets in touch with you."

He promised, then hung up.

Anne shook her head. They couldn't give up. There had to be something, some way.

She lifted her face to the others in the room. "I need to talk to the folks at that gas station in Deshler myself," she said. "Right after I talk to Mitch."

* * *

"What are you doing here again?" Mitch said when he saw Anne and Alex at his door.

"Have you talked to Lucas at all since he left town?" She didn't ask to come in. She needed answers and she needed them immediately.

"No, man." He sized Alex up. "Is this your boyfriend?"

"Can you track with me please?" Anne didn't have time for his nonsense.

"I said no." He lifted a thin shoulder.

"What about Marta? Has she called you, talked to you?"

The hesitation in his answer told her what she needed to know.

"Where is she?" Anne was in his face, leaving him no option but to answer her directly.

"Last I heard she was staying at a hotel in Butler."

Butler! Charles Marley's hometown.

"Do you know which hotel?"

He gave her the name of the place.

"How long ago was this?"

"This morning."

Anne prayed the woman was still there. "Why did she call you?" Anne asked.

"She was worried about Lucas, thought he might've called me."

Anne and Alex were on the road within minutes.

"Where to first?" Alex said, driving.

"Let's stop at the gas station, then we'll head to Butler."

"It's a long shot. You know that, right?"

"What choice do we have?"

"If only we had Lucas's phone number," Alex said.

The comment jarred an idea. She looked up the number for Homer's Coffee Shop and dialed it, asking to speak to the owner.

"Hello," the man's familiar voice said.

"This is Anne Gibson. I spoke to you about Lucas Miller earlier this week?"

"Oh, sure."

"Do you have a phone number for Lucas in your file? Maybe a cell number?" Why hadn't she thought of it before?

"I'm sure I do. Let me check."

Anne waited.

"Here it is." Anne wrote the number down, then once she said farewell she dialed it. The line rang several times, but it went to voice mail.

"Lucas," Anne decided to leave a message. "This is Anne Gibson. I need to find you immediately. I can't say over the phone but it's of utmost importance. Please call me!"

When she hung up, she shook her head. "Now if one of them would just call me back."

The gas station where Lucas had purchased gas was right on the highway, a busy spot with a pie shop that brought in diners, as well as those needing a fill-up from the highway.

Anne knew it wasn't likely that anyone would remember him, as many customers as they had in a day, and especially since the police had already come around questioning people, but it was all she could think to do. She showed Lucas's photo to several employees before she found someone who recognized him, an older gentleman who'd just arrived at work.

"A likeable guy," he said, "he came in for pie, struck up a conversation."

"Did he say anything about where he was staying? Or where he was headed?"

The man scratched his gray beard. "He had a red Ford Mustang convertible. I remember because that was what got us talking in the first place...." He paused to try to remember. "You know, I think he did say something about one of the motels in town. There aren't that many so..." He pointed to the motels surrounding the off-ramp from the highway. "Those are about it around here."

Anne and Alex drove around each of the motels looking for a red Mustang, but there was no such vehicle in sight. Anne even stopped in the front desks to ask if Lucas Miller or Lance Martin were there, but that brought about only blank looks and shaking heads.

Anne felt herself sinking into despair.

She checked her phone. No calls from Marta or from Lucas.

"I don't know what to do," she confessed to Alex.

Alex ran a hand across his stubbled chin. "I wish I had some answers for you." He met her gaze. "Other than to pray."

Together they bent their heads in prayer.

When they looked up, Anne's phone buzzed to life.

"This is Alex," he said without bothering to look at the display.

"We have a lead on where that cell phone is, the one that called Anne."

It was Michael Banks on the line. Alex handed the phone to Anne.

"Michael?" Anne said.

"What, you think just because Joyce told us to go away we'll actually stop looking?" He repeated what he'd first said to Alex.

"I'm sending a squad car, but, Anne, you need to know—they're following you!"

Anne lifted her head. Her eyes scanned the surrounding parking lots. There. A van at the edge of the next lot—Anne could make out someone in the driver's seat.

Anne pointed it out to Alex. He turned the truck in that direction.

The van peeled out of the lot and sped toward the highway. "Could they be listening in on this call?" she asked, motioning for Alex to follow them.

"Not as likely on Alex's phone as yours," Michael said. "My guess is Judd Bentley got your cell number when he was scamming you. You didn't give him Alex's number, did you?"

"No." Anne felt a measure of relief.

Alex gunned it toward the Interstate, but the van ahead of them went even faster.

"Where is it now?" she asked Michael.

"Their signal just went out," he said.

"We have to go," Anne said. She distantly heard Michael's protests before she hit the *end* button.

Alex sped up, trying to find the van in the surging traffic. He wove in and out of cars. "I don't see it!" His eyes moved back and forth.

"There!" Anne pointed ahead and to the left. The van was moving past a semitrailer.

Alex punched it up to eighty miles an hour. Anne reached for the door's armrest, holding on for dear life.

He swerved around a slow-moving station wagon and made for the semitrailer. But when they came around it there was no sight of the van.

"Do you think they pulled off at that rest stop?" Anne said, pointing to an exit as they passed, too far on the left to get there now.

Alex slapped his hand against the steering wheel, his lips a thin line.

At the next U-turn spot in the Interstate, Alex made a quick turn and moved back toward where they had come. He managed to get off at the rest stop, but minutes had passed. There was no sight of the van, no sight of Bella or Remi.

Dusk settled across the landscape as they made their way into Butler for the second time that day. They passed the exit where they'd gone to Charles Marley's home. Anne wondered if police were still scoping out the place. A part of her hoped so, yet another part worried that it would get Bella and Remi hurt. Or worse.

The bright neon sign for the motel came into view, looming over the landscape. Alex took the exit that led to it, taking several more turns before parking in the crowded lot in front of the place.

He shifted into park and met Anne's gaze. "Want me to go in?"

Anne unbuckled. "We'll go together."

The lobby was quiet. A boy of about twelve or thirteen was playing a video game in the room behind the check-in counter. When he saw them he called, "Da-ad" toward a room behind him. Then he said to Anne and Alex, "He'll be right out."

A man who looked to be of Middle Eastern descent came out a few minutes later offering apologies for making them wait. "We're all full up," he said.

"We're not here for a room," Anne said. "We're looking for Marta Henshaw." She pulled out the photo she'd printed off of Facebook. "Or if she's not using that name..."

"I'm sorry," he said, "I can't give out information about our customers. I can ring her room for you, if you'd like to speak with her on the phone."

He reached for the phone and dialed. There was no answer.

Anne felt on the verge of tears.

Alex leaned his muscular arms against the tall counter and said, "Here's the deal. I'm going to start knocking on every door in this place looking for Marta Henshaw. I won't be quiet and I won't stop till I find her. I'm sure your customers won't mind that. But you see, we know she's here and we're going to find her tonight. Do you understand?"

The man's face fell. Then he said, "No, sir, that is not acceptable."

"What's not acceptable is that you won't help us," Alex's face was red, the veins in his neck bulging. "You see, we're here because a woman's family is in trouble and Marta Henshaw is the only person who can help her."

He looked from Alex to Anne, then back to Alex again.

"Okay." He held up his hands. "She's in 2C. But I didn't tell you." He raised his hands like Pilate absolving himself and returned to the back.

Never had Anne felt more grateful than she did at that moment. It was all she could do not to give Alex a big hug.

They climbed the stairs, then moved down the dimly lit hallway toward 2C.

There was no sound coming from the room. No TV or music. Anne knocked tentatively at first, then when there was no answer with more vigor. Finally, a shadow moved across the peephole, then the knob turned.

"What are you doing here?" Marta hissed. She glanced up and down the hall then motioned them to get into her room quickly.

Once they were inside, she locked and bolted the door. The shades were drawn and the only light came from the small bathroom. It felt dark, oppressive.

"We've been looking for you," Anne said.

"I know that," she admitted with a sigh. "I'm sorry I couldn't call you back, but I'm pretty sure Marley has someone watching me and he's hacked into my cell. If I'd returned your call, he would've been able to pinpoint both of our locations."

"Do you think that's why Lucas hasn't called?" Anne said.

"Probably."

"So what is this?" Anne turned to her. "Why are you here?"

Marta moved swiftly to the windows, moving them a fraction to look outside.

"I don't know how much time we have." She was gathering her things, shoving them into her suitcase. She shook her head. "I can't risk it."

"What are you talking about?" Alex said. He stood with his arms crossed, studying the jittery woman.

"I took a photo...it's a long story," Marta said. "Anyway, the FBI enlisted me and Lucas to bring Charles Marley in."

"Charles Marley is holding Remi and Bella Miller hostage."

Marta turned to her. Her eyes widened.

"Him and Judd Bentley. You remember him from our interview, don't you?"

"I didn't know who he was till after I talked to you," Marta admitted apologetically. "He was never at the casino when I was there."

"He trashed your place," Anne said.

"Tell me about it."

"They want me to bring them Lucas in exchange for the Miller girls. You've got to help us find him!"

"I have no idea where Lucas is. Hey, I even tried calling Mitch Bach to try to find the guy. My guess is Marley's been tracking him for a long time. It's not safe."

"But you have to have some kind of idea where he would have gone. Or at least know someone who does know."

Marta shook her head. "Who would that be?"

"How would I know?" Anne said. Marta slipped her jacket on and grabbed her small bag, zipping it shut. "We've gotta get out of here and fast." She moved to the door. Glancing out, she gave the all clear and walked quickly toward the far exit, away from the lobby. They moved down the staircase in the same way, watching at each door, making sure no one was there, then burst out onto the back parking lot.

"Where did you park?" she asked.

"Up front," Alex said.

Marta shook her head. "You're gonna need to ride with me. You can get your car later." She opened the door of her Ford Focus and the three of them piled inside.

"Nice Ford Focus," Alex said as he climbed in the backseat.

"Really, Alex?" Anne said. "Now is not the time."

"It was just a comment." He shrugged and Anne shook her head.

"Buckle up," Marta said, bringing the car to life and flying out of the back lot and toward the Interstate.

CHAPTER EIGHTEEN

Anne was back to pacing back and forth when they got to her place. She called Joyce immediately to come join them. She knew the waiting would be maddening for the woman. She glanced at the clock. It was nine.

She could hear Alex and Marta talking with Joyce at the dining table, but she couldn't be still at that moment. She had to move. Hershey followed her around the apartment, looking up at her, concern in those big brown eyes.

Anne moved to a window and closed the curtains. As if that would change anything.

"What matters right now is figuring out where Lucas is."

"You're going to drive me crazy with that pacing," Alex said from his spot at the table. "I'll make coffee if you'll point me to your supplies."

Anne moved into the kitchen and got down the coffee and filters, while Alex set about making a pot.

Once the sounds of brewing came from the machine, Anne turned back to Joyce and Marta. Now that the truth was out the two women seemed at ease with each other.

"Let's go back to when Lucas left that night," Anne said. "You obviously knew he was on the run." She took the chair adjacent to Marta's.

"I knew *something* had happened," she admitted. "But that night someone had been following me. That's why I missed the writers' meeting. I knew something was up. Then Lucas called and said someone had run him off the road and he needed to get out of town. So I called my dad. I figured whoever was on my tail would just find Lucas if I went to him. But my dad..."

"Lucas never told you where he was headed once he got to Deshler?" Anne said.

Marta shook her head. "No. That was on purpose. He didn't want a trail."

"Just how big an operation does Marley run?" Alex asked, joining them at the table, a tray holding three cups of steaming coffee with cream and sugar in his hands. He set them down in front of the ladies, handing one to each.

"His operation is vast," Marta admitted. She lifted the cup and took a sip. "That's why the FBI enlisted my help. I'd been at the casino doing a photojournalism piece on gambling when I took a photo of two men making an...*exchange*. It was in the background of another shot, but when I blew it up I could see that something fishy was going on. I contacted the FBI...and they asked me to work with Lucas on bringing Marley in. Lucas had a way—he was able to get in places that I couldn't."

"So you used his manuscripts to send each other information," Anne supplied.

Marta nodded, meeting her gaze, before glancing at Joyce. "Only I didn't get that last manuscript."

Anne was already rising from her chair.

"What are you doing?" Marta said to her back, but it came to Anne then, the connection. The next place they needed to look. Probably the place she should have been looking all along. She'd found the codes as well as the initials that pointed to the perpetrators, surely Lucas had included some sort of clue as to where he would be if something went awry.

Moving to her bedside table, she pulled the drawer open and retrieved Lucas's manuscript. She never had read it to the end. It was about time she did.

Anne could see that Marta and Alex were curious about what she was doing. She motioned toward the draft with her other hand. "This is where we need to look," she said, taking a chair at the table alongside Marta.

"You have the manuscript." Marta couldn't seem to believe it.

Anne flipped toward the end, finding the spot where she'd left off.

She'd read several pages before a passage caught her eye. It read: *Victor knew where Larry was at all times. His office was housed in a downtown building in Altonia.*

"Listen to this," she read the section out loud.

"Victor," Anne said, looking to Marta for confirmation, "that's your boss, right? The FBI agent that hired both of you?"

She nodded. "He works the blackjack table at the casino sometimes. Big greasy looking man. He's the one who hired Lucas, the one coordinating the Marley sting."

"But you didn't know where he kept an office?" Alex said.

"You have to understand—we had to keep things moving. If we'd stayed in one place for long…bad things would happen." She reached for her phone from her pocket.

"What are you doing?" Alex said.

"The night Lucas left he sent me a text. I locked it so I wouldn't lose it." Her gaze was on the screen of the smartphone. "1100 Main," she said.

"The address," Anne guessed. Marta nodded.

"We knew that if both were in the manuscript it could be devastating to our mission."

"Is there an Altonia, Pennsylvania?" Alex's arms were crossed over his chest. "There's no such town near here."

"Altoona," Marta said.

* * *

Before the sun came up the next morning, the four of them climbed into Anne's car and headed straight for Altoona. Alex had punched the address in to the GPS. It was a short drive compared to some of the drives they'd made recently. Yet, Anne couldn't wait for it to be over. She checked her phone. No messages.

She hadn't slept a wink the night before. How could she? Exhaustion tugged at her body, yet she forced herself to go on.

Anne wove through the streets of Altoona and finally the address came into view. She parked in front of the three-story brick building on a corner on Main Street. The first floor was a store front. A narrow glass door to the side led to the offices above. It fit Lucas's description to perfectly.

Climbing out, Anne glanced up and down the street, asking the Lord to use this lead to take them to Lucas.

Marta led the way to the cramped offices. The sign on the door read *Vincent Barrio, LLC*. That seemed indistinct enough.

The hallway smelled musty like carpet that had gotten damp and needed a good airing. It was still early, not quite eight o'clock so the man might not be in yet. Anne knocked on the door.

A man's voice immediately said, "Come in."

His back was to them when they first entered, then, when he turned his chair, recognition dawned. Anne and Alex had spoken to this man at the casino—that drooping mustache was hard to forget and the way he tilted his head back to look at them. His gray eyes narrowed at first. Then when his gaze turned to Marta he was on his feet.

"How did you find me?" He looked from Marta to Anne and then Alex. Marta turned to close the door. There were only two chairs opposite the desk so Alex and Marta stood in the back while Joyce and Anne sat.

Vincent waited for them to settle, his brow furrowed, his gaze moving from one to the next. So this was the man Anne had read about in the newspaper article from so long ago, the one who'd discovered his captain was a bank robber. He looked much older than the photo she'd seen online. She never would have connected him to the blackjack dealer she'd met. "We need to know where Lucas Miller is," Marta said.

"I can't give you that information," he said. "Let the FBI do their job. They'll find those girls."

"I kicked the FBI off the case." Joyce said.

"What!" he was almost shouting. "That's ludicrous."

"If you know where Lucas is…," Anne said.

But Vincent was shaking his head. "We risk everything—the whole operation."

"The whole operation is already blown, sir," Marta said. "We'll still get Marley."

The man turned in his pacing behind the desk, chin in his hand.

"Sir, do you know where Lucas Miller is?" Anne said. She couldn't keep the desperation from her voice. "You have to tell us."

"I know where he is," he finally admitted. "He called in last night." His eyes met theirs each in turn. "He said someone was onto him." He shook his head. "I doubt you'll beat Marley's men to him."

* * *

"This is maddening!" Joyce said as they left the city limits of Altoona.

The day would be a warm one. Already she had to turn on the air conditioner in the car.

"We're not going to fail," Anne assured her.

"What will they do if we don't take him Lucas?" Joyce shuttered visibly.

"Don't think that way," Alex cautioned. He looked as exhausted as Anne felt. He and Marta hadn't gotten any more sleep than Anne had. Who knew how long it had been since Joyce had slept.

"We have to think clearly, move forward," Anne said. "That's all we can do."

Alex turned in the front passenger seat to face Joyce. "You can't give up."

Vincent had given them a name. An agent Lucas had been staying with in Punxatawney—Christopher Jones. They headed west on 22, then cut north toward the town made famous by a groundhog.

The house was out in the country, on a dirt road that wound through the Pennsylvania hills. Anne caught a glimpse of the quaint town as they came around a bend.

Then, after a few more turns, the ramshackle place came into view.

"We have to make sure this location isn't compromised," Marta said. "I'll get out here and check it out."

Anne nodded as she pulled the car to a stop a couple hundred yards short of the house and they got out.

They watched as Marta approached the house that looked at least a hundred years old. Any paint it had once had on its facade had long faded, leaving a gray exterior and curling shingles. Several windows were boarded over and the porch looked like it might fall off at any moment.

Marta motioned for them to stay to the side, then she moved quickly, stealthily forward.

Ancient oaks shaded them—Anne moved from one to the next with Alex and Joyce doing the same.

Then, up ahead she saw a red Mustang. It was parked off to the side of the old farmhouse. The same kind of car the man at the gas station had mentioned. "That's Lucas's car," she whispered to Alex.

He nodded and moved on. Marta disappeared inside the house. Anne saw her form pass the front windows. Then a few minutes later she was back on the porch motioning them forward.

When the three of them met her there she said, "No one's here."

But Anne pointed to the Mustang. "That's the car Lucas was last seen driving. He's got to be nearby."

Several outbuildings surrounded the abandoned place. They leaned every which way, old chicken coops and machine sheds, ghosts of a former life.

Anne ducked inside the first one, taking a moment for her eyes to adjust to the darkness. Cobwebs and fallen beams filled the space. Dust motes floated in the sunshine that split the rafters overhead like swords of light stabbing the interior. A rat scurried into the corner of the cluttered space. No one was here.

She went back outside and saw Alex up ahead, coming out of the faded barn. He shook his head. No Lucas. Then she noticed a trail that led off into the woods. Where did it lead? Searching the ground she saw footprints. Recently made.

She motioned to Alex then followed them down the short path, between thick ferns. She'd gone a good hundred yards when she saw the shack. A shed of no more than ten by ten feet. She quickened her pace, pressing her body against the wall to peek in its lone window.

Inside was dark, but she could see the form of a man. It had to be Lucas. His head was bent away from her, reading, as he sat on a cot or a bed of some kind.

Once Alex was alongside her, Anne knocked.

The floorboards creaked.

"Who's there?" Lucas's voice said.

"Lucas," she said as joy filled her. "It's Anne Gibson. Please open up."

Lucas didn't respond at first. She waited in a moment of timelessness.

Finally, the door opened and Lucas was there. He was a specter. His skin was pale, almost translucent. Dark circles ringed his eyes. The look he sent Anne was furious, scared, before he tugged her into the shed. *Hovel* seemed a more apt word. Trash was everywhere. A foul smelling odor stung Anne's nose. Lucas cleared a place for her to sit on a folding camp chair in the corner.

"Did you get my message?" Anne asked.

"I couldn't call you back. You don't understand what I'm up against here. Why did you come? The police should be handling this—it's just going to get more dangerous for everyone. Is Joyce okay?"

"No, she's not okay," Anne said. "She's been devastated since you left. And, Lucas"—she met his gaze, waiting for him to realize the scope of their problem—"Marley has your daughters."

Lucas's mouth dropped open in shock. "My girls? It's my fault." He grimaced. "I never should've agreed to help the FBI. It's become a huge, tangled mess."

"They want you, Lucas," Anne went on. "Marley says he'll return the girls if you come."

Lucas was shaking his head. "The monster. There's no telling what he'll do…" His words fell away and the man began to weep into his hands. "Does Joyce hate me?" he asked. So much pain in his face. "I miss her and the girls so much."

"They want you back," Alex said.

Lucas shook his head. "I want to go back!"

"Then let's do this thing," Anne said.

"Okay," he finally said, meeting her gaze. "You're right."

When they came out of the woods, Marta looked at Anne in wonder. Joyce was nowhere in sight. "How did you know?" Marta asked Anne as they headed toward the car.

She shrugged. "A hunch."

Marta moved to Lucas, checking him over. "You okay?" she asked.

"No, Marta," he said honestly. "I'm not okay." Then he looked at Anne. "But we have a job to do and I'm going to do it."

When they reached the car, Anne saw the way Joyce straightened in her seat upon sighting Lucas. Disbelief filled her face. Then tears. She opened the door and climbed out.

She was shaking by the time Lucas got to her.

"I'm so sorry, babe," he said, standing back as if he were afraid she would have nothing to do with him. He shook his head and closed his eyes. "I was a fool to think I could handle this all on my own. And the person I hurt was you—the one I didn't want to ever hurt. If you hate me—"

But Joyce was there then, in his arms, holding him, stroking his back, whispering her forgiveness. Then they kissed for everyone to see. It was a kiss that spoke of true love, the kind that persevered, the kind that believed the best.

* * *

"I have him," Anne told Marley when he called later that day. They were back at Anne's apartment. Mildred had stocked the refrigerator with sandwiches so they were filling their stomachs.

"I knew with enough motivation you'd be able to find him," Marley said, sounding smug. "My boy Jared told me you were pretty clever when it came to that kind of thing…" Jared—Judd. That still took some getting used to.

"So where do we need to meet you?"

"There's an old steel factory outside of Deshler. You know the place?"

"I do." The factory had closed in the late seventies. Decay had taken it over, along with pigeons and rats no doubt.

"How long will it take you to get there?"

"I can be there in half an hour."

"Sounds good. Just you and Lucas, got that?"

"Of course."

"If I see anyone with you, any sign of a cop…"

"I understand," she paused. "But if you want me to bring you Lucas, I need proof that his daughters are all right."

Within a few minutes Remi was on the line. "Hi, Mrs. Gibson."

"Are you okay?" Anne asked.

"We're okay. They haven't hurt us."

At least she had that. Finally, Marley came back on the line. "Satisfied?"

"Yes," Anne said. "We'll be there in half an hour."

Anne and Lucas drove alone to Deshler. The others would follow in an unmarked car. They promised to park far enough away that no one would catch sight of them. The police would be there if anything went wrong, Marta assured.

"I don't like this, Anne," Lucas said when he climbed out of her car. "Who knows what you're walking into."

"We'll be careful." Anne looked up at the towering factory. "We have to do whatever it takes."

He sighed, meeting her gaze. "Thank you for this," he said.

Anne had no words to reply.

"You should be blaming me."

"No." Anne shook her head. "That's not how I see it." She waited, watching him. "It's not how Joyce would see it either."

He shook his head. "Joyce..." The name fell from his lips like honey. Sweetly. "After everything, she forgave me."

Chapter Nineteen

The building that had housed the old steel factory had been abandoned a long time ago. Enormous tubes tangled toward what looked like a grain elevator in a hodgepodge of confusion with an enormous warehouse at the other end. High windows ran the length of the building to let in light. Many were broken, victims of disuse and vandals.

"He's trying to intimidate us," Anne whispered to Lucas as they made their way toward a side door.

"That's what this guy is all about," Lucas said, "intimidation."

Trying to be soundless, they moved toward the yawning door that hung on broken hinges. The old parking lot was overgrown with weeds that pushed against the weakened asphalt. There wasn't a car or a person in sight. Most of the buildings in this neighborhood were abandoned as well, giving it the feeling of a ghost town.

"If we can at least get a lay of the land before Judd or Charles sight us we'll be better off, be able to formulate an idea of how to escape," Lucas said.

Anne nodded. Her heart was thumping in her neck. She could feel every beat pulsing.

They were within thirty yards of the door when Anne heard the echoing sounds of a girl crying. Then the bark of a man to "Be quiet!"

Anne must've made a grunting sound because Lucas lifted a finger to his lips as they moved inside.

She'd expected darkness, but the cavernous space was girded by an intricate web of metal and glass. Light flooded in through the windows overhead, giving the place a bright feel. A bird flew up, swooping down the length of the long building.

They moved toward the sound of the voices, careful to keep to the side, in whatever shadows they could find.

Then she saw them. They sat in a pool of light. Chairs were set up in a semicircle—Lucas's daughters sat on these. Men were positioned around the area keeping watch with Judd and Marley at the front. No doubt with guns at the ready.

Anne studied the girls. They didn't seem to be in immediate distress. There was no evidence of having been beaten or injured, though they were tied with thick ropes around their hands and feet.

Who would tie up innocent young women? The thought sickened Anne.

Bella moaned. "How long are you going to keep us here?"

"I told you to keep her quiet," Judd barked.

Remi shushed her sister. Both girls looked so frightened.

Never in her life had Anne wanted to hurt a person, but in that moment that was exactly what she wanted to do to Bentley and Marley—get these children away from the monsters and give the monsters the justice they deserved.

Lucas turned ahead of her and met Anne's gaze. He pointed to an exit not far from where the family was, to the right. Anne nodded and he stepped out into the open.

"I'm here, Marley," Lucas said. His hands were in the air, showing that he had no weapons.

Both girls gasped immediately. They wanted to run to him.

"Let my daughters go. You got what you wanted." He moved toward them tentatively, slowly, while Anne stayed in the shadows.

She didn't know if Judd or Marley saw her till Judd barked, "You come up here too, Anne. I see you."

Anne lifted her hands, following Lucas's lead.

When they were about twenty feet from the girls they halted.

"Please let them go," Lucas said again.

"You're not giving the orders around here." The man had a gun trained on them, yet Anne felt oddly calm, as if she were watching this all on a big screen and weren't a participant.

"Get Miller. Bring him here." He motioned to one of his goons to tie Lucas up. A burly man with a shaved head brought a rope and began tying Lucas's hands behind his back.

"You have me now," Lucas said. He was pleading. "Untie them. Let them go."

Judd nodded to his other men around the room. "Go ahead," Judd said. They did as he bid, pushing Bella and Remi to their feet. Anne could see that they wanted to run but were too afraid to move, too afraid to leave their father to this man.

"Go!" Judd barked. They moved quickly to Anne who ushered them to the door that Lucas had pointed out earlier. Once they were outside they took off at a run. Then, when they were a good one hundred yards away, they stopped to catch their breath. Everyone was crying.

"What are they going to do to Daddy?" Remi sobbed.

"How did you find him?" Bella asked.

"We have to get out of here," Anne said. When she lifted her head she saw the police officers arriving, a whole SWAT team surrounding the building, silent as night. The lead officer motioned them to move out.

"Are you all right?" Anne whispered to each of them as they made their way down the street. She couldn't bring herself to talk at a normal volume quite yet. Not till they were far away from this place.

"We are now," Remi said. She met Anne's eyes. "Thank you for coming."

She stopped and hugged the girl. "How could I not come? You're like family to me."

By the time they reached Alex, who was pacing three blocks away alongside Anne's car, it was clear that the building was under assault. Marta had gone in with the police, he told them.

They turned to watch as the scene played out. Gunshots sounded. Sirens blared.

Within minutes it was over. A handcuffed Judd Bentley was shoved into one of the waiting police cars. His eyes met Anne's and she wondered how she could have been so fooled by the man. Anne watched, hoping and praying that Lucas wasn't hurt in the attack. There was no sight of him.

Marley was brought out, flanked by two officers. He'd obviously been shot in the leg. A bandage covered the spot that oozed red. The man's face held a dark scowl, and he looked at Anne with narrowed eyes that sent a chill down her spine.

Where was Lucas? Anne felt anxiety rise within her as echoes of those gunshots fired in her mind.

Then he came. Marta was beside him. He was limping and he looked awful. His hair stuck up in every direction and deep circles lined his eyes, but the grin on his face overpowered all of that. Joyce ran to him, taking up the other side, helping him walk.

"What happened?" Anne asked when he was near enough to talk.

"Marley tried to use me as a shield, the coward, but when my leg got caught on a board I tripped and he lost his grip." He laughed at the irony of it. "I hadn't even *tried* to trip, but it was the opening the police needed to get him." He pointed at his ankle. "I've never been so happy to have a twisted ankle in my life!"

Remi went up to him first.

As soon as Lucas saw her, tears filled his eyes.

"Sweetie," he said.

"I didn't think I'd ever see you again," Remi confessed. "Oh, Daddy!" She fell into his arms and he stroked her hair. "Don't ever leave us again."

"I'm not going anywhere, babe. I'm so, so sorry." Their tears mingled, till Remi finally pulled back, wiping her wet cheeks with her hands and sniffling.

Bella came next. Her face was blotchy and red, but Anne didn't think she'd ever seen the girl look more elated. She too held onto her father. Joyce stood back. Watching. Her face was lined, her eyes rimmed in red.

After hearing that her parents were worried about her, Marta headed to Lock Haven to see them and to assure them that she was well. Then everyone else gathered at the Millers' home in Blue Hill sitting around with cups of coffee and tea.

"So," Anne said to Lucas, "I'm interested to know how this connection with the FBI and Charles Marley all came about.

Lucas gave his wife a timid look. "If you're comfortable telling, that is," Anne amended, not wanting to cause a rift.

"No, honey," Joyce said. "It's really okay. We're just glad that you're home. Tell us," she urged.

They held hands, sitting close together on the sofa, looking like a much younger couple, unashamed of their love for each other.

Lucas paused for a long moment before he began.

He stroked the back of Joyce's hand, then kissed it before he told them what happened.

"I took the job at the casino to research an upcoming book—that's truly how I got caught up in this. That's not always the best strategy, by the way." He squeezed Joyce's hand. "I recommend using Google and lots of imagination."

Everyone chuckled.

"I knew Joyce didn't like the idea, but I did it anyway. I figured if our girls didn't know about it at least they wouldn't think their old man was a poor example." He looked at his daughters. "Some example."

"Dad," Bella scolded, and Lucas smiled.

"I should've listened to your mom." He looked Joyce in the eyes. "I really should've. I'd been working there several weeks when Vince Barrio approached me about helping the FBI find the bookie who was working out of the casino." He shrugged. "Marta had taken some incriminating photos, so they knew something was going on there. I was flattered. How often does a boring novelist get to take part in a sting operation?" He cleared his throat and added, "How often indeed?" Lucas shook his head.

"But things started to get too hot. I could sense Marley and Bentley were onto me. Especially when things started happening to the other book club members. Those break-ins…" He lifted his gaze around the room. "They were trying to figure out who I was working with. I was sure of it.

"I had quit the job at the casino. But it was too late by then. I'd crossed the line. I was getting pressure from Barrio to see the operation through to the end, but I desperately wanted out. I knew I was putting innocent people in danger yet I didn't see how to get out of it. I even took an online course on how to disappear if it came to that." He paused. It was obvious that this information was difficult for him to share.

"I didn't want to leave," he finally went on. "You know that, right?" He looked from his wife to his daughters again. "It was just that I knew these men would stop at nothing to get to me, and I didn't feel the agents had my best interests at heart. I knew I had put my family in danger, and I couldn't see any easy way out." He sighed and ran a hand through his hair. "I didn't want you to know what I was doing for the FBI. I figured if you didn't know then they'd have no reason to come after you. That was naive of me!" Lucas drew a deep breath.

"Marta and I had a system—I'd place my bets, write my discoveries, any odds they were laying, into my novel, then pass them to her at the writers' meetings and a couple times at the

Keystone Café." He shook his head. "The night I left, I'd had no intention of leaving. I was coming home from our meeting when I saw Jeremiah Briggs—Judd Bentley—peeking in the windows of our house. You were all in there!" His tone rose in urgency, his need for them to understand strong.

"I knew what his intentions were, so I let Judd know I was there, then I led him away. It was the only thing I could think to do. But then I skidded off the road and crashed into that tree—that wasn't part of the plan. I managed to hide while Judd searched for me and then I wrote that note." He turned toward his wife. "You have to know how hard it was to write that note."

Joyce merely nodded, her eyes shining.

"I managed to get to Fowler's Auto Repair and find Scott Milhouse still working. I left the pen there. I knew you'd know that was something I'd never leave behind. Not unless there was a really good reason."

His gaze moved across the whole room. "I guess I wanted you to find me, to figure out what Marley was doing to me, but I just didn't know how to lead you to me without my pursuers finding me first. Or what would happen when you did find me. I still wasn't thinking straight—I was endangering you. But then, when I saw the newspaper photo from the *Gazette* online of all of you and that the police were giving up their search for me, I saw Jeremiah! You don't know how much fear that put in me—seeing that he was right here in your midst and you had no idea. You were still in danger and there wasn't a thing I could do to protect you! So I wrote a note and sent it to Anne. Then I made the deposit. I figured if you were still trying to find me"—he looked at Anne— "you'd make the connection and come to Wilkes-Barre, hopefully bring Judd with you...though that wasn't how it all worked out, was it?"

He cleared his throat and took a sip of his tea before he went on. "Judd was hot on my tail then, anyway, but I knew he was trying to find me, didn't really believe he would go so far. I should have known the depths of his evil. I'm sorry for being so gullible, so naive."

"Don't apologize for being naive," Joyce said. "That's a good thing. Just...no more secrets, okay? None. We could've figured something out if this had been brought into the light."

"No secrets," he agreed.

* * *

The lumbering motor home pulled up in front of the library around eleven the next morning. Anne had never been so glad to see her family. Marlene reached to give her a hug. "Everything okay?" she whispered into Anne's ears.

"With you here—more than okay," Anne said, giving the woman a tight squeeze.

"What was that all about?"

"I love you."

Byron followed, saying, "We missed you, kid."

"Not as much as I missed you."

Ben was quiet as Anne hugged him.

Liddie talked on and on in great detail about the sites they'd seen in the past several days, from Philadelphia to Washington, DC. "Oh, Mommy, we had so much fun. We didn't get to see the president at his house, but I know he was in the next room. I could hear him talking!"

They tugged luggage up to their private apartment where Anne had set out lunch for them.

Finally, when there was a break in the conversation, Anne asked Ben, "You okay, buddy?"

He lifted his thoughtful nine-year-old face and said, "Yeah, I'm okay, Mom." Suddenly he seemed much older. Hershey's toenails clicked on the hardwood floor as he padded over. He gazed lovingly at his master. Ben patted him on the head. "I'm sorry I've been such a brat lately."

She opened her mouth to tell him it was okay, but he wasn't finished.

"I was being selfish. But you weren't selfish at all—you could've gotten really hurt, but you looked for Mr. Miller and his daughters anyway."

"Well, of course," Anne said.

"If you want to find a new husband... Well, that's okay with me."

"A new husband!" Anne exchanged an awkward glance with Byron, who sat on the other side of Ben. "Honey, I'm not..."

But Ben was shaking his head. "I was worried that if you found a new husband I wouldn't get to see Grandma and Grandpa Gibson anymore. That you'd forget about them."

He looked at his grandparents.

"Forget about them? They're your *grandparents*," Anne said. "They will always be in your life. Nothing will change that."

"Really?" He glanced at his grandparents.

Marlene moved next to him and gave him a squeeze. "Of course we will," Marlene said. "We just want your mom to be happy. You'll always be our grandson."

Ben looked up at his mom. "That's what I want too. I want Mom to be happy." Then he looked at his grandpa. "I really wanted to take Mom fishing."

Byron said, "You know…" He paused. "Grandma and I don't have to hurry back to Ithaca." He glanced at Anne. "What do you think, Anne? Could you spare a few days of camping and fishing? We could head out in the morning."

Anne said, "Why not? I'll just close the library for a couple of days. Some things are just more important."

* * *

The next morning, Liddie and Ben were buzzing to go on an adventure with their mom. Anne picked up the bag that she'd packed before the ordeal and hoisted it into the motor home.

Things had changed in her relationship with her in-laws, she realized, in the past two weeks. They had become more than Eric's parents to her, they'd become *family*. As much hers as they had been his.

Byron and Marlene had proposed the idea of an annual "Grandparents' Camp," where they would plan a week or two of uninterrupted fun time with Ben and Liddie, traveling in their motor home or doing whatever came to mind. The kids thought that was a great idea and whooped when Byron proposed it.

They were blessed to have such grandparents.

Anne climbed back upstairs and checked the apartment to make sure she hadn't forgotten anything. Hershey was downstairs with Ben, eager to join the road trip. Anne realized she was excited about the idea too. She'd already taken down the tackle box and poles that had once belonged to Eric. He would've loved the idea of three days of fishing.

She turned off the lamp in her bedroom, then paused at the dresser. She bent and looked at her hand. Eric's rings glimmered there, memories of very good times, as well as the hardest time of her life. Losing him.

She wanted to live again. She needed to live again. A deep longing filled her. But it would never be filled, could never be filled. So she tugged the rings off and placed them gently, reverently, in the ring box she kept in the top drawer. She could always look at them if she wanted, but they were a tie to the past. A past that was over. Someday, if Ben wanted to offer them to his future bride he could have them.

But for now she would look ahead with confidence to the God Who was still there by her side. He could bring her even things she thought impossible.

ABOUT THE AUTHOR

Emily Thomas is the pen name for a team of writers who have come together to create the series Secrets of the Blue Hill Library. *Without a Trace* was written by Traci DePree. Traci is the author of eleven novels, including the best-selling Lake Emily series, six books in Mystery and the Minister's Wife as well as another book, *Off the Shelf*, in Secrets of Blue Hill Library, both Guideposts series. She has five children, three adult daughters and two younger ones whom she homeschools in a rural town in southern Minnesota. She and her husband, John, have been happily married for twenty-nine years. To learn more about Traci and her upcoming titles join the conversation on her Facebook page at facebook.com/traci.depree. She loves getting to know her readers.

A Conversation with the Author

Q. What makes your hometown library special?

A. I, too, live in a small town, and my little library is a second home to me. I always see people I know there. The librarians are well read and always ready with wonderful reading suggestions. There's a sense of welcome and camaraderie, and if I'm on a writing deadline, my librarian will set me up in a private corner to write. She's my biggest supporter—I'd be lost without her.

Q. Have you ever solved a mystery in real life?

A. I can't say that I've solved any mysteries like Anne's mysteries, though my family does call me "The Finder." I'm able to find just about anything that's lost in our house, you name it— keys, glasses, remote controls. I'm your go-to girl if you want to find it.

Q. Aunt Edie had a lot of adventures in her life. Can you tell us about the most exciting adventure you've experienced?

A. I've had a lot of wonderful adventures with my family. One that comes to mind happened the first year of our married life. My husband and I lived in the U. S. Virgin Islands. One night we went snorkeling with flashlights under the pier in

Fredericksted, St. Croix. At first the swim was pretty uneventful...until the jellyfish started floating in. There were jellyfish everywhere we turned. We couldn't get away from them! They were beautiful, translucent, shimmering in our flashlights' beam. By the time we'd swum to the end of the pier I was covered in jellyfish stings. It was extremely painful. Needless to say I don't recommend night snorkeling under the Fredericksted pier!

Q. *If you could visit Blue Hill, where would you go first? Why?*

A. The Blue Hill library of course! It's the hub of life for the small town of Blue Hill. I'd like to see how my descriptions compare to the real thing!

Q. *Anne moves back to her hometown after years in New York City. What do/would you miss about your hometown?*

A. The thing I miss most about my hometown is my family. None of my family still lives in the town I grew up in. Now it's a place of strangers, totally rebuilt from when I lived there. I can't visit it as it was, because it's a place of memory not reality. Everything I recall is gone for the most part.

Q. *What is the most memorable photograph you have on your wall?*

A. I have an old photograph of my grandmother, who was a surgical nurse at the turn of the century. The shot is of her and the entire surgical team in the middle of an operation! No face masks or gloves, the only light came from the window behind them.

Q. *Which character in* Secrets of the Blue Hill Library *are you most like? Why?*

A. Liddie! That kid likes to have fun, she's uninhibited and expresses herself freely. She's joyful, thoughtful, and spunky. I like to think I'm that way too.

Q. *What characteristics of Anne's personality do you see in yourself? In what ways are you a total opposite of Anne?*

A. I'm the type of mom Anne is, taking care of others, careful not to hurt feelings yet earnestly seeking to live in the truth. But I'm not nearly as fastidious as Anne is. She's more logical than I am. And more curious.

Recipes from the Library Guild

Marlene Gibson's Cream Cheese Brownies

Filling
4 ounces cream cheese,
   softened
1 egg
3 tablespoons sugar
¼ teaspoon vanilla

Brownie Batter
2 squares (1 ounce each)
   unsweetened chocolate
⅓ cup shortening
1 cup sugar
2 eggs
½ teaspoon vanilla
¾ cup flour
½ teaspoon baking powder
½ teaspoon salt

Beat filling ingredients together in a small bowl and set aside.

Heat oven to 350 degrees. Melt chocolate and shortening over low heat, stirring constantly till melted. Remove from heat. Add sugar, eggs, and vanilla till blended, then add dry ingredients. Spread three-fourths of brownie batter in pan. Spoon filling evenly onto brownie batter. Spoon the remaining brownie batter over the filling. Cut through mixture with knife several times for marbled design. Sprinkle with chocolate chips. Bake for thirty minutes or until toothpick inserted in brownies comes out clean.

FROM THE GUIDEPOSTS ARCHIVES

This article by Tommy Webb originally appeared in
Guideposts magazine.

Fridays are always hectic at my auto-repair shop, and this Friday had been no different. I'd put in a full morning before glancing up at the clock: ten o'clock in the morning. Where's Burke? I suddenly asked myself. It wasn't like my nineteen-year-old son to be late for work. Not like him at all. He knew the customers all wanted their cars ready for the weekend.

In my first spare minute I made some quick calls. Burke had set off from his mother's house in Taylorsville at eight the night before, headed back to Asheville, where he lived with me. I dialed our house. He wasn't there.

Taylorsville is about ninety miles away, nearly a straight shot on I-40, a trip Burke made frequently since his mother and I split up. There must be an explanation. Burke wouldn't just disappear.

All afternoon I tried to concentrate on mufflers and spark plugs. But finally around four in the afternoon I slammed the hood down on a repair job. I'd take a ride over to Taylorsville.

"Burke probably just had him some car trouble or something," one of the mechanics reassured me as I left the shop.

But why hasn't he called? I asked myself over and over, my eyes darting from one side of the interstate to the other. Had he pulled over and fallen asleep, maybe got tied up helping another motorist? I half expected to see his white truck parked on the shoulder, the truck he'd bought with his earnings from the shop.

But there was no sign of it or him all the way to Taylorsville.

I checked by his mother's house and with some of his friends. Everyone was baffled. *I shouldn't have waited out the day,* I thought guiltily. It was eight o'clock in the evening; Burke had been missing a full twenty-four hours. I tried the back roads, any route he could have taken. Nothing. Now I knew it was something more than a forgotten phone call or a flat tire. My son was in trouble.

Long after midnight I started back toward Asheville on I-40, not able to see much in the pitch black. My eyes ached by the time I got home and looked in Burke's room, which was quiet and undisturbed. I flicked on the porch light and went to my room. I'd get some rest, go out again in the morning. But I hoped to hear something before then. I put the phone next to my bed. "God, help me," I prayed as I drifted off.

I grabbed the receiver in mid ring early Saturday morning. It was Burke's grandfather Bill. "People don't just disappear," he said. "Somebody must have seen him." Bill was in police work, so I felt hopeful when he said he'd be right over to pick me up. "Bring along a recent picture of Burke," he advised.

We asked at gas stations and convenience stores off the highway. We showed the high school graduation picture to one stranger after another. Our waitress at the truck stop where we had coffee studied Burke's face, thinking she saw something familiar in his smile. But no, she couldn't be sure. The truckers all promised to keep an eye out. But we still weren't any closer to finding Burke.

Just past noon we walked into the highway patrol station. I told the desk sergeant I needed to fill out a missing persons report. "Who's missing?" he asked.

"It's my son. No one's seen him since eight Thursday night."

"How old's your boy?"

"Nineteen."

"Well now," he said slowly, eyeing me. "That could explain it. You remember what it was like being a teenager." The sergeant leaned back in his chair. "While you're out worrying yourself half to death, he's at the beach having a good time. I can't tell you how often I've seen it."

"Maybe the sergeant's right, Tommy," Bill said. "Burke wouldn't be the first kid —"

"He's not at the beach, Bill! I know my own son!" I was trying to control my frustration. But I knew I was right. Didn't they understand?

"Tell you what," the sergeant said. "If your boy's not back by tonight, we'll file that report. Nothin' I can do till then, seeing as how we're required to wait out the forty-eight hours."

I walked quickly out of the station house and stared at the empty police cars lined up in front. The only possible explanation was that Burke was in such trouble that he couldn't get to a phone. Time is running out.

God, please help me find Burke. I wanted to pray, really pray — out loud — not just think the words. I wanted to tell God how desperately I needed Him. But I wasn't sure how.

I hadn't made much time for prayer in my life. Some of the guys at the car dealership next door to my garage met Wednesday mornings for prayer. I went once or twice when I'd first opened. Then business picked up, and I quit. Who had time for prayer meetings when you're trying to make a living? Now I wished I'd made the time. "God, I'm sorry ..."

Suddenly I felt Bill's hand on my shoulder. "The officer's just doing his job, Tommy. Might as well head on back to Asheville. You drive."

I got behind the wheel. My thoughts wandered to what we'd do in Asheville—go to the police, check the hospitals. By then we'd only have a couple hours daylight left...

I tried to keep my mind clear, open to any clue we might be passing. The terrain was now so familiar. Our eyes had been over every inch—farmland, cornfields, tall pines. We came to a section just before a curve, where the land to our right rose from the road, reddish land with patches of bushes and weeds, a few wildflowers sticking out of the brush...

Wait a second—what was that? Something up there off the road, glinting in the sun. I slowed down. No sign of an accident. As we got closer, the angle obscured my view. I almost lost sight of it. What could it be?

"Bill, look up there." I rolled onto the shoulder, pebbles crunching under the tires, and got out. "I thought I saw something glinting in the sun," I said, suddenly unsure. Bill followed me up the incline, where I scuffled around in the bushes. Were my eyes playing tricks on me?

Then I saw it, a piece of metal embedded in the soft earth. I walked around it, pulling back the bush that hid its shape. "What's this, Bill?"

"Can't really tell. But it's mighty busted up."

And then, with a sharp pang of alarm, I recognized it: "Bill, this is a fender off Burke's truck! But where's his truck? Where's he?"

I tried to keep my mind clear, open to any clue we might be passing.

I looked out toward the highway, then down the other side of the incline, where there was a steep drop-off. My eyes were drawn to something twisted and bent in the trees growing out of the murky ravine below. I could just make out a door...

"That's his truck!" I shouted and started down.

"Wait, Tommy!" Bill lunged and grabbed my arm. He pulled me back. "You go to the highway. Flag down a car. Get them to call an ambulance. I'll go to the wreck. I'm trained..."

I knew what he meant. He was experienced with accidents, accidents where people die. Not my son.

There wasn't time to argue. Bill struggled down the drop-off toward the dark clump of trees. I ran back to the highway and waved my arms wildly. Several cars stopped and one motorist called for help.

I dashed back up the incline and froze at the top. My eyes fixed on the dark green trees. What were they hiding? I'd never been so frightened in my life. *God*, I finally prayed, *I trust in You and will accept what waits for me. But please...*

Just then Bill emerged from the clump of branches. He stared up at me, breathing hard. Tears stained his dirt-smeared face. "He's alive, Tommy. Burke's alive."

I raced down toward him, stumbling, sliding, crying, branches tearing my clothes. Then I was crouched on the ground by my son.

His face was bloody, his leg twisted under him. Dried blood and dirt had caked over a gash under his arm. "Dad ... thank God," he barely whispered.

"Easy, Son," I shushed him.

"Easy."

I cradled his head in my hands until paramedics arrived. They gingerly maneuvered Burke onto a stretcher and over the incline. I rode with him in the ambulance to the hospital, where Bill and I spent a nightmarish thirty minutes before the nurse came out and said, "He's going to make it."

"I knew you'd be looking for me," Burke said groggily when they let me in the room to see him. "I prayed God would help you." He'd fallen asleep at the wheel and his truck had enough momentum to vault over the incline. He was afraid the accident couldn't be seen from the highway. I told him about the fender glinting almost imperceptibly in the sunlight.

It's a real helpless feeling, searching for something you can't find. But I discovered that even in our most lost moments, when it seems there's no hope, there is something we can do. God is never deaf to our prayers, no matter how imperfect they seem.

I'm still busy down at my auto-repair shop. And Fridays aren't any less hectic, even with Burke helping out now that he's back on his feet. But these days I always make time for something else — those Wednesday morning prayers with the guys at the car dealership next door.

Read on for a sneak peek of another exciting book
in Secrets of the Blue Hill Library!

Stagestruck

A nne Gibson stepped back from the Victorian mystery novels
display she was setting up in the Fiction Room of the Blue
Hill Library and viewed the effect. She turned to her helpers, her
five-year-old daughter, Liddie, and her nine-year-old son, Ben.
"Well? What do you think?"

Ben tilted his head sideways. "I think the lamp is crooked."

Anne straightened the fake oil lamp suspended from the wall.
"Anything else?"

Liddie had her arms full of crocheted lace doilies from the
attic. "I think it needs more of Aunt Edie's lace."

"It doesn't need more lace," Ben objected.

"How about this one?" Anne held up a doily with several
holes where the thread had broken and the crochet unraveled. "If
I drape it over the candlesticks, it'll look like spiderwebs."

Ben grinned. "Cool."

Liddie made a face. "Yuck."

After arranging their "cobwebs," Anne turned to Liddie.
"Now I need Aunt Edie's hat." She untied the purple ribbons
under her daughter's chin and removed the bonnet-style hat with
white feathers and silk violets decorating the crown.

As the hat was removed, Liddie blinked her chocolate brown eyes. "Now I can see."

"You always could see," Ben said. "It didn't cover your face."

"But I couldn't see on the sides." Liddie turned her head from side to side.

"Over one hundred years ago, women wore these all the time." Anne perched the bonnet on a small nail in the wall. "I wonder if they ran into lampposts a lot?"

Ben and Liddie giggled.

Ben pulled the black silk top hat from his head. "Can I stop wearing this now?"

"But you look so handsome," Anne teased him.

Ben rolled his eyes. "Mo-om…"

Anne hung the hat on another nail. "There. A perfect pair."

Ben scratched his hands through his scalp, ruffling his brown hair. "How did they wear those things? It itches."

"Wasn't it just like when you wear a baseball cap?" Anne asked.

"No. I felt like I had a building on my head."

"I suppose it was heavier than a baseball cap." Anne looked at the display with satisfaction. The decorations drew the eye, and she had displayed cozy mystery novels set in the Victorian era. "It looks like we're done. How about some raspberry spoon bread?"

"Yeah!" Both kids were delighted with that suggestion, and they headed through the doorway to their living quarters on the second floor of the library. In the kitchen, Anne served up the new recipe she'd tried last night, using the spring season's earliest raspberries. The fruit-studded cake melted in her mouth.

"Can I have more yogurt?" Ben asked.

She gave Ben another generous spoonful of raspberry Greek yogurt on top as a healthier alternative to whipped cream.

After their afternoon snack, Anne stood. "I'm going to wash the dishes and then go back downstairs. Ben, did you take your dog out?"

"Yes, I took Hershey out when I came home from school."

Anne was proud of how responsible Ben had become about his chocolate Labrador retriever, but his eyes seemed to slide away from hers, so she asked, "How about your homework?"

Ben groaned. "But school's almost out for the summer."

"And what does that have to do with finishing your homework or not?" Anne hid her smile. She could remember the antsy feeling she'd had in the month before summer break. Homework had been especially onerous.

Ben heaved a dramatic sigh and slid off his seat to head to the living room.

"Finish up quickly," Anne told Liddie, who still had a few bites of spoon bread. "It's almost time for story hour."

"Okay." Liddie shoved a gigantic piece into her mouth.

Anne washed their dishes and then sent Liddie to the Children's Room where kids were gathering. Anne was surprised that her friend Wendy Pyle wasn't yet there to do Story Time. Wendy had a flair for it, with lots of fun props and crafts.

At the checkout desk on the first floor, fraternal twins Remi and Bella Miller were checking books and stacking them in a cart to return to the shelves. As Anne reached the desk, the front door to the library opened and Wendy breezed in, bringing the fresh air and the scent of new leaves from outside.

"Sorry I'm late." Wendy shucked off her cardigan. "I was at the community center. Looks like that spring storm last week was the last straw—the roof over the theater caved in."

"Oh no!" Anne said.

"Oh no!" Remi and Bella echoed. The twins belonged to the community theater club. "What happened? Was anyone hurt?"

"No, thank goodness, but the hole is right over center stage."

"You were planning your next production, weren't you?"

Wendy was on the planning committee, and she'd told Ben and Liddie she'd help them get small parts in the next play.

Wendy nodded mournfully. "We'd almost decided on the play too, but now we'll have to postpone and figure out how much it'll cost to repair the roof. The director was calling Alex just as I left."

"I'm sure he'll give a fair estimate." When Anne's aunt Edie had left her lovely Victorian home to Anne, she had stipulated that it be renovated into a library for Anne to run, and Alex Ochs, Anne's old high school sweetheart, had done a wonderful job on the renovations.

"I'm sure he will," Wendy said, "but the community theater group simply doesn't have a lot of money. We'll need to figure out some type of fund-raiser we could do."

"I suppose a bake sale wouldn't bring in quite enough?"

Wendy laughed. "That might pay for a few shingles. We need something really big that a lot of people would be interested in."

"We'll put our heads together and come up with ideas," Remi said.

"I'd better run to do Story Time." Wendy grabbed her bag to head upstairs. "The kids must be climbing up the walls by now."

As Wendy left, the front door opened again and Reverend Tom Sloan entered. Anne smiled. "Reverend Tom, you're just in time to see your Victorian mystery novels display upstairs."

His hand smoothed the graying hair at the top of his head that had been blown about by the spring breeze. "Surely it's not *my* display. I only gave the suggestion to you after reading that Sir Arthur Conan Doyle biography."

"It's definitely your display." Anne pulled him upstairs to the Fiction Room. "Your idea was great."

Reverend Tom's eyebrows rose as he saw the display. "That's wonderful. I recognize that purple bonnet too. Edie wore it one Easter."

"All the decorations were from the attic or Aunt Edie's closet."

"I had no idea there were so many Victorian mystery authors." He bent over the stacks of books on the table.

Anne nodded. "There were Victorian writers such as Sir Arthur Conan Doyle, Wilkie Collins, and Charles Dickens, but in the past decades there have been more contemporary mystery authors who set their books in that time period, like Emily Brightwell's Mrs. Jeffries series and Elizabeth Peters's Amelia Peabody series."

Reverend Tom had picked up the first book in the Mrs. Jeffries series. "Now, this looks interesting…"

Anne left him happily perusing the books as she went to peek into the Children's Room. The kids were doing some sort of twirling dance, led by an enthusiastic Wendy, which made Anne dizzy just watching it. She wondered which book Wendy was reading to them as she went downstairs.

Bella's mouth drooped as she and Anne shelved books in the Nonfiction Room. "I can't believe the roof to the theater caved in. I was looking forward to the next production."

"How often does the community theater club put on shows?"

"Usually once a year, or once every eighteen months, because of the cost."

Anne was surprised, but maybe she was spoiled because there had always been plenty of new shows when she lived in New York City.

"Maybe for the fund-raiser, we could do a play here in the library," Bella said as they moved to the History Room next door. Her blue eyes sparkled. Couldn't you see this room as perfect for some play like *The Maltese Falcon*?" She gestured to the dark cherry wood furniture and upholstered chairs in rich tapestry colors.

"It's nowhere near as large as the theater," Anne said.

"If we did a small play, we could fit in more people for the audience."

"Do you know any plays for only a few people?"

Bella grimaced. "No. But do you know who probably would? Ms. Sanchez."

The name was familiar to Anne. "Do you mean Flores Sanchez? The nurse at the elementary school?" She had called Anne about Liddie or Ben a few times for minor things like rashes and coughs.

"Yeah. When she's not working, she writes plays. She's got an agent and everything. She's hoping one of her plays gets produced off Broadway or in London."

"Wow, she's really serious about it."

"Remi and I acted in at least one of her plays a few years ago." Bella shelved a book on railroad history. "It was a family drama, sort of like *The Glass Menagerie* but with more people."

Anne shelved a book on Lewis and Clark. "I'm still not sure the library has the space for a large enough audience."

"Maybe Remi and I can come up with a really great fund-raiser idea."

When they returned to the checkout desk, a woman was speaking to Remi. "I'm looking for Anne Summers."

"I'm Anne Summers Gibson," Anne said.

The woman looked at her from beneath a very fashionable turquoise-green velvet toque hat, which Anne wouldn't have been surprised to have found in Aunt Edie's hat collection. She had soft green eyes and straight, fine, ash-blonde hair with subtle lowlights pulled back from her round face into a smooth chignon. She smiled when she saw Anne, and then Anne recognized her.

"Tami?" Anne said in amazement. In high school, Tami Bates had been quiet and shy, dressing in loose clothes and drab colors that seemed to enable her to fade into the background—a completely different style from the fitted tweed jacket with turquoise-green velvet trim to match her hat, her turquoise silk blouse, and cleverly tailored tweed slacks that she wore now. "Tami Bates, is that really you?"

Tami laughed. "In the flesh! Although it's Tami Bates O'Brien, now."

Anne gave her a hug. "I haven't seen you since high school. You look amazing!" Anne felt distinctly underdressed in her slacks and pullover.

"You don't look like you've aged a day." Tami grinned.

The years fell away and Anne was sixteen again, roller skating with Tami and Jennifer at the park, laughing and teasing each other. "I heard you were living in London now."

"Yes, I'm a theater producer's assistant, and my husband is an actor. I'm back in Blue Hill to visit my folks since it's in between our spring and summer productions."

"You work in the theater?" Bella's eyes were the size of saucers. "That's so cool!"

A faint blush appeared on Tami's cheeks, reminding Anne of the shy Tami she'd known in high school. "It's not very glamorous being a producer's assistant, believe me."

"But your husband's an *actor*." Remi's expression was as awed as her sister's.

"And he's quite good, if I do say so myself." Tami winked. "He'll be arriving in two weeks, as soon as the play he's in finishes its run, so you'll probably get to meet him."

Bella and Remi grinned at each other in excitement.

Tami leaned closer to Anne and touched her sleeve. "Anne, do you have time to talk privately?"

Anne looked at her in confusion. "Of course. Let's go upstairs."

As Anne led Tami through the connecting door into their family's living quarters on the second floor, Tami started in surprise. "You live here in the library? I didn't know that."

"When Aunt Edie left her house to me to turn into a library, we renovated the third floor and half the second into our home." Anne peeked into the living room, where Ben was doing his homework, the tip of his tongue poking out of his mouth. "How are you doing, Ben?"

"I'm almost done."

"This is my friend Mrs. O'Brien. Tami, my son, Ben."

"Hi, Mrs. O'Brien," he said.

"Hi, Ben." Tami tilted her head toward Anne. "He looks just like you."

"I also have a five-year-old, Liddie, who's in the Children's Room for Story Time. She looks more like my late husband." Anne waited for that same pang to hit when she mentioned Eric, but she realized that it wasn't there. She wasn't sure if she was relieved that she no longer felt the rawness of her grief, or if she was sad that his memory was fading ever so slightly.

"I'm sorry about your husband," Tami said.

"Thank you. It's been three years, and our family has been blessed to have this opportunity to move here to Blue Hill." Anne put a kettle on for tea. "Tell me, how did you meet your husband?"

"Aiden was chosen for a play produced by my boss." Tami sat at the kitchen table. "We immediately hit it off. By the time the play ended, we had fallen in love."

"How romantic."

"My husband is the romantic one. I'm actually rather practical. It makes me a good assistant for my producer."

Anne put the serving container of raspberry spoon bread on the table in front of Tami. "I have to admit, Tami, I had never thought you would work in the theater."

"No one is more surprised than I am. But in college, my roommate was a theater nut. I didn't want to act, but the logistics of putting together a production were really fun. It appealed to the organizational side of me, but it was still creative."

"I can see how that would be." Anne took out cups and tea bags, as well as plates and utensils for the raspberry spoon bread.

"I applied for a prestigious study-abroad program, and no one was more surprised than I was when I was accepted. I loved Great Britain, and I met my future boss, Gideon Rossiter, during my year there. When I graduated, I went back and applied for a job, and he hired me right away."

The water boiled, and Anne filled the cups and brought them to the table, sitting across from Tami. "I've got lots of different tea bags to choose from."

"I'm English now." Tami laughed. "Do you have any Earl Grey?"

After tasting—and praising—the raspberry spoon bread, Tami put her fork down. "Actually, that study-abroad program relates to why I need to talk to you. The program was created by Roy Underwood. Have you heard of him?"

Anne shook her head.

"He grew up nearby in Deshler, but he was a well-known theater director in London. I met him when I won his study-abroad program, and over the years our paths crossed in London. He always remembered who I was and had a smile for me. I've always been grateful to him for the opportunity that allowed me to do what I love."

"He sounds like he's a nice man."

"He was wonderful, but he died only a month or two before your Aunt Edie did."

"Oh, I'm sorry, Tami."

"He had wanted his things auctioned off and the money set up to support his study-abroad program for western Pennsylvania students, and so I attended the auction. Oh, Anne, some of the things that were auctioned off were amazing. Antiques you wouldn't believe, famous costumes and props. I couldn't afford most of it, but I did manage to win a couple costumes from a lesser-known production of *Henry IV* that he did shortly before his passing."

"That's terrific you were able to get a memento of a man who did so much for you."

"Actually..." Tami reached into her purse, a classic leather handbag that looked Parisian, and withdrew a small white envelope. "I've had the costumes since the auction, but I was storing them until I could figure out how to display them. A couple of months ago, we moved to a bigger house, so I unpacked the costumes. That's when I found this hidden in an inner lining pocket of the man's costume."

Anne took the envelope from Tami and was surprised to recognize Aunt Edie's flowing handwriting addressing the letter to Roy Underwood in London, with her return address here in Blue Hill. There was a card inside with a lilac design that was exactly like the cards Anne had seen in one of Aunt Edie's desk drawers:

Dear Roy,

Thank you so much for calling me last week. It made the anniversary of my mother's death a little easier to bear.

I know you always tell me that what you did for my mother all those years ago was something anyone would have done, but if anyone else found my mother after she fell in that Deshler parking lot, they would have simply taken her to the hospital and left her there. I will forever be grateful to you for taking care of her when I was not able to because of my work overseas.

But now I think I can finally repay your kindness. I was in the attic the other day, cleaning up some water damage from a leak in the roof, when I found a play I had tucked away for safekeeping. It is the famous "missing" script by Hugh Bettridge. I'm afraid I can't tell you how I managed to get this script, but I want to lend you the play to produce. All I ask is that you return the script to me when you are done with it since it is very precious to me.

The next time you come to Deshler to visit your family, come visit me and I will hand it to you. I would prefer not to send something so valuable to you through the mail.

I look forward to seeing you again, dear friend.

Edie

Anne looked up in astonishment at Tami. "A missing script?"

Tami's green eyes sparkled like emeralds. "I recognized the name Hugh Bettridge as soon as I read Edie's note. He was a famous playwright who died about twenty years ago. I did more research on him and found that in the months after his death, there were rumors that he had an unproduced script, but no one ever found it. Tami reached over to grasp Anne's hands in an excited grip. "If this is really the 'missing' script, Anne, it could be worth thousands of dollars today."